IN
Enemy
ARMS

A STRIPLING WARRIOR NOVEL

MISTY MONCUR

IN
Enemy
ARMS

A STRIPLING WARRIOR NOVEL

MISTY
MONCUR

EDEN BOOKS — STANSBURY PARK, UT

Cover photo © 2015 Heather Waegner
Cover design by Sherry Gammon

Published by Eden Books, Stansbury Park, UT

ISBN-10: 0-9898959-5-5
ISBN-13: 978-0-9898959-5-8

Moncur, Misty Leigh, 1978-
In Enemy Arms/ Misty Moncur
Summary: Stranded in enemy lands, Ava tries to uncover Dare's secrets.

ISBN: 978-0-9898959-3-4

Library of Congress Catalog Control Number

2015951733

IN MEMORY OF

Becky Paget

AND WITH SPECIAL THANKS TO

Tamarha

CHAPTER 1

My feet were light on the soft ground, but my breaths were coming in heavy pants. Tec was stronger and faster, but I kept him in sight. I had to. I didn't know where we were running to or why we had to run so fast, but I knew it had something to do with those stinking, vile Nephites.

Tec was tearing across the terrain. He was deliberate and exacting, and he did not waste movement, especially when there was urgency. Through the dense pines, over fallen logs, up inclines and down their opposite slopes, my brother had traversed these hills many times, and he led the way with confidence.

As I slowed to duck a low hanging branch, I saw Tec draw his bow on the run and reach back for an arrow. Then he disappeared from view.

What was over that next rise?

"What are you doing here? Protecting Nephites?"

I stopped, skidding on the dirt, catching my breath for a different reason.

Josiah.

"These are not the men who killed Zaaron," Tec told him.

No of course not. We had already led those Nephites through our lands to safety. We had already helped them escape. I scanned the group of people below me. These were just more Nephites—but it was becoming clear that Tec had become entangled with them, too.

Josiah glanced around at the foreigners surrounding him and the men from my village. "A Nephite is a Nephite. You betray the Order to protect them."

I stood still, breathing hard, and watched the scene below me. The men from my village had their weapons drawn, and they faced off against a band of Nephites. My brother stood between the two groups with his arrow trained on Josiah, a man he had looked up to, learned from, fought beside, and who was now pointing an arrow right back at him.

"These men are under the protection of the Order. They are under the protection of Zaaron," my brother lied.

"Zaaron is dead," Josiah's emotionless voice accused.

"And you would dishonor him?" Tec shot back. Then, he lowered his voice and sneered, "You have a habit of dishonoring the wishes of the dead."

A lump rose in my throat. Why did he have to bring that up now?

They stared at each other in silence, and after one of the Nephites had interpreted my brother's words for his kinsmen, everyone in the small clearing fell silent.

It was nearly imperceptible, but Josiah increased the tension on his bow string.

"Honor his wish. Go home." Tec spoke as if he had a right to command Josiah. He definitely didn't, but Josiah owed my brother humility—deference at the very least—and they both knew it.

Morianton jolted forward and growled, trying to cajole

his leader. "He is no longer our brother, Josiah. You don't need to listen to him. Kill him! Avenge Zaaron's death!"

Neither arrow moved.

I didn't think I could face down Josiah, but I had to. I could end this quicker than anyone.

Because Josiah owed me something too.

"Stop it, you big babies!" I yelled as I finally got my feet moving again. "Zaaron was not dead when I left the village. There is no need to avenge him."

Everyone turned to look at me, and I hoped they would believe my bravado. My heart was racing, and when my eyes met Josiah's, I almost couldn't breathe. I'd had more breath when I was running.

"Put your weapons down," I said as calmly as I could. I hoped my terror was not showing. "Tec is working under Zaaron's orders."

A lie.

Josiah's eyes filled with suspicion. "Is this true?"

"It's true," Tec affirmed.

"These are not the men you're looking for. Those men have already passed into Nephite lands. We tracked them." *A lie.* "Tec is to spy among these." *Another lie.*

But it was not as if Josiah had never lied to me.

Finally, Josiah lowered his weapon a notch. "Is this true?" he asked Tec again.

"Yes, what Ava says is true." *Yet another lie.*

I made my feet move again until I was between Tec and Josiah. I knew Tec would drop his weapon, but I had no idea what Josiah would do. I tried to ignore the sting of the insult when he did not lower it. Willing tears not to form, I reached up and put my hand on Josiah's bow until at last he released the tension on the string and allowed me to push the weapon down. His infallible pride remained in the set of his jaw and the stiffness of his shoulders.

"I need you to take Ava home," Tec told Josiah. "She is interfering with what I must do."

I whirled on Tec. "No! I can help! And I'm not going with *him*."

I would never agree to go with Josiah. Not him, not his rude men. I would rather be bound and sacrificed at the great temple in Ishmael.

Josiah laughed, and I might have imagined a note of hurt in it. "She got herself here. She can find her way home. Come on." He motioned to his men, and he turned and left the little clearing without a backward glance at the enemy warriors gathered there, without a backward glance at me.

I tried to catch Tec's eye, but he wouldn't look at me. What had he done? What had I done? Slowly, we turned to face the Nephites we had just saved. I didn't care about saving them. I had only wanted to save Tec.

Despite the fact that all the men had their weapons trained on him, Tec spoke to them in their own language. I thought he may have introduced us, for I recognized my own name.

First he saved them and now he was being polite to them?

From the looks on their faces, the Nephite travelers believed it about as much as I did, and they did not lower their weapons.

Just great, Tec.

4

Tecumeni stayed completely still as he told them something about Lamech and Kenai, men from the band of Nephites he had led to the border city of Amulon. His words were calm, but his utter stillness showed he recognized the threat. The men held their positions for another moment, but they simultaneously lowered their weapons.

Tecumeni stepped to the one who looked to be their leader, positioned in the middle as he was, and held out his arm, which appeared to be a Nephite custom he had learned somewhere.

While they talked in the strange foreign tongue, I took a breath and looked at the Nephites.

The men all looked the same to me, and several of them were openly regarding me. I scowled at them and turned toward the women, who cowered behind their men. At least two of them had Lamanitish blood, which was a shock. What were they doing with these despicable men? One of the dark women was wrapping the wound of Josiah's arrow, high on the arm of a man with hair the color of Ponderosa bark. He had been shot before I entered the clearing, but I knew it would have been Josiah's right and honor to shoot first, and a quick view of the arrow on the ground confirmed it.

It served them right, being on our land as they were. And if they were here with the Nephites who had fought in our village, it would serve them right if they all had wounds, and much more severe. Even I could see that man's wound was nothing. Their conversation continued on, and though I wondered what was happening, I was uninterested in the foreign words until Tec said something about Sarai, the Nephite girl who had betrayed us all.

"Sarai!" I exclaimed and marched up to Tecumeni. He was taking this too far. "I knew it! I knew this was about her!"

"Be quiet," Tecumeni said. "Do you want to show these men more of your bad manners?"

I crossed my arms and glared at him.

"You interrupted my conversation with Josiah," he complained.

"I saved your life!" I indicated the Nephites behind him. "And theirs."

"I had it under control."

At this, their leader laughed. He sent two of the men out of the clearing, probably to make sure Josiah didn't circle back, and then he spoke to one of their women.

She looked so Lamanite as she stepped forward that I felt instantly at ease with her, though I didn't want to because she was willingly consorting with these Nephites—our enemies.

"I am Melia of Ishmael," she said. "Thank you for what you said to that man, Josiah."

"I want that arrow," I said, motioning to Josiah's arrow on the ground. "It is mine."

She looked to the arrow and said easily, "Then you shall have it. Now, how did you and your brother come to know my kinsmen?"

"Those Nephites cannot possibly be your kinsmen," I said. It was too disgusting to fathom.

She actually laughed. "But they are. My father married an Ammonite woman, though Leah is Lamanite by birth to be sure."

"A traitor?"

"Of course not," she laughed again as she drew me to the side of the clearing. She spoke brief words to the woman who had bandaged the wound, a beautiful woman with coal black hair, and then she stooped to retrieve the arrow. When I saw that she intended to use the water from her water skin to wash the Nephite blood from the arrow, I placed a hand over hers.

"Leave it," I said.

She regarded me silently for a moment and then returned her water skin to her belt and offered me Josiah's arrow.

We sat together and watched the other women prepare venison for a meal and for travel, and I tried to slow the beating of my heart as she explained how she had come to be a dirty Nephite.

"Leah's husband was the king of the Ammonites. Perhaps you have heard of them. They call themselves the Anti-Nephi Lehis."

"Traitors," I repeated.

"They joined the church of God," she agreed. "A Nephite religion. And they received much persecution from our people in return."

"They deserved it."

She shrugged. "My father killed Leah's husband in battle, but when he saw the man held no weapon, that his people had come out in peace, he felt great remorse. From that day forward he began making reparations to Leah's family— four small children and herself. The youngest was still a babe in the womb. The way Leah tells it, Father made himself such a nuisance, she couldn't help but fall in love with him."

Lamanites falling in love with Nephites? It was unthinkable.

"You will come to the Land of Melek with us and you may stay with my Father and Leah. You could stay with my husband and me," she indicated the handsome Lamanite man in the clearing—the only handsome man in the clearing, "but we travel a great deal for my father's business."

She didn't want someone like me in her home while she was away, she meant.

I had impulsively tracked Tec out of our village the day he left with Sarai, but I wasn't going back. Not without Tec. But these people? The widow of the Ammonite king and a man of the upper class?

"I couldn't stay with them," I said. And if they knew of the humble village where I came from, they wouldn't let me.

"They would welcome you."

"No, they wouldn't."

"You will see," she said. "Now, are you hungry?"

I had endured the mortification of eating Sarai's corn cakes. I could endure this venison. The deer had been shot on Lamanite ground, after all. But from now on, I would do my own hunting.

I hadn't known Tec didn't plan to return to our home in Ani-Anti, so I did not have a large travel pack like the others here—only provisions for a day that I had long since used. But I tucked the arrow into my small pack, the fletching sticking out the end, and followed Melia to the fire where the prepared food was warm and fragrant.

And then I stood stone still and appalled while the people said a prayer over it. A prayer to their Nephite god.

Chapter 2

The waterfall in Melek reminded me of the cistern at home where the women took their wash and the boys snuck away on hot days to swim. The churning water calmed and pooled before wending its way back into the lower river. It was perfect for swimming, and a swim, I thought with a sigh as I stepped into it, was just what I needed.

Tecumeni came with me sometimes, swam through the cool water with me, but today I was alone.

Together we had walked away from our village. My brother and I had been in Melek for six moons now, and I often wondered how Mother was getting along without us to shoulder our portions of the work. Guilt was not a sufficient word to describe my feelings about leaving, but if it was coupled with helplessness, it might come close.

Caleb would be a help to her, I knew, but feeding a family was a lot to put on the shoulders of a fourteen year old. I was all too familiar with the weight of it. Tecumeni and I had been just fourteen when Father had been killed in the battle at Cumeni. Father's death—it had made my mother a widow and my twin brother the head of our family.

I listened to the rush of water, quieter here than at the base of the falls, as I floated on my back and gently stroked through the water. It couldn't be undone now. I had followed

Tec into the forest, and I could not go home.

I wondered if Uncle Zaaron had survived his wounds from that day. Tec and half the men here had assured me the wounds were not fatal, but I had seen all the blood—on his arm and chest, his leathern kilt, dripping down in a trail as he limped back into the village leaning heavily on Josiah. I had not looked closely at the actual wound—because I had been looking at Josiah. Fatal or not, one of the Ammonite men had struck my uncle with the sword. I would never know which one, and I hated them all for it.

But the Ammonite people had taken me in, cared for me, fed me each day, and it was a bitter herb to swallow. I survived on their kindness, and I hated them all the more for it. But they did not view me as their enemy, and I often wondered why. Had they not been taught to hate my people as we had been taught to hate them?

The tops of the trees were swaying in the breeze, and as I idly floated in the pool, I wondered if Josiah was happy with his new bride. It was childish of me, but I hoped he wasn't. I tried not to think about him, but it was shameful how often I thought of his shaved head and his beautiful dark skin, his brusque manner that, in private moments, could actually turn tender, and the way he held his bare shoulders as if nothing could hurt him—and nothing could.

Josiah was the greatest warrior to come out of our village. He had never been so much as wounded in battle, or so the stories went, and they were practically legends. He was ruthless, decisive, unyielding. He took what he wanted and left what he did not.

I shut my eyes.

He had touched my face once, looked fiercely into my eyes, and said—no, *vowed*—he would return for me when the wars were over.

He did return.

And that was where I stopped myself. I never let myself think beyond that moment when he had walked into the village without my father. It was too humiliating.

I turned my thoughts back to my current circumstances.

Melia had been right all those months ago. Her father had welcomed Tecumeni and me warmly into his home. He and his wife, Leah, had five children between them, and they were all grown and gone from home—all grown and gone but their youngest son, Darius.

I didn't know the other children well, but Darius was...interesting. He lived with Kalem and Leah too, but he was seldom there. He traveled a lot, or maybe stayed with his flock of sheep, but he didn't stay in the village if there was anywhere else he could be. At least, that was how it seemed to me.

"It has something to do with Sarai," Tec had told me once. "He is punishing himself or something, from what I gather."

Tecumeni had been trained in the army to gather information. He had been taught the Nephite tongue so he could blend in and spy on our enemies. Zaaron had seen to it.

Tec could understand everything that went on in this village, and not just the things people said out loud.

As for myself, I could understand only a little, and I chose to understand nothing. But, despite my best effort to keep the ugly Nephite words out of my head, I had learned the language of daily life with its basic phrases and greetings.

I told myself it was traitorous to willingly speak the Nephite words, but the truth was, I couldn't do it. Even when I knew the right words in my head, I couldn't make my mouth form them. I usually refused to even try to speak it, but I didn't know how much longer I could get by.

"Why did you follow me here if you were only going to spend your life sulking about it?" Tec had asked once when we were sitting in the courtyard together. Tec was splitting logs and I was grinding wheat on the milling stone.

"I didn't know you planned to stay here forever! I didn't know you would never go home! I didn't know we would spend our life in enemy lands!"

I had caught Leah watching us from the corner of her eye and been embarrassed for letting such a personal piece of myself be known. Though Leah still understood the Lamanite languages, she was a Nephite now to be sure, and I had to remember to keep my guard up and my mouth shut.

Tec, Kalem, and Leah indulged me and spoke in Lamanite inside the small house, making it easy to ignore the fact that I needed to start speaking the local language. But because I was stuck in the tiny Nephite village, I would have to communicate with its residents.

Eventually.

I guessed I was still hoping Tec would take me home.

Tec was the only one who could take me, and he refused to leave. He was even making plans to stay permanently in the village, to tether himself firmly here.

My brother was going to marry one of the village girls.

That burned hot on so many levels for me.

But when I set aside my anger and jealousy, I was worried for him. Tec had been taken with Chloe from the first moment he'd seen her, and she didn't seem to like him in return. She didn't seem to like anyone. Even disregarding the undeniable fact that Chloe was a Nephite, our people's enemy, she was unpleasant and outright rude. She was inconsiderate, selfish, and disrespectful. She reminded me of Alena back home, a girl Tec could barely tolerate on a good day, though, bless him, he had always tried.

Chloe was beautiful. I could admit that, but only because it couldn't be denied. I just hoped Tec wasn't basing his affection on that. I worried he was, because I couldn't see anything else to base it on.

The worst part of the whole situation was that Chloe didn't know yet. Her father had agreed and everything was in place, but nobody dared to tell her that, minus a ceremony and some documents, she was betrothed. Her father was at his wit's end, I thought, trying to discipline her, so he had made arrangements to hand that all over to Tecumeni.

"It's not that she is bad," Tec had so optimistically explained to me. "It's not that she is doing any harm, only that she is not doing any good."

I'd had a good scoff at that.

"If you won't hear when I speak of the spirit of God—"

"I won't," I broke in.

"Then you cannot understand how I know this is the right thing for me," he finished.

Tec was always so steady. He was always prepared, and he was smart. How many girls could say they actually admired their brothers? I did. I always had. But this issue of the imminent betrothal being the right thing for him? I couldn't support it. But like my very presence in this village, and this was the part that rankled, there was no other choice.

That was how we had left the issue of Chloe, the Nephite girl who was not doing any good.

I understood her father's reasons for arranging an early betrothal for her. She was only thirteen, but the way she went around doing what she wanted with no regard for consequences was not safe.

Tec would become her guardian in the way only a kinsman could. He would be able to accompany her on her wild jaunts. Or, if the situation called for it, he was actually capable of making her stay where she was supposed to.

Hemni had to work. He had to see to his shop and his animals and his fields. If Chloe had stayed home more often than she did, her mother might have had more influence on her. But she didn't stay home, and Dinah was as frustrated as Hemni.

She had done it to herself, but she was going to hate it, and my brother was going to bear the brunt of that hatred.

But Tec had made an agreement with Hemni, and I knew he would honor it in every way.

Unlike some men.

I waded out of the churning pool, feeling the sharpness of the stones on my feet.

I was sitting glumly on the bank combing my hair dry when I noticed two people come into the meadow. I was expecting them, but not here—they were expected in the village. The woman waved. I got to my feet, gave a small wave in return, and waited for them to cross the meadow.

"Do you remember me? I'm Keturah," she said. "This is Gideon."

"I remember," I said, recalling the time we had spent traveling north together into the Nephite lands. Gideon was the reason her kinsmen had traveled to my home near Jerusalem. He had been captured in battle and transported to a prison there to await presentation to the king as a prize of war.

Keturah turned and took in the falls. "I've never seen the river run so high," she said. "And I've been coming here for many years." She shared a look with her husband. "It's kind of a special place for me."

I nodded, not knowing what to say to that. I only understood half of her words. Did she want to swim? Did she want me to leave?

Gideon must have interpreted the look on my face because he spoke to me in my own language. I was surprised, but not because he could speak the language—many here did—but because he could speak it so well. The Ammonites here in Melek were refugees from the southern lands, and had sought religious asylum from the Nephite government. Many of them spoke my language or a similar dialect of it. Kalem and Leah both spoke with heavy accents, each different, but Gideon spoke as if he had been raised in my village.

"We wanted to stop here on our way into the village. It's been a long time since we were here together," he confided.

I nodded again. "I was just going back," I said. "I'll leave you to be alone."

15

Gideon laughed. "We are never alone now." He indicated the baby sleeping in a pack strapped close to Keturah's heart.

I couldn't help a smile and reached out to touch the baby's head. It was covered in hair the color of his father's, woody brown with honey highlights that caught the sun. It was soft. But when I touched him he sucked in a sudden breath, and I pulled my hand back.

Keturah laughed low in her throat. "You didn't bother him. Go ahead."

I didn't understand all the words until Gideon translated them for me, and even then, I didn't reach out for the baby again.

"Did Darius travel with you?" I asked.

"He did," Gideon replied, and I didn't miss the quick flick of his eyes toward his wife.

"I was only asking because..." I tried to think of a reason. "Because Leah misses him so much when he is away," I finished lamely.

The baby, Gabriel if I remembered right, started to fuss.

"Let's get walking again so Gabe will settle down," Keturah said.

Gideon nodded and said, "If you're indeed ready to go back to the village, we'll walk with you."

I bent to gather my things.

"I thought you would understand the language better by now," Gideon said as we started through the meadow. The comment was conversational, not accusing, but I bristled.

"I do understand." I glanced at Keturah. She was

walking next to her husband, but humming softly to the baby and didn't seem to be listening to us. I looked at my feet as they sifted through the meadow grasses, already long from the wet weather. Lowering my voice, I admitted, "I can't form the words. My tongue was not meant to say these words."

He chuckled. "Six months of practice has not made it easier?"

I twisted my lips. I never tried to use the words. It would be like admitting I wanted to stay here, and I definitely did not want to stay here.

He read my expression right, but only said, "The main difference in our languages in not in the words, but in the way we use them."

I snorted. "Easy for you to say."

He was quiet for a moment, and I could sense him studying me. Finally he said, "I was under the impression you didn't want to learn the Nephite language."

The only place he would have gotten an idea like that was if someone had given it to him. I thought of all the letters Leah wrote to her daughter, and I bristled again. Had I been the subject in some of those letters?

"I don't," I bit out but then sighed and tipped my head back to look into the sky. "But I am finding it to be more and more necessary."

He nodded.

"And," I said, my voice sounding embarrassingly forlorn, "I am often very lonely."

I could almost feel his pity, and I looked away, wishing very much that I hadn't said any of that. He was not my friend. He was a stranger.

But this stranger began to explain languages to me in a way no one else ever had. Maybe in a way no one else ever could. He was nonchalant, easy in his knowledge, and readily shared what he knew. As he spoke, a calmness came over me, and I realized he was not always speaking my familiar Lamanite nor the Nephite I had heard so much of, but many languages. He moved between them as easily as breathing, and though it was impossible, I understood him.

"Would you like a blessing to help you?"

I had lived among the Ammonites long enough know what they termed a blessing. It seemed useless and silly.

"Of course not!" I spit out, shattering the calmness that had enveloped me and feeling instantly petulant for being rude. But still, I did not want a blessing. I did not want anyone to put his hands on me and speak the prayer words to their god. I bit my lip and avoided Gideon's eyes.

"God does not want you to feel isolated and alone, Ava."

Why had this turned from a lesson in language to a sermon about the Nephite god? As if he or it would care about my feelings!

"If you will pray to God each evening and ask for help, you will know the language in no time," Gideon said, the calmness almost radiating off him again.

I hesitated, but scoffed.

He looked up into the trees and changed the subject to the only thing that made me angrier than talk of a god I neither cared about nor believed in.

"They say your father was at Cumeni."

I swallowed and was relieved when my voice came out

even. "They say you were, too. Your kinsmen, I mean."

The breeze rustled his hair. "It's been six or seven years since I was last at Cumeni, but that is a battle I will not forget."

There was no response to that—nothing I could say without shrieking at him, so I clamped my lips shut and held the shrieks inside.

"Fiercest, most determined warriors I ever saw," Gideon said, giving his head a shake as if he could not quite believe it.

I was sure he meant it to be a compliment, but what did ferocity matter when my father was dead?

"That's how I know you're fierce and determined enough to learn the language, to learn anything you want. To do anything you want."

A smile broke over my face, and I looked away to hide it from him. "Your wife is the only woman who would think the gift of ferocity was a compliment," I said, the words coming easily in Lamanite.

Gideon's laugh was hearty, and my anger toward him ebbed.

"What is it you have said to make my grumpy husband laugh so hard?"

I looked over at Keturah, astonished that I had understood her words so easily. Then I looked at Gideon and laughed too.

How good it felt to laugh!

Perhaps I could find a friend here. Perhaps I would not always be alone and sad.

We emerged from the thick vegetation into the village,

where we found Tec talking to Hemni in the middle of the road.

The look on Tec's face was a dangerous one. I had seen it before—when he had put Lamech and Sarai behind us in the woods and told me he was not going back home. I had seen it when he had informed me he meant to join with the church of God. And I had seen it again when he had told me he meant to betroth himself to Hemni's beautiful daughter.

Keturah went directly to Hemni and gave him a hug. It was awkward with the baby between them, but they both laughed, and Hemni put his hand on Gabe's head just like I had done.

I went to Tecumeni's side.

"Come on," Tec said. "I want to go check on Dare's sheep before the evening meal." But he was looking past me toward Chloe's house.

"Perhaps I should stay to help Leah with the meal," I said, eying the people who were starting to gather around Keturah.

"I'm sure she has it taken care of. She's been expecting them for weeks."

I looked at the house and could see that the cook fire was already burning in the yard. Leah would come out in a moment and see that her daughter was here in the village with the baby.

"Alright," I agreed. I would feel out of place among the reunion. I could already see the village women looking up from their work in interest. I turned to Gideon. "Will you tell Leah we will be back for the evening meal?"

"If you promise you will be."

It was kind of him to offer an invitation to what would surely be a family celebration, to make sure we felt welcome, but all I could give him in return was a half-hearted smile.

Tec and I walked out of the village along a path that led to the city of Melek, but we turned off onto a smaller trail long before we reached its busy streets. When the pastures came into view, naturally terraced along a small mountain range, I secretly basked in the views. It was pretty and green and open along the foothills, completely unlike the village, which seemed to have been built in a large thicket of trees. The only thing it was missing was a view of the sea.

"Do you want to tell me what's eating you up?" Tec asked as we began to ascend toward the pastures Darius and his oldest brother, Micah, kept.

"What do you mean?" I asked, knowing full well what he meant.

"Don't pretend," was all he said.

I sighed. After a moment, I sighed again.

"Do you miss home?"

Not as much as I should have. "I miss Mother and Caleb and the others. They need us, Tec, and we just left them."

He was thoughtful for a moment. I knew he felt guilty about it, too. "Caleb can supply meat for them, and Zaaron will not let them go hungry."

"Do you really think Zaaron is all right? Do you think he healed?"

"His wound was superficial. I thought I told you that."

"You did."

"It was part of a staged rescue."

21

"No." I shook my head. "Tec, no. I cannot believe Zaaron, our uncle Zaaron, assisted you in that. I cannot believe he helped you break those Nephites out of prison. It is beyond comprehension."

"Believe it. It happened."

"But how? Why would he even consider it? The High—" I cut myself off and glanced around. I couldn't help the habit I had formed so long ago. We were not ever to speak of Zaaron's rank in the Order of the Nehors. I was not even supposed to know about it.

"The High Assassin? That's an honorary title. They don't actually kill people."

"Yes they do!"

"Not people like Sarai."

"And people like Gideon?"

He brushed it off, avoiding the answer—because important chief captains like Gideon were exactly the kind of person they killed.

"Zaaron did nothing but fake an injury."

"The blood was real."

"It was only blood."

I laughed. "You are impossible to argue with."

"Then why do you persist?"

We entered a gate in the lowest of the pastures. The next level up supported a craggy outcropping from which a shepherd could see for quite a distance, and Tec set his path for it. I had been to the fields before with Tec and Micah, once Darius was even there, and I loved the view from the rocks.

"I want to go home," I persisted.

"No you don't."

"Ha!"

I caught a sideways glance from my brother. Here it came.

"There is nothing for you there," he argued.

Not anymore, he meant. And he was right. So starkly right.

I twisted my lips. "At least I would be with my own people. I would be able to help Mother with the children."

"Noble," he scoffed lightly. "Do you really want to spend the rest of your life raising someone else's children?"

I blinked back a sudden sting of tears. "Don't be cruel," I said in defeat.

"Sis," he said. He hardly ever called me that, and it sounded so pitying. "Do you still think it was your fault, what happened?"

"No." I said, but I thought about it as we climbed the outcropping and knew it wasn't the complete truth. "I know it is not my fault," I said slowly, taking a seat on a rock at the top. Tec remained standing, scanning the pastures. "But I *feel* that it is my fault, or rather, that there is some fault with me." I choked on the last part, but said it anyway. "I feel as if I'm the ugliest girl on earth."

He didn't look at me. I had made him uncomfortable. After a moment, he asked, "Did you love him?" I opened my mouth to respond but he said, "I mean really love him. Or are you just angry at what he did?"

Wasn't my anger proof I had loved him?

I looked down and spit out the truth. "I thought I did, but I loved him in the way only a young girl can love, blind and wholehearted."

23

Free, innocent, and so foolish.

Tec laughed a little. "Is that different than real love?"

"I have to believe it is," I said. "Mother said you can only love like that once."

"Ava."

I didn't even want to recognize the tone in his voice, let alone admit what it meant. I turned, shifting my body away from him and looked plaintively at the sheep.

CHAPTER 3

When Tec and I walked back into the village, I could see the celebration for the new baby was much larger than Leah had anticipated. I felt guilty for going to the pastures when I had felt that I should stay and help her.

Leah was holding Gabriel and laughing with an old woman who sat next to her. She looked very happy, even joyful, and the presence of the extra people did not seem to annoy her at all. Mother would have been beside herself making sure each guest was taken care of, or trying to. Leah, it seemed, expected them to take care of themselves.

And they did. I noticed several of the village women, Dinah foremost among them, helping with the food—serving, offering more, and clearing dishes away. I knew Dinah wanted to hold Gabriel too, but she hesitated when Leah stopped her with a hand on her arm and offered the child to her. I couldn't help but wonder what caused her to be wary. Leah and Dinah were the oldest of friends, as close as sisters. Dinah had many children of her own. What was it about this one that put the hesitation in her open, loving arms?

Tec and I observed the gathering from the fringes of the courtyard.

The men spilled out of the yard into the street. They talked and laughed. The young ones played ball. The children ran up and down the street and between the houses. Chloe sat on the sturdy fence in front of her home, watching the gathering like Tec and I were. I didn't think Tec had noticed her yet, but I knew his eyes were scanning for her.

I waited until they found her before I asked, "When are you going to tell her?"

Letting out a breath, he glanced meaningfully around. "Not tonight."

"Someone has to tell her."

"Tomorrow. I'm taking her to the market. I'll tell her then."

"She'll be mad."

"Understatement."

I laughed. "Just try to remember it's not you she's angry at."

"No, she'll be plenty angry at me." But he laughed too.

I started to ask him why he was doing it, why he wanted to marry a girl like her, but I stopped myself. I knew why. Well, I knew what he'd say about the holy spirit. I just didn't understand it.

"Hemni will meet us at the government building after that," he continued.

"Is that what you were discussing today?"

"Yes. We will see the lawyer." He paused. "Hemni does not think she will blatantly disobey him."

"It is not too late to leave it undone."

He let out a breath. "It is already done. I will not go back on my word, nor do I want to. This is the right thing, Ava."

A knot formed in my stomach. I knew he wanted this

very much, but I thought it was a mistake.

"Are you going to talk to her tonight?" He didn't spend a lot of time trying to make friends with her. I thought he was hesitant to be overbearing, but because of his hesitance, they were little more than acquaintances. They were not close friends, though I had to admit they did seem to get along well enough. "Or do you plan to spring the whole thing on her tomorrow?"

Tec crossed his arms over his chest and gazed back over his shoulder at her for a moment. "Hemni thinks it will be best if she doesn't have time to think about it."

I thought of my own betrothal—how excited I had been, the plans I had made, how long I had dreamt about it in foolish anticipation before it all fell apart. I was supposed to wed Josiah when he came home from the war in the Nephite lands. But then, he was supposed to come home with my father.

Oh papa, I thought. *How could you have chosen such a dishonorable man? How did he fool us both?*

"But why won't Zaaron make him uphold his contract?" I had cried to my mother.

My mother. Harried with so many little children under foot. A widow, just barely, and in her own grief.

I had run into the forest to be alone, to cry alone. Mother had followed me and sat beside me on the forest floor. She had let me rest my head in her lap, and I had sobbed into her skirts as she'd undone the tie in my hair and begun to comb through the long strands with her fingers.

"Why would Zaaron force you to marry a man who would not honor a promise? Now that we know Josiah's true nature, why would Zaaron dishonor *you* with such a match?"

"Because I love him!" I had wailed into her skirts, answering in the only way a girl with a broken heart could.

Tec was waving his hand in front of my face. I slapped it away and laughed.

"You should go talk to her anyway." I could see he wanted to. He was already half turned in that direction. "Go," I coaxed.

"You'll be okay?"

Why would he ask that? I was a grown girl. I was as old as he was. I was supposed to be at least as strong and wise. Why did he see only the weakness in me?

Because I *was* weak.

Because I never spoke anymore. Because there was something sad in my laugh and had been long before I ever followed him out of Ani-Anti.

As I watched him walk toward Chloe, I thought I should probably do what anyone else here would do and pray for him.

Anyone else but me. I didn't even know who or what I would pray to.

I watched for a moment more as Tec leaned against the little fence. He said hello. He touched her shoulder. She eyed him for a moment and then hopped down off the fence. She listened to what he said, and she smiled up at him.

How did Tec hold his heart together when the hoyden had a smile like that?

I watched them walk out of the village toward the West Road. They could get to the falls that way, and I wondered if that was where he was taking her. It was strange to think of my brother taking a girl anywhere. But then again, he was the one who was strong and brave.

With so many unfamiliar people in the village, I felt awkward and wished I could go with Tec, but that would have been even more awkward.

There was a pond behind the house, just a short walk through the forest, and I decided I might as well be alone if I was going to feel lonely anyway.

Many of the people smiled at me and said hello as I passed through the yard. I tried to smile, too, but it was completely fake. Couldn't they tell I didn't like them?

The pond was pretty. Kalem had told me it was not always present, but this year the seasonal rains had been so heavy the pond sprang up and hadn't yet dried. The water was not good for drinking, but Leah and I had been laundering clothing there and we had seen many of the village children playing in and around it. I could wade all the way through it, from one side to the other—it wasn't much deeper than my knees—and that was what I planned to do. There was something about the mud in my toes that I liked. It made me miss the sea, but the memories were fond and brought me peace.

When I got to the pond, I had kicked off my sandals before I noticed I was not alone. Sarai and Lamech sat on the bank tossing stones into the water and talking quietly. They were to be betrothed, something I resented, something that cut me nearly as deep as Tecumeni's betrothal. I drew their attention when I entered the clearing, and Sarai smiled.

Unlike the other people in the village, they did know I didn't like them.

"Hi, Ava," Sarai said. She motioned me over, then thought better of it and got to her feet.

She wasn't as timid as she had been when Tec had first brought her home to Ani-Anti. She was no longer the stranger in a village full of her enemies.

I was.

For a moment I stared at her, remembering her in my village, and I thought of how she must have felt there, how frightened she must have been. I thought of walking to the cistern with her, hoping she would like my brother because I could clearly see he liked her. I hated that she had lied to him and been so completely false, but I remembered seeing her hanging the wash with Alena—a guest hanging the wash! That hadn't been false. Her kindness had been very genuine.

Tec had seen that in her. She had secured his friendship in the village. She had been confident of it, but his friendship was all she'd had. Even her kinsmen outside the village hadn't been able to keep her out of the prison.

Tec was all I had, too.

And now he had Chloe.

Seeing Sarai there, smiling at me, clearly willing to offer me her friendship, I made a decision I had been struggling with and hoped her kindness would still be genuine.

"Your people talk of forgiveness." I looked from Sarai to Lamech to include him in the conversation also, but I could tell from his eyes that he did not understand my Lamanite words as Sarai did. "I do not want to be angry with you for what you did. If Tec had been imprisoned, I would have done the same."

30

"I know you would have," Sarai said more gently than I deserved.

"I liked you when we first met. I do not want to be at odds with you. I...I am in need of friends here." It galled me to admit it, let alone ask it of Sarai. "But I do not know how to forgive."

There, now she would understand.

If she only knew the grudge I still harbored against Josiah and the pain over my father's death, she would know I was not capable of forgiveness.

She giggled a little. "It is easily learned."

"One may learn this?"

"Of course."

I expected her to enlighten me on just how simple of a process forgiveness was, but her eyes drifted over my shoulder in the moment before I felt the presence of someone behind me.

Lamech raised a hand of greeting to whoever was behind me.

I turned, and when I saw it was Darius, I flushed. I actually felt my face heat up. He had said nothing, done nothing, scarcely more than glanced at me. In fact, no one said anything and his eyes seemed fixed on Sarai.

There was a tension between these people I didn't understand. Tec had learned of it, but now, standing between Sarai and Darius, Lamech too, I sensed it myself. Sarai kept her smile in place, but something else changed—the brightness in her eyes maybe. Lamech moved closer to her, offering his support or perhaps his protection.

I didn't understand it. Darius was not dangerous. He

was quiet and troubled by something, I thought, but kind of sweet too. For a Nephite. Tec had said Sarai was the reason Darius left the village so much, and I could see now for myself that he was probably right.

"Hi, Dare," Sarai said after a small hesitation. "You're back."

"I wouldn't miss your betrothal, Sarai." There was an awkward pause. Sarai looked briefly down at her hands, and Lamech shifted his weight to the other foot. Darius stood stone still, and I looked between them all, trying to comprehend the words they had spoken. Then Darius spoke again, but the words came too fast and I couldn't understand what he said.

Sarai turned to me. "I think you came here for the solitude." She glanced at the dark-eyed boy next to her. "Lamech prefers the solitude, also, but we should be with our guests. We will talk later."

"But Darius..."

"Darius says he is just passing by."

I hoped I hid my disappointment. "All right. Until later then."

She smiled at me. Every time she did that, I knew why Tec had helped her save her kinsmen. She placed a hand on my shoulder in farewell and then passed me and did the same to Darius. I turned to watch his face and saw what I hoped I wouldn't. He glanced at Lamech before returning the gesture. Lamech just nodded to us both and left with Sarai.

"You can stay," I said, hoping the Nephite words I used were the right ones, and reassured that they were when he didn't burst into laughter.

"I planned to," he said and sat near the pond where Sarai and Lamech had been.

"What is planned?" I asked him.

"Something that never really happens," he said.

I tilted my head to the side, thinking about the words he said, trying to make sense of them.

"You didn't understand that, did you?" he asked.

Confused by that too, I just shrugged. If only Gideon could be by my side all the time. The calmness he had would help me understand everything.

Darius grinned, but gave a small sigh. He indicated the spot next to him.

Taking it to be an invitation, I sat there, blushing again. He took a moment to openly notice it, studying me with a curious eye, but then turned to the pond. We sat in silence for a time, tossing pebbles and twigs into the water like Lamech and Sarai had been doing. I didn't look up at him and only saw his long legs stretched in front of us and his hands as he selected the pebbles from the ground between us. We watched the small stones hit the water and make ripples that grew and reached our feet at the water's edge.

"You have to learn the language," Darius said after a while.

I had heard that Nephite sentence many times. "I know," I said.

I sensed him move back a little, and I looked up at his face. His brows were raised in surprise.

"While you are gone, I learn. I understand a little," I said tentatively. "If you talk slow."

I reached into my bag and pulled out a pitaya Melia

had brought me from her father's tables at the market. I had been so relieved to know I could find the pink fruit here. They reminded me of home and of my mother and father.

"Knife?" I asked him.

He produced one from a scabbard on his opposite arm. I hesitated before I took it into my hand. I had seen him use it before. It was of fine workmanship and very distinctive, set with precious stones he did not seem to even notice. Anyone who had seen him use it once would remember it belonged to him. It was not the knife of a shepherd, but he treated it like one.

After cutting into the pitaya in one long, smooth slice, I offered him half of it.

He took it and thanked me. Politely. Like we were strangers.

As we ate the pitaya together, he pointed to my bare feet. I pointed to my sandals near the bank of the pond.

"I planned to walk on water," I said, making a motion with two of my fingers to indicate walking and thinking of how the mud would feel in my toes.

He looked confused.

"Something that never happens," I tried to clarify.

His grin was swift. And crooked. He took both our fruit peels and tossed them into the forest. Then he got to his feet and held out a hand to me. I stared at it for a moment but let him help me to my feet, too. Then, toeing out of his own sandals, he led me into the water.

Despite everything, the mud in my toes made me smile, and as it turned out, smiling was a language Darius and I had in common.

We splashed through the water together and when we were knee-deep, Darius said, "Ava, I think you're pretty."

I didn't know what *pretty* meant, and I looked at him blankly, hoping he would say it a different way so I didn't have to ask him to clarify.

He sighed lightly again, and I thought he was frustrated or even irritated, but he touched my cheek with the back of his hand.

"Here," he said as he ran a finger over my brow. "And here."

I looked at him apologetically. I still did not know what he meant or why he had touched me. Had I splashed mud onto my face?

He considered me for a long moment, his eyes searching mine, and then he bent and splashed me with a handful of water. I turned instinctively and sucked in a breath as the clap of cold water hit me, but I giggled and heard his deeper laugh behind me.

"Let's go," he said.

I did know what *go* meant, so I waded from the water with him.

I thought he meant to leave, but instead of reaching for his sandals, he pulled a small leather ball from his satchel. Motioning me to stand across from him, he backed up a few steps and began to toss it and hit it, sending smiles my way, showing me how to play his game. But when he tossed it to me, it just hit me in the chest and landed at my feet.

"Sorry," I said and picked it up.

He came to me, and I thought he meant to snatch the ball away and return it to his satchel. I didn't want him to take the ball—which I could see now was a small leather pouch filled with something, probably beans. I didn't want him to put it away. I liked the smile in his eyes. I wanted him to continue teaching me so I held the ball tightly. He tried to take it, so I put it behind my back.

Darius laughed and his eyes lit. I had never seen his eyes look so bright before. Had he never shown a genuine smile in all the time I had known him?

I hadn't intended to flirt with him, but when he reached around my back for the ball, I froze, realizing what I had done. I let my fingers fall open, let him take it with no more struggle. I didn't need to learn the game.

But to my surprise, he began showing me more slowly. Before long, I was getting it and we were both laughing as we simply kicked the ball back and forth.

When the sun began to fall behind the trees, Darius snatched the ball out of the air and nodded toward the village. It was time to go, he meant.

He picked up my sandals and handed them to me. Then he picked up his own, and we carried them back to the village dangling from our fingers, walking over the soft earth without them on.

CHAPTER 4

Tecumeni was back in the village, and Darius walked me over to where he sat with Hemni and his sons.

Tec's new family.

I took in the sight, and the lightheartedness I had felt with Darius vanished.

"Ava."

I dragged my eyes from Tec and turned to Darius, helplessly loving the sound of my name on his lips. But with so many unfamiliar sounds here, how could I not?

He cast a quick glance toward Tecumeni before putting himself between us. With his back to Tec, he touched my cheek again. "Right here," he repeated in a low voice. He held my gaze for a moment more, but then his eyes flicked past my shoulder and he abruptly jerked away as if he suddenly remembered he had something to do or somewhere to be. He nodded to the men and stalked out of the courtyard.

Tecumeni and all three of the others were looking at me when I turned back to them, though Hemni and Zeke were trying not to.

"What does *pretty* mean?" I asked Tecumeni before I could forget the word.

He wet his lips. "Did Darius say that to you? Did he use that word—*pretty*?"

"Yes."

His inquisitive frown broke suddenly into a smile, and all four heads turned in the direction Darius had gone.

"What did he mean?" I demanded. "What did he say to me?"

Was it some kind of joke? I really did have to learn Nephite.

He tried to wipe the smile from his face, but he couldn't. "He thinks you have beauty."

"But that is impossible."

Tec was speaking to the other men, probably telling them the same absurd thing he had just told me.

"That is impossible," I repeated. "What did he really mean?"

"He meant you are beautiful. Now personally, I have to disagree."

He was joking, but I felt my chin wavering, and when he noticed it and jumped to his feet to reassure me he had only been kidding, tears burst from my eyes.

At home in Ani-Anti, I was tolerable to look at. I had seen my reflection in the clear waters of the cistern. I was not hideous. Here, where I was so different, so dark-skinned, so tall and gangly, so old, I was absolutely ugly. And nothing Tec could say would change it.

I wiped my tears with the heel of my hand and tried to keep my head high as I walked away from him. I heard him say something in that dratted Nephite to the men, but he didn't come after me.

I wished all the people in Kalem and Leah's yard would leave, just pack up their gear and go away. I stomped to the rear of the house and found my tent and my travel pack. Maybe I couldn't go back to Ani-Anti, but I could get out of the village for a while.

The path to the waterfall was beautiful and peaceful. All the talking in the strange language had ceased, and it was silent. I was alone in thoughts that came in comfortable, familiar Lamanite—thoughts that centered on one particular, intriguing Nephite.

But my feelings were all mixed up with homesickness for my past and uncertainty about my future. They were mixed up with grief over my father and bitterness over Josiah.

I had tried to be strong about Josiah's callous betrayal, but when that had not worked, I had tried even harder to disguise my weakness. After the day I had cried into Mother's skirts, I had not spoken of Josiah again. I had not complained—not to Mother, not to my friends, not even to Zaaron, the only one who could have forced Josiah to keep his promise.

Because Mother had been right. I did not deserve to be married to a man who did not honor his commitments.

But did I want to be married to my people's enemy instead? To be a mother to Nephite children? To live my life pretending to tolerate their foolish traditions and their silly beliefs? That's what would happen if I didn't go home.

But, I could not go home, and even if I could, there would be nothing for me there. I had left with a traitor, and I would not be welcomed. Tec said Zaaron would smooth things over with the people, would say that Tec had been a spy who was only following orders, but with the prisoners breaking out of the prison and the Nephites fighting their way out of our village, no one would believe him—though no one would ever contradict him to his face. No, Tec would not be greeted warmly by our people, and neither would I.

The waterfall cascaded down smooth boulders upstream, and the mist made the evening air cool. As I drew closer, my face became damp and my clothes clung to my skin.

I stared into the churning water. I wanted to take off my sandals and dive into it, to kick hard and swim away, but instead I sat down on the bank and let the noise drown out all the foreign words and conflicting thoughts.

An hour had passed, maybe longer, when I became aware of voices and looked up to scan the meadow. I had never met anyone here, but today it seemed to be quite the highway.

Three men emerged from the trees at the far end of the meadow. Their voices mingled with the sounds of the water, but as they came closer their voices became more distinct. They wore tunics and looked to be young Nephite merchants.

But they spoke in Lamanite.

I shouldn't have stared as I did, but their appearance so contradicted their words, my curiosity got the better of me. When the one who was talking looked my way, he caught me staring quite blatantly. His eyes flashed with surprise and when the others noted his sudden silence, they followed his gaze.

I glanced around. The sun was well below the trees and dusk had fallen. Perhaps it wasn't safe to be out here alone.

Quickly getting to my feet, I stood tall and straight as they approached me, though I felt anything but confident.

"Shalal," I said, wanting to speak first.

They all smiled warmly and the man who had caught my eye stepped forward and laid a quick hand on my shoulder—the way the Nephites did.

"I'm Ammon. These are my friends, Elias and Kish."

Elias and Kish each took a turn to lay their hands on my shoulder, but they stepped back to a comfortable distance. All three of them looked to be passably Nephite, though I had seen many with similar coloring in my homeland. Elias was the lightest, with fair skin, cinnamon hair, and a friendly, open smile. Ammon had darker hair like Darius and was just as handsome. The darkness in Kish was in his eyes, though he looked completely respectable in every other way.

"I'm Ava," I said in Lamanite. I was obviously not a Nephite. There was little reason to pretend. Either way, there would be questions.

For a moment, no one said anything. Then Ammon looked around the meadow and asked, "Do you live around here?" The familiar language was like a balm to the edginess I had been feeling.

It was a casual question, proper enough, but I sensed something calculating in it, too.

I considered carefully before I answered. "I'm staying in a village this side of the city. My home is near Jerusalem."

The three men looked at each other, deciding how to proceed, and Ammon said, "You're a long way from home then."

"As are you."

Ammon crossed his arms but his tone stayed light. "Are you a Nephite sympathizer?"

I licked my lips. I was on shaky ground. If I said no, they would ask what I was doing here. If I said yes, I didn't know what they would do.

"I have little choice," I decided on. "I cannot go home. I do what I must."

They each nodded, but stayed silent. I didn't like the way Kish stared at me. I couldn't help taking a slight step away.

"Have you been traveling long?" I asked. I reached into my satchel and pulled some pieces of dried venison from it. It was a far cry from the delicious foods at Leah's tonight, but the men accepted it gratefully.

"Tastes like Nephite venison," Elias said, and there was a small note of distrust in his tone. He was likely hiding the rest of it.

"And you are wearing Nephite tunics," I replied. "Give me your water skins and I will fill them."

Again they looked at one another, but they handed me their water skins.

They resumed talking—they had obviously been in the middle of a conversation—but now they spoke to each other in Nephite. Did they think to hide their conversation from me? Did they think I lived here and did not know the language? I smiled because it was so close to the truth.

I was listening idly at first, but when I heard them talk of Helaman, a Nephite prophet at Zarahemla, the prophet of the people who lived here in Melek, I listened more intently. They spoke fast, like they were native to the Nephite lands. I missed much of what they said, and what I did catch, I could hardly make sense of.

I looked up from the last water skin as Ammon went to a knee next to me.

"It's been a while since I've seen a pretty girl." His eyes glittered with humor or mischief. "All the Nephite women look like dogs."

He was teasing and he had insulted the people who had taken me in, but I smiled. It sounded like something Zaaron would say. It sounded like something the old Tecumeni would have said.

I knew his remark wasn't meant to say I was pretty— I wasn't, not really—but was meant as a commentary on being away from home, hidden among enemies. Like I was.

But my mind kept picking up snatches of the other men's conversation, which was becoming heated. They seemed to talk openly, but I had the feeling that Ammon was trying to distract me from it. I didn't know if Elias and Kish's words were honest, but I knew Ammon's weren't, not entirely. Or if they were, he wasn't using them for an honest purpose.

And yet, when he allowed that the Nephite venison was soft and good, I blushed with pleasure because I had worked side by side with Leah to prepare it.

Ammon smiled when he saw my cheeks were pink. "Did you make this?" he asked, raising the piece of venison a little. "You're learning the Nephite ways," he said. It was teasing still, not accusation, but it stung and I stood up. He stood too, and I passed him his water skin.

"I have to get back," I said. The light was quickly fading. "They will be missing me."

"Who?" Ammon's eyes sharpened as he feigned disinterest in where and with whom I lived.

"My brother. We stay with his friends."

An expression of acceptance crossed Ammon's face, his mouth. As if I owed him any explanation where I slept at night. He took the other two water skins and walked them the short distance to his friends.

I had planned to raise my tent and sleep here in the meadow, but I couldn't now, not with these boys here. I didn't think they were from the gathering in the village. Where were they going this late in the evening? Did they plan to sleep here?

"Goodbye. I wish you well on your journey," I said to Ammon's back and then hurried away through the meadow toward the village, glad I had not already set up the tent.

I was nearly to the tree-line when I heard the grasses rustle behind me and turned. Ammon stopped before me, awkwardly reached out his hand to my shoulder, not at all in the composed manner he had used before.

I glanced past his shoulder to see his friends watching us curiously.

"Here," he said.

I froze and looked blankly at his outstretched hand.

"I believe this is the custom here."

In his hand lay a tie made of cream-colored linen and black onyx beads. It was made to tie around the ankle, and he had been wearing it moments ago when he had knelt next to me at the river.

I reached to take it but hesitated with my hand outstretched. I wasn't very familiar with this custom. What would it mean if I took the tie? What could I give to him in return? What would *that* mean?

44

Ammon glanced back over his shoulder as he said, "We have to go. I don't know if I can come back." He swallowed hard.

If he was nervous, the polite thing for me to do was ease his nerves. I didn't need a custom to tell me what was kind.

I took the tie. It was still warm from being against his skin.

My mind went through a quick inventory of what I had that I might give to him in return. I had already given him the venison. Was that enough? This custom, which was a Nephite one and unfamiliar to me and possibly to Ammon as well, required me to return his small gift with one of my own. It was a sign of friendship and trust.

Our eyes met, and I read the question in his. Could he trust me to keep their mission secret?

He probably wasn't sure if I knew, if I had heard their plans. But that didn't matter, because I did know. I had heard their plans.

I slipped the bracelet of hammered copper from my wrist and held it out. It was a piece of fine quality, but it wasn't feminine. Still, I liked it and it was a piece from my home, one of the only pieces I had left. I suppressed a sigh. It would look better on him anyway.

"I will keep your secret," I said softly.

Confirmation crossed his features, and he gave a slight, curt nod.

I have no one to tell anyway, I told myself as I walked back to the village through the trees, feeling the soft weight of Ammon's bracelet on my wrist, but I knew it wasn't true.

There were many people to tell, starting with Tecumeni and Kalem, and I probably should tell them both.

But I didn't care what happened to their prophet.

So why did I feel what I suspected was guilt?

CHAPTER 5

The way to the waterfall was not a secret, but the path was not well-traveled and it was hard to find if you didn't know exactly where it was. I followed it back, placing my feet carefully, as it was hard to see the dim forest floor.

When I was nearly back to the main path, I noticed Darius coming from the direction of the village. He looked to be in deep thought and nearly ran into me before he noticed I was in his way.

Instead of looking me in the eye and greeting me properly, he glanced over my shoulder and said, "What are you doing here?"

The boy I had laughed with at the pond was gone, replaced by this scowling boy who slipped silently through the falling night.

I had been grappling with my conscience, prepared to tell him and his kinsmen about Ammon's plans, but his sharp words, the clear disinterest in his eyes made me bristle.

It would not do to put so much blind trust in another boy as I had done with Josiah. It would not do to trust a Nephite boy. Perhaps the Nephite god would just have to protect his own prophet.

I brushed past Darius so he wouldn't see the hurt in my eyes.

"Ava, wait—"

I made myself turn and answer him. "The water," I said. I used my fingers to mimic a waterfall because I didn't know the word for it.

His eyes narrowed. "But you're heading home now?"

Home? I threw my arm behind me, gesturing toward the village. "Not my home."

It wasn't mine. It never would be.

He didn't reply. We stood on the path staring at each other.

"I miss my home," I said finally, folding my arms across my chest.

"I know." He didn't move, just spoke the simple words.

"I miss my mother."

And my father.

"I know," he said again.

"And there was a boy. At home. I loved him."

His gaze sharpened, but he nodded slowly as if maybe he had known that too. After a moment, he scratched his head and glanced over his shoulder in the direction of the waterfall.

Only the sounds of animals in the forest and the rustle of leaves broke the silence between us. That was the way it should be, I thought. I didn't speak his language, and he didn't speak mine. Silence was all I could ever really hope for.

It was a depressing thought, and I knew I harbored it only because I was homesick and lonely.

But Darius is right beside you, I told myself.

I looked at his strong profile from the corner of my eye. He was turned, poised to continue down the path. He was not beside me out of friendship.

48

He had been at Cumeni. His kinsmen had encouraged Tec to betray his family and lead me here. *He and his people are the cause of your terrible feelings, not the cure for them.*

"Were you with the warriors that came to my village?" I asked him suddenly.

"What? Oh." He turned back to me. I had startled him out of some private thought. "No."

"With the others?" I knew there had been two bands of Nephites, but all of them had come from this village and surrounding towns. The bulk of them had been Darius's family.

"No."

The word was so clipped, I thought he wouldn't elaborate, but he did.

"I started out with the rescue party, but one of my friends needed to come back to Zarahemla. I came with him. I never made it very far into your country."

They claimed they were a rescue party, but a war party was more like it. They hadn't had any trouble fighting their way out of my peaceful village. I had always assumed Darius had been there, wielding a weapon against the people of my village, freeing men who were rightfully in our prison.

"But I would have been there if I could have."

I had been thinking ill of him for so long that his words did not cut like they might have.

"You would kill my people?"

He frowned. "No one got killed."

How could he know?

"I would have done whatever was necessary to get my sister's husband out of the prison."

"Even kill my people?" I asked again, bitterness making it more of a demand.

His eyes found mine. "It wouldn't be the first time."

I didn't know how to take that. Suddenly I felt very petty. I was horrified, incensed even, but the remorse and pain in his eyes were undeniable.

I looked away and said more calmly, "My uncle was hurt."

"He wasn't innocent, Ava."

My eyes shot back to him. How could he say such a thing? He didn't even know Zaaron. Zaaron had a wife and a beautiful daughter. He was respected in our village and did much for it. He had taken care of Mother and the rest of us since Father's death, brought us food and provisions from the markets in Jerusalem, sweet treats for the children. Even the bracelet on my wrist had been a gift from him. He was a good man.

Darius sighed. "Zaaron was..." He took a step back and ran his fingers through his hair. "Never mind."

Zaaron was what?

"Not never mind!" I took a breath. A girl shouldn't show so much of her feeling. "What is never mind?" I asked more calmly.

He sighed again, but there was a note of humor in his voice when he said, "It means I shouldn't have brought it up."

I chewed on my lip, taking a moment to think on his words. I wanted to say he had no proof of what he said, but I didn't know the word for proof. "It means you cannot make me know this is true."

"I only know what Tec told me."

"Tecumeni?"

Would Tec say such things about Zaaron's innocence? About his guilt? Would he betray our uncle to appease these people and justify their actions?

Did I even understand what Darius said? The language was hard for me to use. I was confused and among enemies who masqueraded as my friends. But they were not my friends.

And I was not theirs.

"Listen, Ava. I'm sorry. You should talk to Tec about it."

I most certainly would, even though I knew it would place doubt in my mind about a man I loved and respected. It already had.

"I want to be alone now," I said stiffly. I turned to walk away but stopped when I felt a large hand on my arm. I threw a look over my shoulder at that jaw. Those lips.

And when my eyes drifted up to meet his, Darius said, "Where are you going?"

He nodded at the travel gear I carried on my back. I thought he wanted to know if I was going somewhere.

"Yes. I cannot stay at Leah's."

He looked at me for a long time, long enough to make my cheeks get hot.

"I'm traveling to Zarahemla in a week," he said at long last, almost grudgingly. "After Lamech and Sarai are betrothed. If you can wait, I'll take you with me."

Zarahemla. What was he asking me? Was I going to Zarahemla? Did I want to go?

"Yes," I said tentatively.

51

He backed slowly away from me. "I'll talk to Tecumeni, then."

I didn't know how to say goodbye to him, so I nodded and turned toward the village.

Most of the visitors had settled down into their tents or hammocks in the woods by the time I returned, but Kalem's family was sitting around a cozy fire in the yard. Tec was there, Keturah and Gideon, and Keturah's brothers and their wives.

Leah beckoned me over. Tec's eyes followed me, and though I knew he was wondering what I had been doing out in the dark, he was only quiet and watchful.

I sat near Leah, and when the conversation had resumed, she leaned close and said, "Tec said you didn't eat."

I glanced at him. He was still watching me, but Micah, Leah's eldest son, asked him a question and he turned.

I would have told her I was not hungry, which was a lie, but she continued before I could find the right words.

"Dare hasn't eaten either. He was only here long enough to say a quick hello to his sister. I don't know where that boy gets off to."

I put my cool hands on my cheeks to try to stop the flush I knew would come. I knew exactly where he had been—with me at the pond and out at the waterfall with...Ammon and Kish?

I thought of the purposeful way he had been walking down the path, how he kept glancing back over his shoulder while we talked.

It hadn't occurred to me before—because, like a lovesick little girl, I had been entertaining the idea that he had followed me there—but perhaps those boys had been Darius's friends.

Friends he didn't want his mother to know about.

I stared into the fire, and for a while, I tried to listen to the foreign words the family spoke. But I had spoken more Nephite that day than I had in the six months I had been in the land of Melek, and my head was starting to hurt.

I caught Gideon's eye across the fire. He smiled as if he were encouraging me. I returned his smile, but I did not listen to any more of the foreign words until I heard Kenai call out, "My little brother returns!"

I couldn't help looking up. The tall boy who walked from the darkness into his family's firelight was nearly a man, and the frown on his face made me think he did not appreciate being called anyone's *little* anything.

I had not been listening to the conversation, but I could feel that the mood around the fire had changed. The silence was different, as if maybe they had been talking about Darius. I glanced around and saw many sets of eyes darting between Darius and me. I sat up straighter. Had they been talking about the two of us? Perhaps because of that word Darius had said? *Pretty*?

"You missed the evening meal," Leah said. "But I kept some warm."

Normally, she would get up and fix her son a dish of food, but she must have been worn out from the day because she kept her feet up and looked to me. I often prepared and served the meals, and I quickly got up to serve Darius, dishing myself a serving as well, as it seemed she had saved exactly enough for the two of us.

Darius pulled the strap of his satchel over his head and laid the bag aside when he sat. He was quiet as he watched me, thanking me with a nod when I passed him his food, so different from the boy I had been laughing with at the pool. Different from the distracted boy I had met on the path in the forest.

Kalem's daughter got up and kissed her father. Her handsome husband, Muloki, escorted her to the edge of the firelight with a hand on her shoulder. Leah's sons, Micah and Kenai, bid a goodnight and left with their wives. After a time, Keturah and Gideon retired to their tent which was tucked in the trees a short distance behind the house.

The five of us remaining had spent many nights just like this. Kalem had taught us the gospel of Christ at this fire. Tec had become converted to it sitting right here, just as we were.

I finished my food and reached out for Darius's dish, long since emptied.

"You don't have to—"

"I'll burn them out," I said. "Here at the fire. No trouble."

I turned the dishes over the coals and went to the house for a cloth. When I returned, I knelt and rubbed the dishes out with ashes to clean them, starting with the big pot Leah had used for cooking.

"Ow!"

I sucked my finger into my mouth. I had really burned it good.

Leah's feet went to the ground instantly. "I'll go get you some salve, dear."

Suddenly, Darius was kneeling next to me, pulling my hand from my mouth.

"No need, Mother. I've got mine."

He slipped a jar from his satchel and removed the lid.

"It stinks, I know," he said quietly. "Now, let me see."

Pulling my hand closer to himself and angling it toward the fire, he smoothed the opaque salve, a recipe of Leah's, over a burn at the base of my thumb.

"That will blister," Tec said.

I glanced at him over my shoulder.

Darius shook his head. "Not with Mother's salve." He blew lightly on the wound, and I winced.

"Sorry," he whispered as he retrieved a bandage from his bag.

As he wound it around my hand, I glanced up at the others. Tec was frowning at Darius, but Leah's eyes were bright and she shared a small smile with her husband.

But this was nothing. No one would let me suffer with a burn if he had the remedy in his satchel.

The next morning while I milked Leah's goat, Tec came and sat beside me.

"Darius asked me if he could take you to Zarahemla," he said directly.

"So that's what he was saying about Zarahemla."

"He said you told him you would go."

I grinned at him. "I wouldn't know, but I probably did."

"You can't."

I sat up straight and brushed a strand of hair from my face. "Why not?"

"Do you know why he's going?"

"No."

"Do you know when he will return home?"

"No."

"Do you know why he invited you?"

"No. Tec, what do those things have to do with it?"

We both laughed because the answers to those questions had everything to do with it.

"You can't even talk to him."

"I'll learn."

"In a week?"

"A week? I thought he said something more like...oh, I don't know what he said."

I finished with the milk and set the clay bowl aside so the goat would not step into it.

Tec's eyes narrowed when he saw the small smile I could not quite hide. He rubbed his thumb over his lips to stifle his immediate protest.

"Did he say why he invited me?" I asked.

"He didn't have to."

"What do you mean?"

"I mean you can't travel alone with him."

I huffed. He was overreacting. "It's not up to you."

He studied me for a moment. He crossed his arms over his chest. I expected him to disagree. In the absence of my parents, my father in particular, it absolutely was up to him.

"You're right," he said. "But what business do you have in Zarahemla?"

I looked around the courtyard we sat in. It wasn't ours. I looked around the village. We didn't belong here. At least I didn't.

"You are making yourself at home here," I said. "But Tec, this is not my home."

"Neither is Zarahemla."

"You will have a wife and a home, and I will have nothing."

"And what can Zarahemla offer you?"

Darius.

"This is not my home!"

Tec went silent. He stared at his knees, and I felt bad for making him feel guilty. It wasn't his fault I was here. I was the one who had followed him into the forest.

"I think you should go."

We both looked over to see Leah near the corner of the house. She was pretty in her green and yellow sarong as she walked toward us, and she looked so much like her daughter it was hard to believe she was a grandmother.

"For Darius," she continued. Dropping to her knees in the dirt, she patted the goat's side. "He's not comfortable here because of what happened with Sarai. He leaves often and is gone much." She shifted. "He's never allowed anyone to go with him before. Not even his friends or his brothers. I want you to go with him. I want you to tell me where he goes when he leaves the village."

"Like a spy?" I asked, amused. But when I met her worried eyes, I knew her request was serious.

"Kalem and I have been talking." She turned her eyes to Tecumeni. "We would like to arrange a betrothal between your sister and my son."

"Oh, no," I cut in. "Darius would never agree to that."

Leah laughed a little. "I think he would. But I do not

want him to merely agree. I want him to think it is his idea."

"How would I make him think that?"

Her eyes flicked to Tec. "Go with him to Zarahemla. Be yourself."

I snorted. "I really don't think that would be successful."

"Will you agree to try? If he doesn't speak to Tec on his own when you return, then you wouldn't be bound to any agreement."

"And if he does?"

"I think the rainy season would be lovely for a betrothal."

I laughed and looked at Tec to see what he thought of the offer.

"Can I speak to my sister alone?" he asked Leah.

"Of course, Tec." She rose and placed a hand on his shoulder, almost as if she were offering him support. But wasn't I the one who needed support? Was having responsibility for another person so dreadful?

When Leah had returned to the house, Tec turned to me and said in low voice, "It is a good offer, but do you have any affection for Darius? I respect Kalem and Leah, I even like Darius, but I have no problem saying no."

I must have blushed, because one look at my face seemed to be all he needed to be assured on that point.

He huffed. "Okay, then. My only other reservation is that I don't know what Leah was talking about—what happened with Sarai. People avoid Dare, and I don't know why."

I nibbled on a fingernail, a habit both Tec and I shared.

"Sarai does not seem to be upset with him. I was with them both yesterday at the pond. There was a feeling of awkwardness, but I thought it was because Lamech was there. Sarai was very agreeable toward Darius, and polite— even friendly."

He considered that. "I will ask around about it," he finally decided.

"Wait," I said. "Should we not be straightforward and ask Darius directly?"

"That would only give us one side of the story."

"I suppose you're right."

I didn't say it but I didn't think I needed more than one side of the story. I knew whose side I would be on. Darius had secrets, but I didn't think he was a liar. I knew who I would believe.

"And I suppose you can go." He paused. "But you cannot go alone with him."

I snorted, the kind of sound a girl can only make in front of her brother. "Are you ready for today?" I asked him.

He took a breath and shot me a familiar grin, but it was a nervous one.

"Or should I wonder if Chloe is ready?"

"She's not. That's the problem. I hate doing this to her. I never imagined this would be the way I'd get my wife."

I wanted to place my hand on his arm, but I didn't. Surely he had imagined Father and Mother helping him choose a nice girl from our village.

"Then why do it?"

He sighed, becoming instantly wary. "Look, I know you don't like her—"

"It's not that. I only meant, well…" I blushed a little. "Why not wait until she thinks it is her idea?"

He shook his head, but smiled. "Hemni thinks this is right for her, and I agree. I can keep her out of trouble."

"Or she can get you into it. Besides, Hemni has had no luck up until now. Why should this be different?"

"Because the responsibility will fall to me now. This is his last resort."

"I can't believe a man like that can give up on his daughter, even if she is wayward."

"He's not giving up. He's finally found the right thing for her."

I gave him a wry look, one that said I hoped he knew what he was doing. Then I stood and carefully carried the milk toward the house. "Good luck," I called back over my shoulder.

CHAPTER 6

"I want to go." I heard Chloe's voice during an evening meal at Hemni and Dinah's.

It was the day before Darius and I were to set out for Zarahemla. Tec appeared to be considering her request, but he hadn't yet answered. Hadn't he told her they were going with us? He had already arranged it with Darius. It was the condition upon which he had given his approval for me to go.

"Izz and Sarai got to go to Jerusalem!" she pouted.

I wondered if Tec would pretend to give in to it. He had to know how manipulative she was.

The talking seemed to quiet. Hemni exchanged a look with Dinah, who only glanced at her daughter before getting up to bring more food to the table.

"I want to see the great city Zarahemla before I am an old married woman, and I want you to take me."

Tec returned to his food, seemingly unaware of all the interest in his reaction. He was very aware of it, but I knew he was not trying to impress anyone with his ability to keep Chloe in check.

"Sure," he said easily. "I'd like to see Zarahemla myself." He turned his eyes to Darius. "Mind if we tag along?"

"Not at all." Darius smirked. "Can you be ready by dawn?"

He was playing along, too.

Tec turned to Chloe and raised one brow. She grinned.

I bit my lip and looked down to hide a smile, because she only thought she had gotten her way.

When dawn broke, we were already outside of the village.

"What was that look my mother gave you when we left?" Darius asked me as we cut through the forest on a narrow path.

"What look?"

He pointed ahead of us. "That's the West Road. You didn't notice the look she gave you?"

Of course I had noticed it.

I shrugged. "What will we do in Zarahemla?" I asked him.

"Here." He held out his hand to help me down a steep slope that leveled into the West Road. "I'm meeting some friends."

"Do you always go to the grand city Zarahemla when you leave your village?"

"No."

"Where else do you go?"

He hesitated. "Is there somewhere else you would like me to take you, Ava?"

"No. I care not where we go."

He adjusted the strap of his travel pack and glanced at the sky. "What do you mean?"

I glanced at him, trying to keep my footing secure on the steep hill and all too aware of his hand closed around mine. "If I'm not going home, it doesn't matter where we go."

"Do you want to go home?"

I sighed and glanced over my shoulder when Chloe squealed and nearly jumped over the edge of the hill. I watched as Tec reached out and grabbed her elbow, holding her back, and then proceeded to guide her down the hill as Darius had done for me.

"I wish I had not left Mama with all those small children."

"So it is guilt that makes you frown so much?"

I frowned up at him.

"You would have had to leave your mother's home anyway," he continued.

Tec and Chloe made it down the slope, and Tec rolled his eyes as they passed us and began following the road south.

"You wouldn't have been able to stay with your mother after you married," Darius clarified.

"You're right," I said as I stared after Tec and his betrothed.

Darius followed my gaze. "You don't like Chloe?"

"She is Nephite."

He searched my face for a moment then turned to follow them southward. "We're not all bad," he said.

I laughed a little and followed him. "Some Nephites I do not mind." My cheeks flamed, so I hurried to say, "Chloe is not so bad, but she's like a girl at home, a girl Tec did not like at all. I wonder that he cannot see the sameness in them, and I wonder why he has tied himself so firmly to your people. I like his conviction, but I do not understand what motivates him."

"You like his what?"

"Conviction," I repeated, and then realized I had said the word in my native tongue.

Darius tried it out.

"I do not know the word in Nephite," I confessed.

"Your Nephite seems to have gotten good quite quickly," he observed.

"Gideon helped me."

He nodded. It was all the explanation he seemed to need. "What is the word for road?" he asked me.

I told him, and he repeated it.

"And what is the word for sky?"

I told him, and he continued to ask similar questions for much of the morning.

"Why do you want to know so much?" I asked when the sun was high and its rays were warm on my face.

"I want to speak to you in the way you understand," he said simply.

But there was nothing simple about the way his words made me feel inside.

We caught up to Tec and Chloe. Chloe stood with her hands on her hips looking up into the trees that canopied above us while Tec drank from his water skin. As Darius and I drew up, he tied off his water skin and glanced between us.

What were you do doing back there?

I knew what his expression said, but I couldn't help a bit of a smile that made him frown.

We sat together off the side of the road and ate the food Leah and Keturah had sent with us: cold corn cakes filled with pork and achiotl, raw roots, and a purple fruit that was soft and sweet when ripe but today was slightly tart at the peel. I ate it anyway and tried to pay attention to the conversation.

"Father sent me money to buy Mother a new sarong from the fine silks in the market. It is to be a surprise," Chloe said.

"What will she do with fine silk in your tiny village?" I asked, instantly wanting to withdraw my words. I should have stayed out of it and kept my snipping words to myself, but Chloe didn't seem to notice the rudeness in them.

"She can wear it to church of course."

"I thought your prophets discouraged the wearing of costly apparel."

"One beautiful sarong shouldn't cause my mother to be vain when she has been humble her whole life," she replied. "Besides, there is nothing wrong with looking pretty once in a while."

"I think Dinah is pretty all the time," Darius said as he took the last bite of his fruit and tossed the pit into the trees.

"Like her daughters?" I asked quietly.

He licked his fingers and wiped them on his tunic while I wished again that I could recall my words.

"Sure," he said after a pause and reached over to tug on a piece of Chloe's hair that had fallen loose from her hair clip.

I swallowed down the last of my food, feeling like it caught in my throat. I was saying everything wrong.

"I'll be back," I said as I dusted off the hem of my dress and adjusted my belt.

It was a relief to be alone for a few moments. I was

used to being alone in the small village, and spending the entire morning talking to Darius had my nerves jangling. Why couldn't I just be normal about it? Wasn't it what I wanted? Why did I have to say things that betrayed my petty jealousy?

I found a tree with a thick trunk to lean against. Letting my head fall back onto the rough bark, I allowed my eyes to fall closed and wondered how I had ended up in Melek with these people. They had lives. They had history together. Chloe and Darius had grown up together. They were friends. How could Leah imagine that I could make Darius happy?

I let out a deep breath, opened my eyes, and nearly jumped out of my skin.

"Dare!"

Darius had followed me and was leaning against a neighboring tree with his arms crossed over his chest.

"Sorry," he said, but he didn't sound sorry. He didn't look sorry, either—he kind of looked upset. He didn't move a muscle until finally he said, "Chloe is like a little sister to me."

There was nothing between Darius and me—not yet, maybe not ever. It shouldn't matter what he thought of other girls, especially those he had known long before I ever came to his village. I had no cause to be jealous.

But I was.

Suddenly, he pushed off the tree, and he was standing in front of me in two angry steps. He put his hand on the tree near my head and leaned in close.

"I am done with that family." His eyes nearly blazed.

I swallowed hard. "Jarom is your friend."

"You know I meant the girls."

I couldn't meet his eyes. I let my gaze drop, but he was so tall I was staring at his lips.

"It doesn't matter," I said and tried to duck under his arm to get away. But quick as lightning, his other hand shot to my waist to keep me there.

"If it doesn't matter to you what I think of Jarom's sisters, what are you doing here sulking by yourself?"

"I'm not sulking!"

"I recognize sulking when I see it." A smirk touched the edges of his lips, a look that was annoyingly smug.

"If you care so little for Jarom's sisters, why do you leave your home to sulk by *your*self?"

His smile grew slowly. I couldn't help but return it.

"How do you say 'That is none of your concern'?"

I laughed and told him. He repeated it, tightened his hand at my waist for a moment, and then backed away.

"We need to get moving. In a short time, the trees will thin out and we will descend into a valley. You will be able to see Zarahemla before we descend, but we won't get there for three more days."

When we made camp that night, Chloe and I cooked a rabbit Tec had shot with his bow and arrow during the late afternoon. Chloe found some large red berries and dug some roots to cook as well. I grudgingly admitted she was less of an annoyance than I had thought she would be. She had her wild tendencies, but she was surprisingly kind to Tec and almost friendly with me. It seemed she couldn't help herself. She was just a nice person, and it naturally shone through. It seemed to be such a drastic change from her behavior in the village, I had to wonder which girl was the real one.

"Dare," I said when Tec took Chloe to an outcropping to overlook the valley we would cross the next day. "Why does Chloe put on such an act? Why is she so difficult to her parents?"

Darius leaned back against a rock and stretched his legs out to the side of the small fire that glowed between us. He shook his head. "I'm not sure. She changed while we were at the war. Something happened, I think. I don't know what. No one does."

"The kindness she shows to Tec," I ventured slowly, not sure if I was noticing things right. "Is it real?"

He gave me a puzzled look.

"Is her kindness real or is her wildness real?"

He put his hands behind his head and looked up at the sky. "They are both real. I don't think she will deliberately hurt your brother, if that's what you mean."

I gave him a weak smile. It was exactly what I meant. "Tec is all I have."

"Only if that's the way you want it."

"Hmm?"

"You could have more friends if you wanted them."

"You're right," I allowed, thinking of Sarai and of Melia and Gideon. "But he is my only family."

"You could have more family, too."

"Maybe," I allowed again after a moment.

"You left your village for the same reason I leave mine," he said. "There is someone there you cannot bear to see."

"No, I only followed Tec because—" My mouth dropped closed when his eyes narrowed with skepticism.

"Because you weren't happy where you were. You don't have to lie to me. I've been in the same place. Believe me, I get it."

"Who is she?"

His eyes darted away, and his jaw tightened. He shifted, leaning forward and drawing a knee up to rest an elbow on it.

Tec and Chloe came back into camp, but Darius only gave them a cursory glance.

"I should have been the one to leave." He mumbled the strange comment under his breath as he got to his feet and left.

Oblivious to the tension, Chloe sat beside me and asked, "Did you see the city?"

"Yes." I had seen it when we were in the foothills earlier in the day, when Darius had pointed it out to me. It didn't look so impressive from this distance, but I could tell it was large like Jerusalem and could even make out the large structures within it.

"I can't believe we will be there in just two days!"

After a time, I heard footsteps and looked up to see Darius returning to the small camp. His water skin at his belt was glistening wet as if he had only gone from camp to fill it. Without looking at any of us, he knelt and quickly set up the tent for Chloe and me with an efficiency that spoke to the number of times he had built a similar shelter.

I drew my knees up to my chest, encircling them with my arms as I watched him and wondered if Josiah felt as guilty about me as Darius felt about Sarai.

CHAPTER 7

Zarahemla was vast and busy. When we approached the city wall, Darius stopped to talk to the guards at the gate.

"This is Kimner," he said to us. "And this is Chloe, Tec, and Ava," he told his friend.

Kimner was a light-skinned Nephite with sandy brown hair. He was pleasant but forgettable. I was apparently forgettable to him, too, because his eyes flicked over me and settled on Chloe.

"Chloe is Zeke's youngest sister," Darius very obviously informed him. "And she is betrothed."

"Got it," Kimner said with a smile, but as the two men talked, his eyes kept returning to Chloe. Of course that's where his eyes would fall—Chloe was beautiful and I was not.

But it was becoming harder to stay jealous of her. She was beautiful, there was no doubt, but it became more obvious each day I was with her that she had little idea how to handle it. Even now, it was evidenced when she scowled at Kimner and stomped on his foot as we passed.

Darius led us through the city center and pointed out the government buildings, the temple, and the square where the market would be held the next day. He led us past a large arena where they played ball games, but when we looked down inside, it was quiet and empty.

"Can we go down into it?" Chloe asked.

Darius shook his head. "The games are sacred."

Leading us on, he turned down a street that ran parallel to a high wall. The street was quiet and the noise of the many people of the city had faded so much that I could hear the leaves rustle on the branches that hung over the wall.

"Are those guards?" I asked Darius when we passed two men who appeared to be loitering casually among the slow carts and mothers with small children that traversed the lane.

"What makes you think that?" he asked. Was that suspicion in his voice?

I ignored his question. They were so obviously out of place here. "Where are we going that must be guarded?"

He glanced back at the men. "We are going to the Estate of Alma."

"Who?"

"Where Helaman lives."

Chloe looked over. "We're going to see the prophet?" Her eyes were wide, and I could tell this was a prospect that interested and impressed her.

"The prophet died," Darius said.

I had a sudden sick feeling in the pit of my stomach.

"This is his son, Helaman the younger," he continued. "If he's not too busy, we can see him," he said, but it sounded like a warning, as if he did not think Helaman would have time for us.

And why would he accept us into his home, even if he did have the time?

"But is it not impolite to go there uninvited? To his home?" I asked.

Darius shook his head. "The Estate of Alma is much more than a private residence. Much of the business of the Church of God is conducted here, and Helaman the younger is a judge in the courts."

"And we will be welcome there?" I asked as I eyed the two guards, these ones uniformed, that flanked a gate in the wall up ahead.

"Of course," he insisted. And then, more quietly to me he said, "I come here all the time. It will be all right."

And it was, or it seemed to be. When we approached the gate, the guards simply opened it, greeted Darius by name, and ushered us all through with polite nods.

Darius walked us through the beautiful gardens. We passed several buildings, an open area where children were playing, even a large stream before Darius stopped at a building half covered by a vine that was covered with a fragrant pink flower.

"This is Eliza's, a guest house," he said and dropped his travel gear near the door. He waited for us to do the same, and then he led the way inside.

"Hello?" Darius called out as we entered a large common room, but there was no reply. "Good," he said, turning back to us. "You will have the place to yourselves. Tec and I will stay at the cottage beyond the stream." He turned to Chloe. "That's where Zeke lived when he worked here."

"Oh," she said, only mildly interested in the other building as she looked around at the grandeur of the one we were in.

The boys left and returned with our travel gear, which they set just inside the doorway.

"You can rest for the remainder of the afternoon," Darius said. "We will return for you in time for the evening meal."

When we were alone, Chloe and I went to explore the other rooms.

"There are two beds in this one," she called from a room off the large common area.

"And two in here," I called back from another.

We searched several more similar rooms, and when we returned again to the common area, our eyes met and we both giggled.

"It is enormous!" Chloe exclaimed.

I nodded. "Let's share a chamber," I suggested.

She grinned and hauled her belongings into one of the rooms. Giving a tired sigh, I hefted my things and followed her.

When Darius and Tecumeni came to get us for the evening meal their eyes were bright and I knew they shared a secret. I thought they would bring something for Chloe and me to cook and prepare, some fish from the beautiful stream on the property perhaps, but they didn't bring food.

Darius took Chloe and walked ahead, leaving Tec and me to walk together toward the largest building on the estate. After spending three days with Darius, it felt different to be alone with Tec—familiar and relaxed.

"I'm to interpret for you tonight," Tecumeni told me. "In case you don't catch all that is said."

I looked at my brother for a moment and then rolled

my eyes. "How am I ever going to make Dare fall in love with me," I whispered, "if you never let me spend any time alone with him?"

Tec pinched my neck.

"Ow!"

He laughed, and I punched him and then rubbed my neck.

"I miss you too," he said.

I snorted.

"All day long for three days is not enough time with him? Truly, it borders on improper, Ava."

"As if proper matters for me now," I reminded him, resigned to it.

"Did you not think it might still matter for him?"

My throat went tight, because indeed I had tried not to think of it. Of course Darius would be concerned about what his friends and his family thought of him leaving the village with me.

"Hey." Tec's voice gentled. "No one here knows what Josiah did. No one has to know."

I spoke with bitter humor. "That will make it easier to unburden yourself of me. I get it." I expected him to respond with sarcasm, but his sincerity took me completely off guard—and went straight to my heart.

"I don't care if you live with me and Chloe forever. I hope you know that." He paused. "But that's not what I want for you. What Josiah did, breaking the betrothal, has no bearing on your ability to be a good wife. It is not even worthy of mention."

"You do not think my husband would care that his wife

is divorced?" Because that was essentially what I was. I had been legally betrothed, and Josiah had failed to honor his end of the contract he had made with my father.

Tecumeni's voice was hot with anger when he said, "Josiah didn't even acknowledge the contract existed!"

"And so he didn't legally dissolve it. That is worse than being divorced." Being married to a man who was married to someone else by now was much, much worse.

Tec ran a hand through his hair and glanced ahead at Darius and Chloe as we neared a much smaller building that sat behind the huge estate house. It was a nice home, made of stone and wood and plaster, but more modest—though far from the humble tent lodges in my village.

"Who lives here?" I asked as we approached it, but I was afraid I already knew.

"Helaman," Tec said. I could feel him watching me for my reaction.

Darius had said we would be unlikely to meet Helaman while we were there. I didn't know exactly what this place was, but I knew it was—with its well-guarded entrances and its many tasteful buildings—more than just Helaman's home.

I thought of my home back in Ani-Anti. So far away. So small. So insignificant.

What would Helaman, son of the great Nephite prophet and judge of the people—probably stuffy, pretentious, and self-important—think of an ugly, divorced Lamanite girl?

I tried to step forward with confidence, but I couldn't do it with anticipation as the others did.

We were greeted at the door by a tall man with broad shoulders who smiled warmly at us all and firmly clasped arms with first Darius and then Tecumeni.

Darius turned to Chloe and me. "This is Helaman."

I swallowed hard. Was this man with the warm smile the man Ammon and his friends had spoken of so coldly?

"This is Chloe and Ava," he said as he turned back to the man. "Chloe is Zeke's sister, and Ava is Tecumeni's."

Helaman briefly laid his hand on each of our shoulders. "Zeke is a good friend of mine," he said to Chloe and he turned back to Darius. "Everything is ready. My wife has been cooking all day." He beckoned us inside with the inviting wave of one large hand.

Helaman must have been expecting other guests. Why would an important lady such as his wife be cooking for us? We still had travel dust on our sandals.

He ushered us through the home until we came into a large room at the back of it. I heard giggles as I entered and the sound instantly set me more at ease. Helaman gestured across the room to where a woman sat in the corner among five young children. Two little girls nestled on her lap and one stood at her knee. A young boy sat at her feet and an older boy leaned against the wall with his arms folded. The oldest boy glanced at us and straightened, but the others kept their attention fixed on their father.

The woman set the children aside and rose to meet us.

"Janna, my wife," Helaman said.

I wondered that the rest of the people in the room could talk, because I felt that I couldn't even breathe in this man's presence.

But I managed somehow to make it through more introductions. I managed to return Janna's smile. I managed to bear Helaman's touch when he laid his hand on my shoulder.

Such a busy and important man must have very little time to spend with his children. It was clear they were eager for his attention, and I found that I was as drawn to him as they were. There was something about the man, about being in the same room with him, and I wondered if there was truth in what Tec had been trying to tell me about the holy spirit.

I knew what it was the instant I felt it because, despite how I denied it to Tec, I had been listening to him for the past months. I had heard him bear witness of the things he felt and knew. How could I totally ignore something that clearly meant so much to my own twin brother?

We sat around a large table to eat. Tec sat near me with the intention of translating the things I did not understand, but since Gideon had helped me with the nuances of our two languages, my comprehension had increased rapidly, and I understood nearly everything that was spoken around the table.

There was a fireplace with a stone hearth at the far side of the room, and after the meal I sat near it and watched the others interact. The adults talked to one another and the children played quietly. I couldn't help but compare them to my brood of noisy siblings. Their mother and the oldest boy, whose name I had learned was Nephi, helped the smaller children, but after the first game was over and they started another, Nephi moved to the door and looked longingly out into the yard.

I watched him for a time and then joined him there.

The sun was sinking into the hills beyond Melek to our west, casting a glow over everything I could see.

"This is my favorite time of day," I said to the boy.

He glanced at me and shifted his weight a little, but he returned his eyes to the yard and the beautiful gardens. Somehow I didn't think he was yearning to be out among the flowers.

"I envy you," he said, surprising me with his perfect, clipped Lamanite. "Your grand journey from the lands south. Even your journey here from Melek. You're lucky."

"I never thought of it as luck," I replied in the same language.

He turned to look at me then.

"You speak my language," I said.

"I speak many languages. I have been schooled in many more." He didn't say this proudly.

"You speak Lamanite, but you have not been to the Lamanite lands?"

His eyes looked sad as they drifted back to the outdoors. "I have never been anywhere. I have only heard of foreign lands in stories that Father and my uncles tell, but they only tell the good ones when they think I am asleep."

"Foreign lands are strange and scary to me," I confided to him.

His suddenly smiling eyes shot to me again. "No," he said. "They are wild and exciting!"

I laughed at his wide-eyed innocence, though not to offend. If I had not been such an unusually tall girl, I would have looked him directly in the eyes. As it was, I was a little taller than Nephi, and I considered his features, his hazel eyes lit with mischief, his slightly crooked teeth, and his large nose. Somehow, they all came together to make him a handsome youth, and I knew that in time, he would be not only a handsome man, but outstanding in every way. He would have his adventures—I was sure of it.

"I have a brother your age," I said. "I think he feels the same way."

He glanced over his shoulder at Tec. "He did not come here with you?"

"No, and since we left, he has the burden now of a family to provide for." I gestured to his young siblings. His brother and one of his sisters played a game in which one bounced a rubber ball on the stone floor and tried to swipe up twigs before it bounced again. Another sister watched them closely, and the remaining sister was cradled in her mother's lap. Janna was combing through the child's curly, golden hair with her fingers. "You wish for more excitement than this?"

"With every breath in him." Helaman's deep voice came from behind me. "You have my permission to leave," he said to Nephi. "Be back before sundown."

Nephi grinned and looked to his father in thanks, but he did not even attempt to hurry out the door before bidding me a proper and quite formal farewell. He laid a hand on my shoulder and said, "I enjoyed meeting you, Ava. Thank you for taking the time to speak with me."

I glanced at Helaman, who observed his son's actions with pride. "And thank you for giving me the comfort of hearing my own language for these few moments. You have learned it well."

He nodded and quickly turned to run into the wilds of his fenced-in home. But he stopped and slowly turned around. He cocked his head to the side, brushed a hand across his chest, swallowed hard, and looked to his father. But then his eyes settled on me and he stepped closer. He looked as if he had one more thing to say to me, so I gave him my attention.

"Ava." He looked down at the ground for a moment, possibly a little embarrassed, trying to phrase his words. When he looked up at me, it was with conviction, and when he spoke, it was with a tenderness I could hardly credit in a boy of his age, which couldn't have been more than twelve.

"Ava," he said again. "Jesus Christ will come to earth, and He will redeem the children of God." Stunned, I held his unwavering gaze. "I want to tell you that He will redeem you, too."

"I will think on this," I said, not knowing what else to say, and not wishing to offend him with something I might have said to Tecumeni.

He hesitated another moment, then turned and left.

I marveled at Nephi's sudden change in demeanor. One moment we had been discussing his dissatisfaction with his life here. I had seen that he felt sad and hemmed in. In the next moment, he was—what did they call it?—*testifying* to me of their Christ. What would move such a young boy to say those things to me?

"You grieve," Helaman said softly.

I looked down, wondering why he was saying that, how he had noticed. How obvious must it be?

"You grieve for many things, I think."

"I...suppose. Yes."

He let out a slow breath. "The Lord does not want for you to spend your life in sadness."

I recognized it instantly as being very much like the thing Gideon had said to me, and I pondered it while we stood together and watched Nephi run across the yard and disappear around the corner of the large house. "I wish I were as carefree as that," I said, motioning toward Nephi.

Helaman put his hand on my shoulder, not formally as the Nephites did in greeting, but like my father would have. He meant to console me, and though I had refused much of the comfort offered to me by the Ammonites, perhaps because of it, his words were very dear. "You can be," he said simply with a quick squeeze on my shoulder.

When we left, Tec steered Chloe away to walk in the gardens, a simple delight which was probably wasted on her.

Noticing that my gaze lingered on the couple, Darius rubbed his ear and asked, "Would you like to follow them?"

"What? Oh! No. I mean, the gardens are very pretty, but no." It was something a betrothed couple would do. Or a couple in love might sneak away to steal some moments alone. It seemed much too personal, too intimate, too presumptuous to do with Darius.

"Okay," he said, and it might have been my imagination, but he seemed disappointed.

"Maybe for a short walk," I acquiesced quickly, believing his disappointment to be real, and thinking of Leah, and knowing the chance to prolong the walk with Darius would only last for a moment more before we passed the path that turned into the gardens.

"Alright," he said, and I felt the soft graze of his fingers on my elbow to turn me to toward the path, which was narrower than the one we had been on, just wide enough for the two of us to walk together.

Dusk was falling by the time the path opened into a large park tucked into a wide bend of the stream.

Darius walked to a stone bench and stopped before it. He pulled a leaf from the low-hanging branches of a tree and worried it between his fingers.

I sat on the stone bench which faced the east where the sun would rise in the morning. If I rose early enough, I thought I might come back to see it. It was sure to be beautiful.

"Darius," I said. "What is it to be redeemed?"

"What does redeem mean?"

"No. I believe I understand the meaning of the word. But I do not understand why your Christ will purchase me."

He chuckled a little and sat beside me. "Who told you about that?"

"Nephi."

His brows rose slightly, and his lips moved but not quite into a smile.

"Was he wrong?" I asked.

"No. But that's not the best word, maybe, to help you understand Christ's purpose."

This was one of the things I had been wondering. "What *is* Christ's purpose?"

He looked at me for a moment in the quickly fading light. Shifting, he lifted a hand and touched my cheek in the place where he had touched it before. "Christ can make your sad face go away."

Between us there was only the sound of the stream and Darius reaching out to stroke the sadness from my face with his fingertips.

"He did not take the sadness from yours," I said.

CHAPTER 8

At dawn, I was sitting on the stone bench. As the sun rose behind the massive buildings of Zarahemla, I couldn't help but think of being there with Darius and talking about Christ and redemption and sadness. Darius hadn't preached to me or tried to make me accept something I believed to be false, and for the first time, I was glad I could speak the accursed Nephite.

Smiling, I snapped a leaf from the low branches and strolled back toward Eliza's house. When I arrived, the others were coming through the door.

"Ready?" Darius asked, stepping toward me.

I twirled the leaf in my fingers. "Ready."

Darius led us out through the gates we had entered the day before, past the guards, and onto the lane that led to the busier parts of the city. "It's one of the market days," he said. "The square will be very crowded. Try to stay together. Tec, do you think you can get back to this lane?"

"In my sleep."

"Good then. We'll meet here for the midday meal if we get separated. Bring something from the market to eat."

It was still early, but the market square was already filled with people. Tec and Chloe were separated from us immediately by the undulating crowds, but I wondered if it was by design. When a group of adolescent boys ran between us, laughing and joking with each other, I nearly lost my balance.

"Stay close," Darius said as he took my hand, and except for when he paid for the food we chose for our meal, he kept it firmly in his, and I wondered if that was also by design.

"Choose one of these," he said when we were browsing at a jewelry table. "I'll buy you one if you like."

I admired the bracelets he indicated. They were made of all kinds of fine materials—copper, agate, silver, onyx, amethyst, jade, turquoise, ziff—all of which were much too fine for Darius to buy for me.

"You can't," I said.

A darkness came into his eyes. I had insulted him.

"They are much too fine," I tried to explain. "It is much too generous."

"For a shepherd, you mean."

My words brought him insult, and there was no way to ease it unless I told him the truth.

I glanced around. The shopkeeper stole an interested glance at us as he helped a woman make a selection, but he was the only one who seemed to notice us.

I cleared my throat with a small hum, embarrassed to have to say the words.

"It is only that I fear I might take your gift to mean more than you intend."

"You have no idea what I intend," he said and stared hard into my face. "And anyway," he went on more casually, "I see that you have lost your bracelet." He indicated my wrist. "The copper one."

I hadn't lost it. I knew exactly where it was. At least, I knew on whom it was. I had little idea where he was now, but I glanced around when I realized Ammon and his friends were probably getting supplies at the market like everyone else in Zarahemla.

Slowly, I turned to the bracelets and pointed to the one I liked best, the one that had drawn my attention from the moment we had stepped up to the table.

"I like that one too," Darius said, bending near my ear so I could hear his low voice in the noisy crowd.

The bracelet he picked up and held between us was a gorgeous piece of artistry made from stained mahogany beads in shades of indigo and finely carved jade.

"Should I have it wrapped, or do you want to wear it?"

"I want to wear it," I said, thinking that would please him and seeing it was true when he smiled.

I turned, averting my eyes, as he paid the shopkeeper.

"Here," he said. "Hold out your arm."

I tried not to let my fingers tremble as he worked the clasp. The brush of his fingers on my skin as he tied it made me catch my breath, and it told me I should not have been wearing any other man's jewelry.

"Well," he said, testing the clasp. "That's done."

When the bracelet was securely around my wrist and I looked up to thank him, his eyes were fixed on something in the distance.

Drawing them quickly back to me and smiling, he took my hand and led me toward the lane where we would meet Tec and Chloe, and perhaps I could have found my way back to the estate in my sleep as well, because I noticed when

Darius turned off the main road before he was supposed to. He led me between two large structures, silos for grain I thought, and when Darius gave no indication to why we were there, I became nervous.

"Dare, where are we going?"

"To meet some of my friends." He gave me a tight smile. "I have to talk to them. Then we'll eat."

"Oh!" I said when I recognized the boys he gestured to, boys who loitered in the shadow of the silo. All three of them grinned at us as we approached, clear recognition on their faces.

"Do you know them?" Darius asked, his gaze moving between me and Elias, Kish, and Ammon.

"Do *you*?" I challenged, surprised because I knew who they were and what their business in Zarahemla was.

He hesitated only a second before he said, "Of course."

Darius clasped arms with Kish and Ammon, but when he clasped arms with Elias, they did a strange kind of handshake which they both seemed to know. I averted my eyes again, pretending not to notice it, and when I did, I caught Ammon's grin.

"Didn't think I'd see you again," he said. "I certainly didn't think I'd see you here, and I definitely didn't think I'd see you with him." He nodded his head toward Darius.

I shrugged a shoulder. "The family I stay with," I said in Nephite, which seemed to be the language of the moment. "They are Dare's family."

Ammon's brows rose, probably at the nickname I used for his friend. He nodded his understanding politely, but there was nothing polite in the look he slid to Darius. It was knowing and calculating, suspicious and smug.

My mind was racing to piece together the implications that Ammon was forming in his mind. I was staying with Darius. Darius was friends with these men. These men had plans to assassinate the Nephite prophet.

Back in Melek, when I had overheard the plans to infiltrate the prophet's guards and betray them, I had not been very concerned about the prophet. I had been raised to rejoice in any Nephite killing, though I personally had never given much thought to whether it was right or wrong. And Helaman had been just a name to me then. But now I had met him. I had seen his family, seen his children playing together, seen how he lovingly disciplined his eldest son and his pride in the boy. I had been in the same room as him and felt his hand on my shoulder and the warmth that surrounded him.

And now, knowing the plan to infiltrate the guards and kill Helaman—I looked suddenly over at Darius, still talking amicably with Elias and Kish. The same way—the exact same way—he had talked with every guard we had passed since we had entered through the gates of Zarahemla.

Darius caught my eye and sent me a look that clearly instructed me to keep my mouth shut.

"I said I like your new bracelet," Ammon said, attempting to reclaim my attention.

"You can't have it," I laughed, returning my eyes to him.

He smiled too, reminding me why I had been attracted to him in the meadow in Melek. "I am gratified with the one I have." He glanced at my ankle. "And I hope you are gratified with the trade as well."

89

I pointed my toe and twisted my ankle up to show the onyx bracelet I wore there. "I think it looks good on me," I quipped. But glancing back up, I saw him slowly shake his head.

His eyes flicked to Darius before he said, "Better than good. It looks perfect on you."

Our eyes locked and I couldn't think of anything to say—in either language.

"Ava?"

Darius glanced at Ammon as he approached us.

"Will you be okay here for a minute if I go with Elias and Kish? We're just going up there," he pointed toward a hill beyond the silos. "To look over the grounds of the temple."

"Of course," I said. "But I would like to see the temple, too."

"I'll take you later." He glanced at Ammon again. "Alone."

"Take your time, then," I said. "I think Ammon can protect me from the city dwellers."

Darius's mouth turned up in a smile, one side, as always, slightly higher than the other. He gave a quick nod and turned on his heel to catch up with Elias and Kish, who were already halfway up the rise.

Ammon glanced over his shoulder at the departing men. "So what are you doing here—in Zarahemla?"

I put my hands behind my back and turned a little to look at the surroundings. "It was kind of an impulsive decision to come. The city is so large. I didn't think I would see you."

But we both knew I had known he was coming here.

"Did you want to?"

The smile in his eyes when I looked to him told me it was a silly question, only intended to be flirtatious, but I answered anyway. "Yes," I said, flushing, returning my eyes to the surroundings, letting them rove over the long green grasses, the large granaries, the men at the top of the hill.

He was silent for a moment. "Good," he said so softly that I turned back to him. He held my gaze and then looked down and smiled. "That's good," he repeated.

Actually, I didn't see how it was good. After he did what he came to do, he would return to the wilderness and leave me here. Even though I knew he was not honest with me—how could he be with a mission that required absolute secrecy?—I still felt bereft when, after the others returned, he departed with Elias and Kish.

Darius watched the three men go. "Come on," he said. "It's time to meet Tec."

I followed him, giving one last glance to the silos and the hill beyond them.

"How do you know them," Darius asked casually as we turned back onto the main road.

"I met them in the meadow near the falls." We walked for a moment before I thought to add, "That evening I saw you on the path."

"So you don't really know them?"

"No, but I can see that you do."

"Better than I want to," he said under his breath.

"What is that supposed to mean?"

He didn't answer.

"I thought they were quite nice, and it was nice to hear

my own language in my ears for a change."

"Is that why you wear Ammon's bracelet around your ankle?"

How did he know about that?

"If I am understanding your custom correctly, I wear the gift because it would be rude not to. Would it not be an insult to hide it in my satchel?"

"Those are not the kind of men you should be concerned about insulting, Ava."

They were exactly the kind of men one didn't want to insult.

"And yet you are very chummy with them."

He ignored that.

"Is there a reason I should not give them my friendship?"

He chewed on the inside of his cheek, hesitating. "None that I can give you." He pointed up ahead. "There's your brother."

Chloe and Tec had already found a shady place on the side of the road to sit and eat their midday meal. We sat near them and pulled the food we had purchased in the market from our satchels and began to eat.

I watched Chloe. I tried to be surreptitious about it, but Tec caught me, and I gave him a small smile. Chloe was behaving much better than I had anticipated.

Even their arguing turned to banter now and often became good-natured and even playful.

Tec had always been steady—it was why Zaaron and the other leaders had trusted him so much—but seeing the steadying effect he had on Chloe made me step back and really see him. He had become a man, strong and sure of himself.

And Chloe was coming around. One day she would trust him enough to let herself love him, and I had little doubt she wouldn't jump into his arms the way she jumped into everything else.

Someday she would grow up, and he would marry her.

And suddenly, watching her, I was so very envious of what was happening between the two of them. That was supposed to be mine. Josiah was supposed to love me like that, to teach me and guide me and care for me like that.

To my humiliation, Chloe caught the look on my face and offered me a sympathetic-looking smile. As if jealousy and embarrassment weren't enough, she had to add her pity to them. I wanted to get up and walk away, but it wasn't necessary. Chloe got up instead and as she brushed off her dress, she asked Tec to go with her to explore the small woods behind us.

I glanced at the beautiful bracelet Dare had placed on my wrist and then up at his face, turned away from me as he searched for something in his satchel. I thought of the anger in his voice when he had noticed the onyx bracelet on my ankle. I was still unsure how he had known it was Ammon's.

I did not understand him at all, and I was failing miserably at something Leah had made sound so easy. *Just be yourself.* She either didn't know me, or she didn't know her son.

"Here."

Darius dropped a scroll into my lap, drawing me out of my thoughts.

"What is this?"

"It's a book."

"I know that. What is it for?"

"I thought you might like to read it."

"I can't read it," I blurted out. "I mean thank you for the gift, Dare, but I can hardly speak your language let alone read it."

"You've been speaking fine for a while now."

I dropped my eyes again to the book, inordinately pleased by his compliment.

"Can you read in your language?"

"Only a little," I admitted. Why couldn't he ask if I could cook or weave or wash clothing? Or swim? I could do all those things.

"I—" He stopped short, coughed, and restarted. "I like to read."

I nodded, picking up the book and unrolling it enough to see the first characters inked onto it.

"This type of book is called a scroll," he said, taking it from me and unrolling it fully so I could see more of the characters on the linen.

"Where did you get it?" Not many people possessed books.

"I carry it with me everywhere."

I looked steadily at him. This book meant a lot to him. I knew I should not make light of his offering it to me.

"I wrote it." He pulled on a string of his tunic, and then tugged on his ear. "I mean, I copied it from some metal plates. The people of my church are allowed to do that."

Overlooking the clear implication that this was a

religious book, I asked in surprise, "You made these markings?"

"Yeah." He tried to sound dismissive, as if it was no great thing to have such a beautiful hand at writing—it was plain he did—but instead, he sounded reverent.

I ran my finger over the markings. "They're exquisite, Dare, really."

He scratched his head. Then his ankle. And I smiled because I knew he was nervous to share this book with me. Never mind that I had used the Lamanite word for exquisite.

"Will you teach me to read it?"

"Of course," he said, and he reached over to finger the markings as well, as if he wasn't so sure he wanted to give them to me, all his hard work, these words that were sacred and special and important to him.

When his finger touched mine, my heart sped up, and when he outlined my finger with the tip of his, my breath hitched.

Darius quietly began to explain the meaning of the symbols to me, but his voice stilled when we overheard Chloe speaking somewhere in the woods behind us.

"We are legally betrothed. Why do you never kiss me?"

Tec's reply was toned low, and I couldn't make it out. I knew it was not polite to listen to them, but I lifted my head and tilted my ear so I could hear them more clearly.

"My age makes little difference," Chloe said, sounding coy. She was trying to entice him to kiss her? "I am yours now, and you," she paused for emphasis, "you are mine."

Darius began to roll up the scroll. "We should leave," he whispered.

95

I heard Tecumeni's voice clearly this time. "No, you are yet too young for that. That is my firm answer."

Were they getting closer? I briefly caught Darius's eyes. We gathered our things with swift motions and got to our feet. Darius cast me a funny smile, and I almost giggled, but then we heard the hurt in Chloe's voice, and it quickly turned to anger. Surely she was embarrassed, and if we didn't move down the road fast, she would know we had heard her and become even more embarrassed. Wishing to spare her that, we quickly moved away.

But her next words were too loud to miss. "Selfish! You are a conniving bully, and I hate you! I will never kiss you! I will never love or honor you! I hate this all! My life is ruined, and you are ruining it!"

Darius grabbed my hand to pull me into the trees on the other side of the lane, but thinking to console Tec, I resisted his pull.

"I want to go to Tec," I said in a loud whisper.

Darius shook his head.

"Yes," I insisted. "That girl just heartlessly insulted him. I need to go to him."

I turned to go again, but Darius grabbed my elbow hard and pulled me back to him. Shocked, I looked up into his face. I saw him assess the scene behind us over my head and then his eyes beseechingly met mine, and he pulled me finally into the trees.

I tried to wrench my arm away from him. "What are you—"

"Shh!" The sound was harsh.

"Wh—"

"I said shh. You can't go to him. Not now. Not ever—not about this."

"But…"

The look in his eyes silenced me.

His posture changed and he sighed. "Look," he said. "He will never gain her trust if she thinks he tells their business to you."

"But I am his sister! His twin. You do not understand what it is to be a twin!"

"I know what it is to be a brother." Was that pain in his eyes? "I've watched a lot of people fall in love. Tec is doing it right. She is too young."

"She is not too young."

"She is too immature."

"How does he know what is right? He is just a know-nothing kid like the rest of us."

"While you were at home sewing hems into tunics, he was in battle." He glanced through the trees at Chloe and Tec. "He has much more worldly knowledge than you do and is far better equipped to function in the real world than you are."

I gasped. I couldn't help it. Then I did manage to yank my arm out of his grasp. I felt my eyes flash with anger.

"That's not what I meant," he said quickly.

My throat was tight. "You did not mean to say that I am stupid and useless?"

"Of course not, and if you think so you're as childish as Chloe."

I glared at him.

"That's not what I meant, either." He raked a hand through his hair and gripped the back of his neck.

I glanced behind me. "What do you care if Tec's wife respects him?"

"I don't. I care about Chloe."

I sucked in a breath.

"I care about her, Ava, and I don't know what your problem with that is, but you're going to have to deal with it."

I shut my eyes. Why was I so readable?

"I care that Chloe can respect her husband. Tec knows what is right for both himself and those he has stewardship over—that's Chloe—because he heeds the direction of the Spirit."

Still upset by his thoughtless words, talk of their so-called holy spirit did not bring me the comfort I thought he intended it to.

"The spirit," I sneered. "The spirit? It is only attraction he feels for her! Nothing more. Nothing they can build a life together on. It's foolishness!"

Darius didn't respond. Not verbally. When he stepped closer to me, I was determined to hold my ground. But he stepped even closer, and edged closer still until he was so near I could feel the heat from his body. I kept my eyes straight forward—I would have to crane my neck to see into his face—and I studied a tiny hole in the fabric of his tunic at the shoulder, thinking I could mend it for him, as he dropped his lips toward my ear. I expected him to speak, but for long moments he only breathed. I could feel his breath softly stirring wisps of hair at my temple.

"Do you feel that?" he finally murmured

Did he mean his breath on my skin, the butterflies in my stomach, or the mix of fear and wonder in my heart?

"I do not know what you mean," I said.

Oh, but I did.

He spoke slowly. "You loved a man back home in your village. Does this feel the same?"

The mention of Josiah put me immediately on guard, but standing so close to Darius and feeling it ever so much deeper in the fact that he was not touching me anywhere, I couldn't lie.

"No."

He lingered for another moment. "Leave Tec be," he said and stepped abruptly away.

CHAPTER 9

Despite their fight, Tec and Chloe were good company in Zarahemla. Maybe forgiveness was as easy as her sister said it was.

We spent a week on the Estate of Alma, exploring and laughing together. Tec gave me much time alone with Darius, but though I was finding myself more besotted with him each day, there were no lingering touches or fiery glances. Darius treated me much the same as he treated Chloe—like a sister.

On our last morning in Zarahemla, Darius was to take me to view the temple grounds as promised while Tec and Chloe went to the market for supplies.

The air was cool in the morning when Darius and Tecumeni came to Eliza's for us, but the light was pretty and I could hear a bee in the pink azaleas near the door. I recalled the azaleas near the door of her home in the village, and I wondered if Eliza had planted these too in the years she had lived here.

When we were out on the lane, Tec and Chloe hurrying away ahead of us, I said, "I'm glad we have time to see the temple grounds."

"Ammon won't be there this time."

He said it with a teasing smirk that only thinly veiled his feelings. He did not like that I wore Ammon's onyx, but it wasn't because he wished me to be his instead.

I thought about Leah and her offer and what she wanted for her son. I thought of how inadequate I was, how her plan would not work.

I glanced up at him. With the rising sun behind him, his features were in shadow. Maybe he wasn't the untouchable youngest son of a righteous Nephite family. Maybe he was just a confused and lonely person like me. I was skittish and angry, but somewhere inside me there was a girl who was confident and clever, a girl who had turned the head of the village's fiercest warrior.

I took a breath. I would have to be myself.

"I think you have a bit of a jealous streak," I laughed as I punched him in the arm.

He grinned down at me, easily, as if I had not just bolstered all my courage to tease him.

It didn't take long to reach the grassy area between the granaries. We walked beyond them up onto the knoll that provided the view over the temple grounds. As we looked below, we could see people moving about in the courtyard.

"What do you use it for?" I asked, truly curious about the unique layout below us.

Darius squinted one eye closed for a moment while he considered how much to tell me. He folded his arms over his chest. "I'll tell you all about it sometime."

"Why not now?" I wanted to know.

"It's complicated. I think it might be too much information for you right now."

I feigned offense. "Are you saying I'm stupid?"

"Not too much for your mind to comprehend," he

clarified. "Too much for your heart to accept."

"Oh. Then thank you," I mumbled.

His eyes softened. "Come on. Let's get moving."

I nodded, but when we turned to go I noticed something peculiar, something that sent shivers down my spine. I stared at the back of Dare's neck as I followed him down the hill.

The crest of the hill that had such a perfect view of the temple also had a perfect view of Helaman's entire estate— Eliza's tenant house, Helaman's family home, the large manor house where Helaman conducted business, the pretty gardens, the bend in the stream where Darius and I had sat together as dusk had fallen into night.

Darius pointed out various things to me as we passed through the city, but I stayed quiet, thinking about the temple and the estate of Helaman and trying to remember back to a week before and which direction the men had been looking. Again, Ammon had done well his job of distracting me.

We met up with Tec and Chloe at one of the west gates of Zarahemla, but they were involved in a conversation and drifted ahead of us, leaving Darius and me to walk in silence, but it was comfortable silence, better than it had been when I couldn't speak to him in his language.

Darius surprised me when he cleared his throat and said, "You mentioned there was a man at home."

"I did." I didn't see a reason to lie about it. There was the embarrassment, but that was fading with time. And then there was the more difficult subject of my questionable marriage status, but I hoped he wouldn't ask that deep of questions.

"Tell me about him."

"What do you want to know?" I asked cautiously.

"His name?"

"Josiah." I was glad I didn't trip over the word.

"You said you loved him."

"I thought I did." I licked my lips. I didn't want to tell him the truth, but I didn't want to lie to him either. Despite keeping secrets that were not his to share, he valued honesty, and knowing him had caused me to value it too. "I mean, yes, I did. But...it was not the right kind of love. At least, that's what my mother said."

"Did he love you?" Dare asked quietly.

I didn't know. I wanted to say no—to lash out in bitterness and accuse Josiah of lying and hurting and dishonoring me—but I just didn't know. A vision of Josiah's earnest face appeared in my mind. "He said he did," I allowed.

Dare nodded politely, as if he were really considering what I said. "I guess he did you a favor then."

Before I could deny that—vehemently—or ask him what he meant, the strange idea took root in my mind. I had thought Josiah acted out of meanness. Had he fallen in love with another girl? Had he done us both a kindness by refusing to begin a doomed marriage? And had he done it out of love? I had never—not once—thought of those possibilities.

"Sometimes," Dare said, "boys fall in love with girls they're not supposed to."

I frowned. "Dare, are you okay? Did something happen to you?"

"I don't know how to answer that," he said. Then he reached over suddenly and adjusted the strap of my travel pack. "That will chafe," he said.

I glanced at the strap. "Because you don't want to lie," I persisted. "You don't know how to answer because you are not a liar, but you don't want to tell me the truth."

One side of his mouth quirked up, and his chest rose and fell with another deep breath. His large hand went through his hair, but his eyes didn't leave my face. He was considering telling me what was bothering him, why he left the village so much, why he couldn't let himself trust me—or anyone.

"I won't tell," I urged gently. "It's clear you need to talk."

He squinted, began to speak, and then stopped. I could see he wanted to continue, but he remained silent.

I searched his face for a moment. "Would you like to hear more about Josiah?"

"Can you talk about it?" he asked.

"I don't like to. But maybe it is time." And maybe it would help him open up about whatever was bothering him. I knew it was a girl. I thought it was Sarai. I didn't want to hear about it, to know what he felt for her, but I had to admit that I was very curious.

"What happened with him?"

I took a deep, silent breath. "When your kinsmen arrived in my village our men were returning from a year-long duty in Laman. The king requires it of all men. We...I thought it was unfair because they had already gone to the wars and returned."

"Gid said your father was at Cumeni."

"They all were, but my father died there."

He nodded. "Someday," he said quietly, "I could take you to the gravesite at Cumeni."

I frowned. "I never thought of Father having a grave."

"It is a mass grave, but we spent a lot of energy burying the dead. It would be nice if someone got to appreciate it."

I shut my eyes and tried not to picture it. "Father kissed us all and left with a smile. I think he was truly honored to fight for what he thought was right."

"Which was?"

"Oh." I shook off the memories of the last time I had seen my father. "He believed, as we all do, that Laman's younger brother, Nephi, had no right to take his people under separate rule. He stole the brass plates from our forefathers, taking our history, genealogy, and language with him."

"That's true," he agreed. "But he didn't steal the plates, and he was directed by the Lord to leave for his own safety, so he did have the authority to rule his people."

"Authority from a god my people do not recognize. But that is something I will not argue with you, for I do not know the truth of it. I only know what my kinsmen have told me."

"So, you were young when they left."

"Yes." I bit my bottom lip. This was the hard part. "In the weeks before that, Josiah and I shared a betrothal ceremony."

"Ah."

"He had been courting me for some time, and he was quite determined about it. He was nice to me. He…" I smiled. "He made me feel special."

"At least he did that right."

I felt my face flush with color but kept talking. "He was older and so strong. The best warrior our village had. I never could figure out why he wanted me, but becoming his betrothed made me so very happy."

I got lost for a moment in the memories of the good times with Josiah, before the war had changed him, but Dare's disbelieving snort pulled me from them.

"You couldn't figure out why he wanted you?"

"No."

"You were young," he said, as if that explained, or even excused, why I had allowed myself to feel so betrayed.

I shrugged. "But it was not just that." How could I explain? "I mean, Josiah was the greatest warrior, the boy every girl wished for, but I was not special in any way." I twisted my hands together. "I guess he finally realized that."

Darius gave me a dubious look. "So what happened? You're not still betrothed are you?"

"That's the hurtful part."

He looked at me with brows raised, waiting.

"He is married to another girl now."

"So you are not betrothed."

I took a breath. "He did not legally complete a divorce. Or at least, I have no papers to prove it."

"Perhaps he gave them to your mother."

I frowned. "Perhaps. I had not considered that. But Tec knows nothing of it if Josiah did."

"She would have insisted. I'm sure he did."

"She was mourning my father at the time. She may have overlooked it."

He gave his head a hard shake. "No. She did not

overlook it, Ava. Your kinsfolk would have seen to it."

I sighed. I really wanted to believe him. "I hope you're right. I was much too hurt to see to it. Too young. Too stupid. Too naïve. Too everything."

"Hey."

My eyes sought his.

"Don't talk like that. No wonder you couldn't see why Josiah courted you with such determination."

I shrugged again.

"Haven't you ever noticed how men stare at you?"

I had noticed that. "Of course. Because I look so different and act awkward and uncomfortable."

He burst into a deep laugh.

Offended and wanting to change the subject, I asked bluntly, "What happened with Sarai?"

He stopped laughing, sobering instantly, and I couldn't help but feel guilty for it. I wanted the smile back in his eyes, not the stormy look that took its place.

"She saw me kiss Isabel." Darius set his mouth in a deprecating smirk. "On the day Izz was to wed my brother."

It was so terrible I giggled nervously. "Oh, Dare," I said, reverting to my native tongue in my surprise. "I think you had better keep talking."

The smirk remained as he went on—smoothly, as if he had not noticed my words had been foreign. "I always thought I would marry Isabel. She was the daughter of my mother's best friend, the perfect age for me, and we had been friends since we were children. I would run through the forest with her and Jarom and I would look at her and know our parents meant for us to wed when we became of age."

"I understand," I said. What I understood was that this was the thing, the reason he kept leaving his village. "You believed you would fulfill everyone's expectations."

"Right," he mumbled. "When Keturah didn't wed Zeke, everything changed. It set a precedent, I guess. And then Kenai came home from the war and he was so sad and angry all the time. He wouldn't eat. He wouldn't talk to anyone. He spent all his time alone—until Isabel took a notion to…befriend him. She became his only link to the rest of us for a time, and gradually, he fell in love with her."

"And she fell in love with him."

He sighed deeply with a resignation that sounded long-since entrenched. "I think she always loved him, to tell you the truth. She looked at me as a brother. She looked at him—" Had his voice caught? "She looked at him with stars in her eyes. When I saw the way things were, the way her eyes followed him, the way she *breathed* when she was thinking of him…" He shook his head. "I made a decision. It was impulsive, but I stuck to it, except for just that one time when I wished her well with a kiss."

"Oh, Dare."

"I gave Izz my blessing." He scoffed. "Not that she needed it, but I needed to give it."

"Because you loved her."

"No." His voice had a soft rasp. "Because he is my brother."

I let him ruminate in his thoughts for a time and then said, "So it was not Sarai who broke your heart."

He scoffed again. "Who says my heart is broken?"

Oh, Dare. "Nobody has to say it."

109

CHAPTER 10

As we turned from the West Road onto a path that led to the village, I said, "Thank you for taking me with you Dare. I had much…it was…I mean, I had fun."

He studied me for a moment and said, "I did too."

"You don't have to sound so surprised."

That earned me a broad grin.

Many of the villagers were tending to their evening meals when we emerged from the thick trees into the familiar clearing. Chloe was already in her mother's embrace, and Tec waved to us from Hemni and Dinah's yard. Darius escorted me straight to his mother's home where Leah was standing in front of the little house with a smile.

It might have surprised us all when she came first to me instead of to her son. She embraced me warmly and then insisted on helping me slip out of my travel pack.

"Kalem and I have eaten already, but there is plenty of food still warm."

When we were sitting and eating, Leah retrieved her own satchel from a peg near the door of the house and stepped to the little gate. "I will be back later," she called to us, and we watched her walk across the lane to Dinah's home. Her abrupt departure was somewhat puzzling. Usually, she kind of hovered.

Dinah met her between the two homes and they walked out of the village together, pulling their shawls around their shoulders.

My eyes fell to the two dusty travel packs that leaned against the side of the house. "When you unpack, leave your tunics. I will wash them for you."

"You don't have to do that."

"You didn't have to take me to Zarahemla. I appreciate it."

He was quiet for a moment as he finished up the last of his food. He seemed so hungry for his mother's food, so eager for it, I thought of passing him the remainder of my own, and after a moment, I did. He hesitated, but accepted it.

When he was done, he fingered a chip in the rim of his bowl, a silence falling between us unlike the easiness we had experienced on the road.

I reached over and eased the bowl from his hands. I could feel his eyes on my back as I walked away to rinse the dishes, but when I returned, he was gone and the yard was quiet, so I took my satchel and went to the waterfall to bathe in the churning pool.

It was nearly dark when I returned. Kalem, Leah, and Darius were relaxing near the fire. I was about to walk into the light when I heard my name, so I stayed in the shadows at the corner of the house.

"Ava seems no worse for wear after your journey," Leah was saying.

"She is a strong traveler," Darius allowed.

"That is a nice compliment," Leah replied.

Darius had his long legs stretched before him and his

arms crossed over his chest. His dark hair gleamed in the firelight like polished obsidian. Recognizing her tone, as I had, he turned his head to look at his mother.

"After a week together you must have sweeter compliments to give."

Leah!

I clutched my satchel closer to myself and felt my wet hair dripping onto my dress.

"I do."

Darius's answer surprised me, but apparently it did not surprise his mother.

"And have you taken the opportunity to give them to her?"

"It is not the time for me to be involved with a girl," he said, his eyes settling back on the fire.

Kalem shifted forward in his seat. "You're over twenty."

"I am busy."

"Doing what?" Leah's voice was almost pleading.

"Doing what is necessary," he grumbled. "Do not build your hopes up for a betrothal, Mother. You will know disappointment." With that, Darius got up and left the fire.

When he passed me in the shadows, our eyes met but did not hold. I shifted out of his way. I thought he had passed when I felt his warm hand on my wet shoulder.

He didn't speak. He was probably trying to find the right words, the right lie.

But the right lie came from my mouth. "Do not trouble yourself with my feelings, Dare. We understand each other."

"Av—"

I shrugged out from under his hand and walked into the firelight.

The next morning, I woke early to take the wash to the pond behind the house. My hands stilled on the tunics that lay across the table, but I had offered to wash them, and I bundled them into my arms.

It was quiet at the water's edge. I was days late for the village wash day when most of the women washed together. I didn't hurry through the chore, but I was thinking I should go when the sun had burned off the pink from the sky and the air was turning warm. I leaned back to stretch my back, and Darius appeared.

"Hi," he said and ran a hand through his hair. He glanced back the way he had come and then looked toward the water.

"I was just leaving," I said.

He worried the fingernail on his thumb and nodded, but he went to his heels next to me. "I wanted to ask you something," he said.

I pulled the last tunic from the water to wring it out, but Darius took it from my hands.

"You don't have to," he said, his voice quiet, as he efficiently squeezed the garment until it was only damp.

I took it from him to fold down into my basket.

He let out a breath. "Kalem said a messenger came through with news of a wedding. My friend's wedding."

"A surprise?"

He rubbed the back of his neck. "Not really, but I didn't know the date. I would like to go." He paused. "I don't want to be at the wedding alone."

114

I studied him a moment—the mottled red creeping up his neck, the way his eyes darted away. There were some things I did not need to speak his language to know.

"Do you want me to come?"

He breathed out. "Yes. But I was kind of hoping…do you think we could…" He tugged on his ear and then rested his arms over his knees and folded his hands. "I mean, I know we are only friends, but do you think we could just not mention that?"

Mislead his friends? He would have more trouble with that than I would.

"You want them to believe there is more than friendship between us?" I wanted to be sure I understood his intent.

The red crept into his cheeks. He nodded.

"I have no objection to that. And quite honestly, I don't see how it could look any other way if we show up together."

He nodded again slowly. "We will travel with some of my friends from Orihah."

I bit my lip. "When?"

"The end of the season."

"Alright," I agreed. For a long moment his dark eyes met mine, and I saw that what I thought were just blue eyes, were instead cerulean like the deepest sea. When he did not look away, I felt my face heat.

I think you're pretty.

He didn't have to say it because his voice whispered through my memory. But the feel of his fingertips on my face was not a memory. That was real.

Darius disappeared from the village two more times

before the rains came to an end and we made the preparations to go to Antionum. Leah worried, but she tried very hard not to show it. I never heard her broach the subjects of either Dare's absences or his marriage, and she did not revisit our agreement with me, though she did with Tecumeni.

"She still hopes very much for a betrothal," he said often during the long days we endured inside while the rain poured down on the little village.

And during that time, I avoided Leah's eyes because I had failed her. She believed her son would take me to wife, but I knew it wasn't what he wanted. There was something else he wanted more, and I thought his heart was still bruised over Isabel. Did she think I could heal it? I couldn't even heal my own.

It felt like a long time before the rains ended and the ground dried enough for travel.

One evening, Darius said, "We can leave tomorrow, if that suits you."

I glanced at Leah, who was clearly listening though she tried to appear uninterested. After I nodded, he turned and walked from the house. I moved to the door and watched him walk out into the twilight that fell early in the tall trees.

"Let's get you packed," Leah said with a smile she tried to temper.

Darius was waiting for me at dawn by the little gate to Kalem and Leah's courtyard.

The ground was not yet fully dry and the air was cool and thick with mist, especially before the sun burned it off. Had he been cold? Had he felt alone?

"Where did you sleep last night?" I asked after we

waved a final goodbye to a hopeful Leah and a skeptical Tecumeni and slipped into the woods.

Darius only shrugged.

"I think it rained," I persisted, seeing that heavy drops of dew rolled off the large green leaves as we brushed past them.

"I stayed with a friend," he said, almost reluctantly, as if to admit it meant he was not brave enough to sleep alone in the wilderness.

But I knew him to be brave.

He was involved in something he didn't want to be involved in, associating with men he neither liked nor respected.

Did he fear what would happen if he didn't?

He gave me his steady hand as we slid down the steep slope to the West Road, and I asked, "How do you know this friend we are traveling to see?"

"Seth? I know him from the war. He was Keturah's captain."

I knew that Keturah had been in the Nephite army, but it was still strange to hear the boys refer to it so casually, as if it were normal for a woman to march out to battle.

"And who will he wed?"

"A girl from Antionum. A Zoramite. I've met her, but only once."

Darius held a bramble out of my way as we skirted it.

"When did you last see Seth? Antionum is quite distant, you said."

"Remember I told you I went to Zarahemla with a friend while the others were in the Lamanite lands? We ran

117

into Seth while we were there." He laughed. "He introduced us to Naomi, who was a very unwanted tagalong at the time. A very old acquaintance, I take it. Look there."

"What is it?"

"A doe, just there behind that large mahogany."

"She's pretty," I said.

"It will be a cold winter for her."

"How can you know that?"

"Can't you feel it in the air?"

"No," I laughed. "And neither can you."

He chuckled and looked up to study the sky. I glanced up too, but it was no different than any other beautiful midsummer day—vivid blue with high, white clouds.

"Sometimes, Ava, you can feel things that have no logical evidence."

"Like I can feel you are involved in something you shouldn't be."

"Let's not talk of that."

"Okay. I just hope you know what you're doing."

He cleared his throat. "You could feel the harsh weather coming, too, if you were in tune to the signs. If it is not a cold winter, we will be in for a very wet spring. Last spring will seem dry in comparison."

I wondered what he meant by cold. Cold in Ani-Anti meant I put on a shawl in the evening.

"But water is good for the crops."

"True, but flooding is bad for the villages. And dangerous."

"Do you think it will be that bad?"

He scratched his nose. "No."

I laughed again. "You're lying."

He snorted. "I am not a liar, Ava."

"More like a keeper of secrets," I suggested, still smiling.

"More like a keeper of secrets," he agreed.

But he had shared many pieces of his secrets with me, ones that weighed heavily on him. It was I who must be the keeper of his secrets.

By early afternoon we were in the foothills of a mountain range on the east of the Sidon river that Darius said ran south and curved toward the eastern sea to provide a natural barrier between Antionum and the Land of Nephi. We ate our midday meal at a crossroads near a spring. The day was warm, and I downed all my water, then leaned back on my hands and raised my face to the sun.

"What is Antionum like?" I asked lazily.

Darius swallowed what was in his mouth. "It is predominantly Lamanite."

I sat up, squinting at the bright sun. "Really?" I hadn't known the People were so close to Melek. "But how is this possible? And why does Seth live amongst them?"

"The Zoramites, the people who possess the land, they allow the Lamanites to live there. It's a great worry to my people. We have an army stationed in Jershon to prevent against attack to the inner holdings."

"And Seth?"

"Seth is following his heart, not political boundaries."

"He stays there for her?"

"I think it's a bit foolish."

"I think it's sweet."

We heard the voices at the same time. It sounded like a group of people coming toward us on the intersecting road. Darius held up a hand to ask for my silence while he listened.

Suddenly, a broad grin spread over his face.

CHAPTER 11

Eight people approached us on the dusty road. It was clear from Dare's grin that these were the friends we were to meet up with. He trotted out to meet them, and I watched with apprehension as he clasped arms with each of the other boys.

I felt their gazes as they came near, many curious eyes darting between Darius and me. It was the suspicion he wished to foster. We were expecting it, but I was suddenly nervous as they all looked to Darius for an introduction.

"This is Ava," Darius said, and added, "Tec's sister."

He proceeded to make introductions. Enos was Gid's cousin, and I could see the resemblance in his features. The youngest girl, Esther, was his newly betrothed. I swallowed down my jealousy and smiled at her. Zachariah was next and his wife, Beth, who had rich brown hair and kind eyes. A tall man named Lib with tanned skin and fair hair stood awkwardly near a girl who Darius introduced as Miriam. Her pale skin had a light smattering of adorable freckles, and they made me feel dark and different. Two other men, bright-eyed Corban and short, stocky Reb, completed the group.

"Where are the others?" Darius asked Enos.

Enos passed his water skin to Esther, who smiled and took it to fill at the spring. Beth and Miriam gathered the other men's water skins and followed her.

"Noah's just been given charge of the farm, so he could not get away, and Joshua said he could not come. I think he's busy courting."

Darius laughed with the others and turned to one of them. "And your cousins?"

"Cyrus and Mathoni have been fishing off the coast of the East Sea, but I expect they will be at the ceremony. Gid and Keturah didn't want to travel with Gabriel. I don't blame them. And with Jashon gone, Lamech so often in your village courting Sarai, and Shad in the city, Gid is the only son left on the farm. But they sent their best wishes."

"Well, when you've all had the chance to rest, we'll set out."

Enos nodded and went to Esther at the stream, where he put a foot on a rock in the center of it and bent down to splash her. She gasped and splashed him back. Beth smiled at them, but quickly gathered the water skins and returned them to their owners. They each found a stone or a log to sit on to rest as there were plenty that had been left there for travelers.

"Will you be uncomfortable traveling with my friends?" Darius asked softly.

I would, a little. "Why should I be?"

He shrugged. "They were soldiers. They fought in Cumeni." He paused. "They might ask questions about us."

He had asked me to accompany him to this wedding. He didn't want his friends to think of him as lonely. He didn't want them to pity him, and I understood that all too well. But I caught another glimpse of Enos and young Esther and wondered if perhaps Darius wasn't as concerned with looking alone as he was with actually being lonely.

"Is there anything you don't want me to say to them?"

"Like what?"

"Do you want them to know we are not in love?"

"We're not?"

I laughed and shook my head. "I may be too blind to see when a boy does *not* love me, but I think I know when a boy does."

"Don't be so sure," he teased.

When we started again for Antionum, which Darius said we wouldn't reach until the next afternoon, he naturally fell into step with his friends. The blond one seemed to be holding himself back from the others, however, and I decided to try out my Nephite on him.

"Darius says you are to sail off on a grand ship," I said to his back as I tried to catch up to him.

He turned and grinned when he saw me.

"She's grand all right."

"Your ship won't sail without you?"

He shook his head. "We've time yet. And I am just building the ship. I haven't decided yet if I will sail." His eyes darted to the blond girl.

"I imagine such a grand endeavor takes a lot of time to organize."

"Aye, it does. And many legal papers to keep up to date. Signatures and the like."

I nodded, though I didn't really understand how difficult that must be.

My eyes found Darius walking among his friends.

We've time yet.

Lib followed my gaze, but I said, "I think your Miriam is feeling alone."

His blond brow rose, and I pointed to where Miriam was walking, separate from the other girls—as if she were making herself available for someone to join her.

"My…?"

I laughed at him. "She can't keep her eyes on the road for darting glances at us. I fear for my safety while I sleep."

His eyes went to her.

"She is the reason you won't sail." It was clear as the day. "Did it not occur to you that she might enjoy your company?"

"She knows everyone here," he said, a tad defensively.

I caught her eye for a brief moment before she looked away again. "I'd wager there is not one person here she would rather talk to than you."

He shook his head. "It's not really like that."

But it was like that.

I sighed. "Even if it isn't, she is alone. Go. Make her feel comfortable. Your friends can be quite intimidating."

He looked around at the men as if he had never thought of them that way. When his eyes returned to me, they were soft.

"Go on," I urged.

It took him a moment to decide. Was he bolstering his courage? Miriam was pretty, if you liked fair-haired girls, but intimidating? Finally, he gave me a smile and a small wave and loped off toward her.

But I only walked alone for a short time before I felt

a presence on either side of me as Beth and Esther flanked me.

"You would think they hadn't seen each other in a year," one of the women said. I thought it was the one named Beth.

The other giggled. "I think it has not yet been one cycle of the moon."

For a moment, I thought they were talking about Lib and Miriam.

But Beth said, "They are like brothers."

"Do you see Dare a lot?" I asked her, realizing they were talking about the boys, how they were so intent on catching up with each other.

"He comes to Orihah all the time."

"What does he do there?" I asked. I couldn't tell Leah what Darius did in Zarahemla, but perhaps I could tell her something of his time spent in Orihah.

Beth frowned a little, as if she had never thought it strange that he spent so much time in a place that was not his home. "He stays with friends, helps them with their work, and when they no longer need him, he finds another friend who needs him."

"Unless Lamech and Sarai come into town," put in Esther. "Then he leaves Orihah and we don't see him again for a while."

"Why?" I asked, though I knew.

"Well," Esther lowered her voice, "Enos says he goes out to the barley farm and watches Sarai. He's in love with her, but she is betrothed to Enos's cousin, Lamech."

I knew that. I had been at the betrothal in the village.

"Watches her? Do you mean he spies on her?"

Esther giggled again, and I had to wonder how old she was.

Beth laughed too, but at the absurdity of the story. "Something happened between them for sure, but I do not think he is in love with her."

"I don't either," I said quickly, hoping Esther would latch on to the idea. "I asked him about her, and he told me, very straightforward. It was Sarai who loved him, but he was unable to return it, and that hurt him because he does care for her. He would never want to hurt her."

The girls were both silent and I could feel them staring at me. I wondered if I had used the wrong words or perhaps slipped back into my own language as I sometimes did, but then Esther giggled again.

"Enos says he doesn't talk about what happened," she informed me.

"He doesn't," Beth confirmed. "It makes me wonder why he told you." Her smile was knowing.

"He told me because I asked him to."

They exchanged a glance.

"Don't you think others have asked him?" Beth asked.

Surprising me, Esther said, "Perhaps he was not ready to talk about it before. It can be hard to talk about matters of the heart, especially for boys. If what you say is true, Ava, and he had no choice but to hurt Sarai's feelings, he probably feels very guilty."

I looked at him ahead of us, surrounded by his friends. "I think he feels a great deal of guilt," I agreed. "Now," I said, taking a deep breath. "In my village, it is not polite to talk of someone behind his back. We should find something else to talk about."

"Tell us about your village then," suggested Beth. "The men invited me to travel there with them when they went in search of Gid, but I didn't go. I was too afraid, and I kept Zach from going to help. He's a quiet man anyway, but he gave me his silence for a week. It was selfish of me."

"No it wasn't," Esther immediately protested. "You did what you thought was right."

"Well, if I had gone, I would've met Ava in her village."

"But you are meeting her now."

The way the two talked, I could tell they had known each other a long time. Perhaps they were even related.

"You wouldn't have been allowed into the village," I told Beth. "My Uncle Zaaron made the Nephites stay outside the village. The only one allowed in was Sarai, and that was because we thought she was Lamanite."

"Sarai?" laughed Esther. "How could you possibly mistake her for a Lamanite? She is so fair!"

I shrugged. "My uncle said she was, so we accepted it. Besides, she speaks perfect Lamanite, like she was born in my village"

Their eyes went round. "She does?"

"She said Muloki taught her when she was little."

Esther's eyes lit. "Muloki! Isn't he the best looking Lamanite you ever saw?" Esther's voice was wistful and a dreamy look came into her eyes.

"Are you not betrothed?" I asked cautiously.

"Well, sure, but that doesn't mean I can't daydream about a handsome man."

"That's exactly what it means," Beth told her firmly.

Esther sighed. "I didn't mean anything by it." She looked at me. "I have not been betrothed for very long. I am still...adjusting."

I smiled at her. When I had been betrothed, I'd had eyes for no one but Josiah.

"Well, in that case," I said and fanned myself with my hand. "Muloki *is* the best looking Lamanite I've ever seen."

All three of us giggled then, and when I looked up, I caught Dare's approving eye. I grinned at him. If only he knew what I was giggling about with the wives of his friends.

I liked these two women. Even Esther with her youth and her innocence gave me a feeling of hope and happiness that I couldn't explain. So I spent my afternoon with them and enjoyed it.

When we camped for the night, Miriam, joined us to help prepare the meal. Her hair and skin were as light as mine were dark, but she was both pleasant and intelligent, and I couldn't help but like her, too. A year before, I would have hated her on sight.

"I see you have come with Darius," she said. "I am a friend of his sister."

"Keturah?"

"You know her?"

"I live with Leah."

"Ah, then of course you know her. I live near her home in Orihah."

"Gid taught me to speak your language," I offered when we fell into a small silence.

"You speak it well."

128

The compliment made me flush, because once Gideon had taught me how to hear the language, I *had* been making an effort to speak it.

We cooked a quantity large enough for everyone and then we sat together at the fire until exhaustion sent us all to our bedrolls. Zachariah came and held out his hands to help Beth up. Then he turned and helped Esther up, and I wondered again if the two women were related.

Beth turned to me. "Goodnight, Ava."

"Goodnight," I told them and watched the three of them walk into the twilight. Enos came to meet them. He put his arm over Esther's shoulder and the four of them talked for a moment before separating.

"I set your tent up over here."

I looked over my shoulder to see Darius standing with Lib. Lib said nothing, but Miriam gave me a small smile and left with him.

"Thank you," I said to Darius when they were gone, but I made no move toward the tent.

He sat beside me. "Looks like you hit it off with Beth and Esther."

"Are they related?" I asked.

"Sisters."

"They don't look at all alike."

He shook his head.

"They don't even act alike, but the way they act together, it reminds me of home."

I could almost feel him frowning in the silence between us, and when I looked over at him, I saw it in the play of shadows cast by the fire.

He kept his eyes trained on the fire and asked, "Do you ever think you could make a home here?"

I watched him for a moment and then turned to look into the fire too. "Tec says I may live with him and Chloe for as long as I want."

"I'm not talking about living with your brother, Ava."

My heart caught on the low timbre of his voice. He may have come to some kind of understanding with my brother that allowed for me to come on this journey with him, but he and I had come to nothing. He had offered me nothing. Whether it was because he didn't want to or because he didn't feel free to—it didn't really matter.

"Then what *are* you talking about, Dare?"

He looked down into his lap and then back up into the fire before responding. He rubbed the side of his nose. He sighed. "Nothing. No, well, Tec will see you provided for, but I know you miss your family and your old life. Do you think you could ever be happy here?"

"There is nothing left for me there. It wouldn't be the same if I returned."

"And if there was? If you could return and marry Josiah?"

"No," I whispered into the night, the denial blending with the soft crackle of a dying fire. "No," I said again more loudly. "I am not the same person I was. The things I have seen and felt, the people I have met..." I slid my hand over until the outside of my smallest finger touched his on the ground between us. It felt like lightning. He didn't move, and I wondered if he felt it too. "The people I have met and the experiences I have had, all of it makes me feel like a different girl than I was in Ani-Anti. I don't know if that makes sense."

"It does."

"If I am going to be happy, it must be here."

"So you're just going to make the best of a bad situation?"

His tone made me frown. I had at long last resigned myself to staying with the Ammonites. Making the best of it was my only choice. I almost said so, but I sensed it was not what he wanted to hear. But why wouldn't he want me to make the best of my situation?

Speaking slowly and carefully, following some prompting, I said, "I never planned to come to your land, Dare, but I was meant to come here. I know it. There is something for me to do here, to feel or know or experience here, that I could not do in Ani-Anti."

Adding a deep thunder to the lightning I felt, Darius slid his hand over mine and interlaced our fingers. He held it firmly but did not interrupt me.

"I may have been disappointed at first, and even now I do not yet understand why, but I was compelled to follow Tec out of the village. I was intrigued by Sarai and her people in a way I can't explain. If it was your holy spirit guiding my footsteps, I hope that it continues to guide me until I can understand what it is I am supposed to do and how it is I am to be happy."

Darius was still and silent.

"I am not disappointed with where my footsteps have brought me."

Slowly, Darius turned to meet my eyes.

One of the other men poured sand on the fire and the

camp plunged into darkness, lit only by a few embers left glowing for the night guard. I felt Dare's fingers tighten slightly around my hand.

Everyone was headed to their bedrolls, but Darius didn't move, so I didn't either. With the fire out, the stars shone brightly above us. The clouds shifted over the moon, and I could sense a fragrance on the breeze, a flower maybe.

Darius chuckled into the darkness. "Your brother looks at me as if he will draw his sword at any moment."

"Tec?" I laughed, wondering at the change of subject.

"Tec," he repeated.

I didn't believe him. Tecumeni? The boy who had saved all of Dare's kinsmen because he fell for Sarai's pretty face? The boy who had taken on the horror of Chloe's temper and recklessness because some unseen spirit told him it was right? Tecumeni—who prayed morning, midday, and night because of a feeling he could not describe to me? The boy who had been there for me from the very beginning of this life-altering journey, not because he had to, but because it was his very nature to stand between his loved ones and danger?

But had he been standing between me and Darius? He had told me he approved of Dare. He was much better than I deserved, and Tec had been sabotaging it?

Anger and confusion swept through me, making my face heat and my ears ring.

"He thinks I am not moving fast enough to marriage."

It took a few moments for Dare's words to sink past my fury and disappointment, and when they did, not only was my face hot with embarrassment, but my heart began to pound and a lump formed in my throat.

132

I had been feeling quite good about my ability to speak in the Nephite language, but when I couldn't formulate a response to Dare's words, he told me the same thing he had so staunchly told his mother.

"This is a really bad time for me to become involved with a girl."

I knew that. Oh, how I knew it.

CHAPTER 12

"What is that?" I asked.

I was standing with a group of the men on the summit of the pass into Antionum. I was the first to notice what looked to be a dark cloud floating over the ground far to the southwest. No one spoke for a moment as they all stared in the direction I pointed. One of them let out a low whistle.

"What is it?" I asked again, alarmed by the quality of their silence.

Dare looked down at me. "That," he said, "is the dust kicked up by an army of men."

"An army?" I asked stupidly. I knew the word, but what would an army be doing way out here?

In an instant, they were no longer a group of friends, but a band of warriors. It was a change I could feel in the quality of their silence and the prickling of hairs on my neck.

Enos spoke with an authority that none of them questioned when he clipped out, "Reb. Corban."

"We'll catch up before you reach the city," Reb said with a cold resignation that worried me. Reb was always laughing, never like this. The two separated themselves from the others, and then they were both running toward the cloud of dust.

The rest of us trailed Enos's purposeful stride down

the hill toward Esther and Beth, where they knelt together cooking the midday meal, talking with the ease of sisters and occasionally sharing a secret smile. Enos stepped to his pretty, young betrothed and placed a big hand on her shoulder. The smile in her eyes dimmed when she saw the look on his face.

"Finish quickly. I'm going to put out the fire."

She glanced at the other men, but didn't argue. Zach already held a shovel full of sandy dirt, ready to smother the fire the moment the women moved the food from around it.

"What's going on?" Beth asked.

"Looks like a possible attack on Antionum," Zach told her. "An army—to the southwest, a day's journey away."

"How—?"

"Nothing short of tens of thousands of men would kick up a cloud like that," he told her grimly. "Now hurry, get those corn cakes off the stone. We don't want to invite a spy party to the midday meal."

She finished up efficiently, and having nowhere else to set the cakes, passed them out to the men. Each of them thanked her and set to eating with quick, deliberate bites. This meal had become for sustenance and nothing more. No savoring the delicious warm cakes and no talking warmly with their friends while they ate.

When the midday camp and fire had been hidden well, we moved quickly down the mountain. Darius watched me carefully and took my hand when I crossed streams or steadied me at the elbow when the slope was steep. Some of the men wanted to abandon the road and its switchbacks, arguing we could get there faster if we went as the crow flew, but Enos sent one meaningful look toward the girls, and there was no more mention of running recklessly down the hillside.

"Why do we want to get to Antionum so fast if it is to be attacked?" I couldn't help but ask the question that had been on my mind all afternoon.

He glanced at me, then back to the road ahead. Rubbing the side of his nose with a knuckle, he said, "I don't really think Antionum will be attacked. It's half full of Lamanites already. It is more likely that the Zoramite governor has allowed them to assemble in the land and fortify themselves for an attack on the Nephites." He was silent for a moment. "It does not bode well."

"But why? I don't understand."

"The war is not over," he said. "The Nephites have retaken and fortified our outer holdings, but as long as one side wants to fight, the war will never be over."

"It is madness!" I said. "So many die! And for what?"

"My people die for honor," he said hotly. I was taken aback at the venom in his words. "We die to protect our families. We are all that stand between them and the wickedness of this world. I do not know what *your* people die for."

My people. His words stung.

"I see," I said tightly. "How noble of you."

"Ava," he almost growled. His tone might have been apologetic, but if he was trying for that, he didn't achieve it.

"Don't," I said, and I left him to watch after me, if he even bothered to, as I hurried forward to walk with Beth, Esther, and Miriam. They each smiled warmly, though I could see the swift pace Enos had set made them all uneasy.

Thank you for your friendship, I thought fervently as I smiled back at them, and I thought if there was a god, he had surely sent these friends to me. And tentatively, silently, I thanked him too.

"Do you think Seth will go forward with the marriage ceremony with the Lamanite army approaching?" Beth asked her husband.

"We don't know it's Lamanites," Zachariah said calmly from somewhere behind us.

Darius scoffed. I couldn't help turning to glare at him. He was *in league* with *my people*. Hadn't Elias, Kish, and Ammon spoken Lamanite with the ease of natives? Was his disgust just an act to throw these men off his true intentions?

Enos chuckled in clear contrast to the prevailing mood. "Seth won't let anything stop his marriage. That guy was born to be married."

Esther giggled. "What do you mean he was born to be married?"

Enos shrugged. "He's just the type. He wants a home, a wife, and children. Always has, very much."

The type to marry. Did that mean he was not the type to consort with assassins or betray his own people and his god?

It didn't matter. Dare's secret business was none of mine. Men did what they wanted to and didn't have to explain their reasons to women. That was the way things were.

I didn't care what he did, I didn't care if he was duplicitous with his friends, but it would have been a lie to say, to even let myself think, he hadn't hurt me with his thoughtless words.

But he has always been so kind.

I tried to push the thought from my mind. It only confused me more. But when he approached me hours later, as we descended out of the foothills and turned toward the gates of the city, with a hang-dog look, the thought still repeated in my head. *He has always shown you kindness. He has been nothing but kind.*

"I hurt your feelings," he said when he had drawn me to the rear of our traveling companions and the chance of being overheard was minimal.

His candor surprised me.

He tugged on his ear, and the animosity I had been feeling instantly melted away.

"I don't know what I said," he admitted, fiddling with the strap of his satchel, stretching it out in front of him and letting it slide back against his chest.

I turned to study him. His words were true. He was being honest about his feelings.

"You are a contradiction," I said.

His eyebrows shot up.

I wet my lips and took a breath. "You claim disdain for my people, and yet you conspire with them at the expense of your own."

His mouth parted slightly and he shot a glance to his friends.

"I am starting to question whether my people are right in their traditions. I am starting to question if we have a valid reason to hate the descendants of Nephi for what he did. I am starting to question whether or not what he did was indeed wrong."

His eyes lit as he listened to me.

"My feelings come from years of being immersed in the traditions and ideologies of my parents and family, but you, a Christian, hate just to hate." I put a fist to my chest. "But they are my people, Dare. They are good and loving and rich in heritage. They are knowledgeable and skilled. The husbands love their wives, and the wives honor their husbands. Our children are happy and provided for and protected diligently. Your unfair disdain of my beautiful people offends me."

His expression hardened.

"What I do is for my people!" he hissed, sending another glance toward the others. "Do you think your unfair disdain of my people has not offended me?"

I had not thought of it. I had not seen past my own suffering.

"The others of the village think you are only shy, but I saw you when you thought no one was looking. I saw the hateful way you looked at my mother, even as she offered you her home and all that she had. You think she is traitorous to her countrymen. And for what? For seeking religious freedom!" He took a step closer, and his voice gentled on my name. "Ava, I saw the sneer you tried to hide when you looked at Chloe. You thought a Nephite girl was not good enough for your brother." His words were harsh, but his tone took much of the sting from it. He was right, and we both knew it. He reached out to touch my cheek, but he stopped short of it. "How is that different?" he asked softly.

It wasn't, and it was no wonder he hadn't chosen me over whatever he was doing for his people.

"I am trying," I said.

"I know," he replied simply.

When we approached the gates of the city, the guards made Enos tell them why we were there, but they let us through easily enough.

As the rest of us passed, Enos stepped aside to talk to the guards. "There is an army a day's journey to the west," he told them. "It is thousands strong and moving this way. We saw it from the summit."

The guards glanced at each other and one of them nodded. "We know."

I didn't hear any more.

I turned to Darius. "How will we find Seth's home?"

"I have directions."

"Oh. And when is the wedding to take place?"

"Tomorrow."

"What will we do tonight?"

He turned to me with a smile. "Do you always ask so many questions?"

"It is nice to be able to ask them," I admitted. "I was lost in your language for so long. It gave me a headache to listen to it."

"How did you learn to speak so it quickly?"

"Gid's instructions. And it took me six months."

"True, but one day you understood nothing and the next you understood everything."

"I understood so little you thought you could tell me I was pretty and I would not know."

His grin was crooked and sheepish.

"Gideon made me see what I didn't want to acknowledge, that I was comprehending it long before I tried to speak it. I was just being stubborn. I guess I was hoping Tec would take me home before I had to learn it."

"You never considered it might be the spirit helping you?"

I laughed. "If there is such a being, I doubt it would help someone like me."

"You know there is such a being," he said earnestly.

I knew no such thing, and if I did, I certainly wouldn't admit it.

"But I am not part of the church of God."

He shrugged. "We are all children of God."

"Children?"

"Yes. You are a daughter of God, Ava."

A warmness spread over me when Darius said that. It was kind of like the heat I felt in my face when I blushed, but it was inside my chest. In the past, when any of these Nephites talked to me of their church, their god, their holy spirit, or their testimony, I hadn't listened. But I had felt it, I had let Tec tell me of the gospel, and this time I entertained the idea. I really thought about what Darius said, and what its implications were.

"God is my father then."

"Exactly."

Suddenly defensive, I said, "I have a father. I loved him and your people killed him."

I felt instantly sorry for reminding him we were enemies. I didn't want to argue it with him again, but no person or unknown being could replace my beloved father.

Darius didn't respond for a moment. I expected him to adjust his belt or bite on a fingernail, but he didn't and I found it so odd, the fact that he didn't fidget, that I looked up at his face.

He kept his eyes forward, either not wanting or unable to look back at me when he said, "My father died, too, Ava, without a weapon and without reason and at the hands of his own people, the same people you so staunchly defend. It was senseless and brutal and I never knew him. The only father I have known is my Heavenly Father."

Tears pricked at my eyes at the sadness in his voice. I was sad for him too, never having even met his father. I thought about the many years I had shared with mine, and I felt very ashamed of the bitterness I had been feeling and my rash words about having a father when Darius had none.

None unless you counted his Heavenly Father, which he assuredly did.

"You are a son of God," I said quietly.

His jaw tightened.

"I'm sorry I was so insensitive." I hadn't realized I needed to be sensitive with boys. Weren't they supposed to be strong in all things?

"Forget it."

But I wouldn't. I wouldn't ever forget what he had said.

We had passed through the busier portion of the city and moved into more rural communities that resembled Dare's village—huts with thatched roofs, goats tied up in yards, children running in the streets—but much bigger. It seemed to go on and on. The forest had been cleared better and it felt more open than the village. At long last we turned down a street, and I realized Darius was counting the homes.

"This is it," he said to the others when we neared the end of the street.

Enos called out for Seth and went through the courtyard up to the door. There was no answer.

He looked to Dare. "You're sure this is it?"

"No," Dare said, but he pulled me into the courtyard and motioned for me to sit. The others followed us in. Beth and Esther came to sit by me and we talked while the boys milled about the yard and explored behind the house.

Seth still hadn't appeared when it was time to begin preparing the evening meal, but Enos built a fire and took supplies from his pack.

"You can start making the rice and the beans," he said as he approached us and passed a tied bundle to Esther.

"You don't think it would be rude?" she asked, glancing around.

"Of course not. Seth is a good friend. He would want us to make ourselves at home."

"But are you sure this is his home?"

"Dare says it is, and it matches the directions we obtained."

She looked into his eyes for just a moment and then got up to prepare the meal. Beth and I got up to follow her, but Darius came from where he had been leaning against the side of the house and touched my elbow to get my attention.

"There is a garden behind the house. Come. We'll pick some vegetables."

Like Esther, I was concerned about being at a stranger's home, or even at the wrong home, but the men all seemed so confident. I followed Darius around the back to a surprisingly large vegetable garden.

After surveying it, I decided to harvest some carrots. They would still be somewhat small, but anyone could see they needed to be thinned. Darius watched me for a moment and then picked several moderately sized squash.

I stood and stretched my back. "And some beans, I think."

"Esther is making dried beans."

Laughing, I said, "That is nothing like fresh green beans." I studied him for a moment. He stood with his hands on his hips, his mouth set in a boyish pout.

"You don't like green beans," I guessed.

He tried to hide his smile when he shook his head.

We heard shouts of greeting from the front courtyard, and so we collected the things we had harvested and went around to meet Seth.

I liked Seth immediately, though I could never have explained why. He wore different clothing than the other boys—a leathern kilt, short linen tunic, and knee-length leather boots. His eyes were lined in black, permanently inked on if my guess was correct, something I had not seen much of since I had left home. His smile was genuine and welcoming. His forearms were strong, his grip clearly solid as he clasped arms with each of the boys in turn. When he came to the women, he politely touched us each on the shoulder and greeted us warmly.

"This is Ava," Darius said.

"Tecumeni's sister?"

"You know Tec?"

"I've heard of him."

We had traveled a week's distance from Melek, and this man had heard of my brother. "What have you heard of him?" I asked, truly curious.

A teasing grin spread over his lips, but I wasn't sure if he was teasing me or Darius when he said, "I've heard he has a pretty sister."

Darius cleared his throat. "I hope you don't mind that we started the evening meal."

Seth shook his head. "I'm glad you did. The sooner we eat the better because I need to talk to you all when we're done." He gave me a quick glance, indicating, I thought, that he only meant to talk with the boys.

"Is it about the army to the west?"

Seth's eyes widened for a second and then he just nodded and sighed. "You saw them."

CHAPTER 13

We camped in Seth's yard that night, but after the girls had all gone to our tents, the boys went to their heels around the coals of the fire and talked in low voices.

I watched them through the small slit in the flap of my tent, which I moved aside with my fingers so I could pay particular attention to Dare's strong silhouette.

"The army is led by Coriantumr," Seth informed them. "And though the government leaders insist he is here to guard against invasion into their own lands, of course he plans to attack the Nephites."

"The pass is the only way through, right?" one of the other boys asked.

"Strategic," someone else breathed almost as a curse.

"This is what the judges have always feared."

"Are you going to stay here in Antionum?"

All heads turned toward Seth, who stared into the glowing coals, elbows resting on his knees, for a long time before answering. "I thought we could. This changes things." He shook his head. "But I can't take Noel away from her family and then leave her alone while I fight a war."

They were all silent with not so much as the crackle of a fire between them, only the hot glow of silent coals.

In my village, men went to war when they were

summoned by the king. Everyone took their turn or they were put to death. But it was considered a great honor to fight for our people and our way of life, to try to reclaim what the Nephites had stolen from us centuries ago. But no one had come calling here with orders from the king.

Were they so eager to fight against my people that they would volunteer to fight? To die?

I studied the men in turn, each of them somber and determined. More than they were worried about these new events, they were saddened by them.

"One thing is for sure," said Darius into the silence. "Coriantumr is not here to guard his lands."

There were mumbles of agreement, and as the boys began to make their plans, I curled into my bedroll and tried to sleep.

The wedding ceremony took place under a canopy of trees on the far side of the city, closer to the bride's home. Noel was kind and beautiful, and despite Seth's comment that he could not take her away from her family, she stood tall and straight next to him in her long bridal boots and insisted he return to the army of Moronihah with the others.

When he turned sad eyes on her, she laughed and said, "I will go with you." She wouldn't let him tell her no, and before they had been married a full day, we were all traveling back toward the land of Zarahemla.

At midday we stopped to eat, but we didn't even rest a quarter of an hour before the men were ready to go again. I exchanged a glance with Beth and we both suppressed a tired groan, but we fell in diligently. After a time, I began to notice we had veered off the road toward the west.

"Why are we going toward the army?" I asked my question to Enos when I saw that Dare was deeply involved in a conversation with Seth. Noel walked with her hand in her new husband's, and she listened intently to their conversation. She even appeared to be adding her own ideas to the discussion.

"We're going to separate and send messengers to the neighboring cities. The Zoramites don't seem to think it is important, or they have agreed not to warn the Nephites. But I wish we had better information to give. I wish we knew Coriantumr's plans. Reb and Corban could find out nothing."

I frowned. "Do you think he intends to attack that city on the other side of the pass?"

"Jershon? Maybe. Fortunately, there is a large army stationed there."

"Is it large enough?"

He didn't answer, and I read the answer through the worry in his eyes.

"There is a way to get into the camps," I said. "There is a way to figure out what Coriantumr means to do."

I turned and ran toward Darius.

"Dare!"

Both Darius and Seth hauled around to look back at me.

"The army—there is only one person who can infiltrate it to determine what Coriantumr intends."

We locked gazes, and it only took him an instant to realize who I meant. I saw it on his face. He glanced at Seth and put his hand in the air, calling all the men to a halt with a strange cry that sounded identical to the call of a small, sleek wildcat that lived in the forests near my home.

As the men gathered around us, I wondered if it was hasty to suggest this.

"Ava's brother, Tecumeni, can find out what Coriantumr's plans are," Darius said.

Murmurs went up immediately through the other men. Did they doubt it?

I looked around defensively. "He will blend in much better than your man with the light brown hair," I said, gesturing to Corban who had rejoined the group with precious little information to offer. "He speaks the language. He spied for the Lamanite army. He knows their ways." I turned my eyes back to Darius. "He can disappear in their ranks. You cannot. None of you."

"No one doubts you, Ava. We didn't think of it, that's all." Darius looked at Enos. "We should send a messenger to the judgment seat and one to the camp of Moronihah. I will run for Tecumeni."

Enos gave a decisive nod. "And a man to the camp of Lehi and the border cities."

"And tell them what?" asked Zachariah. "That an army sits on the border? We don't know that they intend harm. Perhaps their purpose is just as they say, to guard against attack."

"They are not here for any good reason!" Reb growled. "They have not assembled an army of that size to offer us peace!"

After a moment of silence, Enos began assigning men to cities and destinations I had never heard of—Manti, Nephihah, Moroni, Ammonihah, Cumeni. When all the assignments had been given, Enos knelt in the dirt and everyone else followed him down, joining together in prayer.

Most of the men had already departed, running in their various directions, making haste and taking this threat with the utmost seriousness when Enos approached Esther. She looked up at him stoically but with her heart in her eyes. Her betrothed tenderly smoothed her hair back, brushing her neck with his fingers. He kissed the top of her head and said, "Go with Zach. He will take you home to Melek. I will meet you there when my task is done."

"If that is what you ask of me," she said.

He smiled. "It is." He looked into her face for another moment, turned, and jogged into the forest.

"You too," Darius said.

Startled, I jerked my eyes from the couple to look at Darius.

"Zach will see you back to Melek with the other girls. You can take your time at a more leisurely pace." When he saw the wild look in my eyes, he gentled his voice. "Don't fear. An army that size could never catch you."

He thought I was afraid of my own people?

"I want to go with you. I want to talk to Tec. And Chloe will need someone after he leaves."

"No." His voice was even. "Seth is coming with me. Tec can get a two day head start if we run."

I turned imploring eyes to Seth, but spoke to Darius. "Send Seth with his bride. I will go for my brother."

The men exchanged a look over my head. Darius was probably rolling his eyes, but I could see Seth wanted to go with Noel.

After a moment, Darius agreed. "Alright. Take what you need in your satchel and give your travel pack to Zach."

I did not wait to be told twice. As I was slipping out of my pack, I noticed he was not doing the same. "You're keeping your gear on?"

"We need supplies, and I can carry them. Can you run?"

I nodded as I hastily rifled through my pack for the things I would most need.

"It's a long run," he warned.

"I said yes." I tied off my pack and looked up at him, determined I would not make him regret taking me with him.

He gave a nod and handed my pack to Zachariah who easily donned it with his. Then, gathering me in a glance, Darius turned and jogged into the trees. I only had time to send a small smile to the other women before I turned and followed him.

We ran, but Darius kept the pace moderate. I would have thought he kept it so for me, but I knew we had a long way to run and preserving our energy was only wise. Darius stayed at my side. At first he continually glanced at me to be sure I was keeping up, but when he determined I was not going to hinder his pace, he didn't give me much more attention. The afternoon was long and quiet between us, nothing more than the sound of our feet on the forest floor and the heavy, controlled breaths we took.

When we stopped to fill the water skins at a small, swift-moving river, he sent a prolonged look over our back trail.

"Are you doing okay?" he asked

"Yes," was all I said, and it was all I needed to say.

He was impressed, I could tell. I had earned his respect. He wanted to tell me I was doing well, but somehow it flattered me more that he didn't say it.

After another minute, I said, "We're going to Zarahemla, aren't we?"

Could he think I hadn't noticed we were running more north than west?

"The judgment seat." The lie was smooth, but he avoided my eyes.

"Is that all?"

"No."

The truth was even smoother, so I didn't ask him more.

"Here." He held out a piece of dried venison.

"I'm not hungry."

"Your body needs it whether you are hungry or not."

"It will give me a cramp," I argued, but I reached out to take it, intending to make at least a half-hearted effort at eating it because I knew he was right.

When my fingers brushed against Dare's, he suddenly wrapped his hand around mine and gave a sharp tug. My tired legs stumbled toward him.

I met his eyes, which were blue like the evening sky, flecked with mischief, rimmed in darkness, and smiling speculatively down at me.

I swallowed hard. "What are you doing?"

"I don't know," he said slowly, his expression unchanging.

I let my eyelids drop as I looked down at our hands,

mine held firmly in his. I raised them a little between us and said, "I do not understand what you mean by this, Dare."

He took a breath. Another. "Neither do I," he said, his voice low. "I don't understand it at all."

I looked up, and he kissed me.

I thought about the sequence of events many times later. How he lowered his head, as if he had only been waiting for me to look up. How he touched his warm, uncertain lips to mine and moved them like the brush of a feather. How I almost didn't respond, my disbelief was so great. And then how, slowly, like approaching a wild animal, I kissed him back, touching him nowhere but his lips and the place where our hands were clasped between us.

He didn't pull me into his arms. I didn't put my hands into his hair or onto his shoulders, but I thought perhaps I had not imagined those moments on the lane near the Estate of Alma, when he had taken me to task over giving Tec privacy, when he had taken my heart with nothing more than the look in his eyes.

Dare squeezed my hand again and stepped back. "Eat," he said.

I looked down at the venison in my hand. Smiling, I bit off a piece and savored the taste on my tongue.

"Feel good enough to run again?" Dare said after he finished his own piece of venison, pulling me from my private thoughts.

I nodded. I needed to run.

It was dusk when Zarahemla came into view. Lights were starting to appear in the windows of homes. Soon they would light the torches on the main streets and at the gates, but we wouldn't reach it before nightfall.

"Let's camp here for the night," Darius said as he slowed to a stop in a protected glen in the low hills east of the city.

"But the judges," I pointed out breathlessly. "Tec."

Darius dropped his pack from his shoulders, but before it hit the ground unceremoniously, he grabbed the top of it and set it down more gently, letting it lean against his leg while he opened his water skin.

"It's late."

"You can navigate at night." So could I for that matter. Tec could be inside the Lamanite camp inside a week if we kept moving. The army was currently camped outside the southern border, but I knew there was urgency. The Nephites needed forces in place for protection, and that took time.

Darius just shook his head as he rummaged in his satchel. He came up with his flint. "I'll get some kindling if you will mix up some corn flour."

Glancing toward the city in the distance, wondering why we had run all day if it was not to get a message to Tec and the judges, I shrugged and set to work.

In a while, maybe longer than I thought, Darius returned with wood for a fire which he efficiently set about making. It was small but sufficient for our needs. I barely glanced up when he disappeared again. The fire was lighting my preparations when Darius returned holding the soft ears of a rabbit.

"How did you get that so fast? And in the dark?" I asked as he made short work of skinning the thing and plopping warm rabbit fat into my dish of corn flour, herbs,

155

and water. It wasn't much fat, but it was the perfect amount.

"Practice. A lot of it."

"That will make a much nicer corn cake," I said.

"I know."

"Ah, something you do know," I teased and then clamped my mouth shut.

He only laughed a little. "Surprise you?"

"No."

He cleared his throat. "Ava, about before."

"Don't apologize," I said. "You didn't offend me. It was nice. We can leave it at that. A lot has happened the last few days. You're worried. We're both worried. We've been spending a lot of time together. We've been pretending to...to..." I paused and took a deep breath which I hoped wasn't audible, not because I needed to, but because I realized I was rambling on. "It was bound to happen."

"Sounds like you have it all figured out."

"Don't you?"

"Not even close. And see, if it was only nice, I think I might have been doing it wrong."

"Don't be too hard on yourself," I managed to quip. "I'm sure you will get it right with practice."

I knew he could see me blushing because I knelt in the firelight. I had tied my hair back for the long run in a way Sarai had taught me, but I wished it was loose so I could let it fall across my face between us, so I could hide behind it.

I flattened the dough up the sides of the dish and settled the whole thing down into the coals.

"I've never seen anyone cook them that way," Darius said.

156

"It's how my mother does it," I told him.

When everything was ready, I passed him a corn cake that I knew, despite my method of cooking, would taste just like it would have if his mother had made it. She had taught me her recipes, and I had listened.

"Ava?"

"Hmm?"

"When Josiah came back, what did he say to you? I mean, how did he tell you he wanted to break your betrothal?"

I stared into the fire as it burned down. The flame was small now and it would soon go out. "I just knew," I said softly. "I could see it in his eyes when he walked into the village and they did not look first for me."

It must not have been the answer he expected, because Darius made no reply.

"I could feel it in his breath," I continued, suddenly wanting someone to know. "I could feel it in the absence of his touch. I could hear him screaming it at me with lips that never moved."

Darius remained quiet, letting me talk through the memories.

"It was Tec who told me, who had to look at me and say the words. He didn't force Josiah to do his duty, because he knew what I could not at that time accept—that marrying me would have been nothing more than a duty to Josiah by that point. Tec wanted more for me—if not love, then respect at least." I finally turned my eyes to Darius, and I gave him a weary smile, though it was the best one I could give. "You were right. Josiah did us both a favor."

"Tec," Darius repeated, almost to himself.

157

"He became the man of our household at fourteen, and he always took it very seriously."

Darius nodded slowly, mulling that over. "My father died when Micah was five. He has been more father to me than brother."

"So you understand why Tec is protective of me…" I let my voice trail off. It was too presumptuous.

"No," he said. "Micah would understand that. The only thing I understand is that Tec intends to make things difficult for me."

The breeze rustled through the leaves and grass around us. My eyes were drooping closed, and I thought longingly of wringing Tecumeni's neck.

"I'm glad Josiah did it," Darius said softly. "I'm glad he broke your betrothal." He shifted, turned away toward his bedroll. "Get some sleep, Ava."

CHAPTER 14

It was the end of the second watch when Darius woke me. I thought he meant for me to spell him off so he could sleep, but there was no fire, not even coals, and he handed me my satchel.

"Did you sleep?" I asked as he led me down the hill.

His reply was a soft grunt, but I couldn't tell if it meant yes or no.

When we approached Zarahemla, I saw that the gates were closed and heavily guarded.

"The gates are closed," a guard called out when we entered the light of their torches, but his voice was almost friendly with recognition when he saw it was Darius.

"What has happened?" Darius asked. "Why are the gates closed?"

The guard glanced around and pulled Darius to the side, into the dim shadows of the wall. I was surprised, but not very, to see Darius turn his back to the other sentries and give this guard the strange handshake he had given Elias at the granaries.

The guard's eyes darted to me, but Darius said, "Pay her no mind. She's just a woman. Now tell me, what has happened?"

Apparently trusting Dare's dismissal of me, the guard

bent close and said in a low voice, "It is just as we hoped. Pahoran has been slain."

Dare's eyes widened slightly. "Excellent."

I knew if Darius was involved in something wicked, then this man, this guard, was not the kind of man I wanted to meet, so I kept quiet and tried to look uninterested in their conversation. *Just a woman.* I smirked. Dare certainly knew how to talk to men of this ilk.

"No one is to leave or enter the city until the murderer is found." The man chuckled. "But he will not be found."

Darius laughed too. "I will take the news of Pahoran on to Coriantumr. He can use the civil unrest here to his advantage."

"So he has come? And with the promised army?" The man was unable to mask his excitement.

"A mighty army, thousands strong, stands ready at the south border," Darius confirmed.

A quick nod. "Then go with god, my friend," the man said and then he laughed in a way that raised the hairs on the back of my neck.

We could not enter Zarahemla, and I remained quiet so Darius could come up with a new plan, because I knew he had to enter Zarahemla.

He led me back into the woods outside the light of the torches. "There is another gate," Darius said quietly. "Hopefully it is still held by the Nehors. Ava, I am going to go into the city. I want you to wait out here."

"What? No."

"You can keep my bow."

"Dare, who is Pahoran?"

"The Chief Judge," he said stonily. "He was the chief judge."

The Chief Judge at Zarahemla. Dare's traveling. His lies and deceits. A secret gate. A bracelet Darius clearly despised. The strange handshake. His familiarity with Helaman, a high ranking city and religious official. What had he gotten himself into?

"How long will you be?"

"I'll be out by dawn. Just stay hidden." I felt him shift. "The city is in complete lock down. I don't know what conditions are like inside. It isn't safe for you to accompany me inside the walls."

It wasn't safe out here either, especially not alone, and he knew it every bit as much as I did. That was how unsure he was about the state of the city and our ability to travel freely inside it.

I had followed Tec and Lamech halfway through the Land of Nephi before they detected me. I knew how to be stealthy.

"No," I whispered. "I am coming with you."

Silence.

"Please."

"Ava." The tone of his voice told me he was considering it. "Tec would kill me."

"You won't let me get hurt."

There was a moment of silence before he acquiesced. "Come on then."

I followed closely behind him as we crept back toward the city. The east gate was heavily guarded, and it was a place we wanted to avoid. Skulking outside of the circle of light cast by the torches there, we moved silently toward the hidden gate.

The west wall of the city was bare, almost as if it had been purposely cleared, but here along the eastern wall, the trees were thick. We ducked under branches as we hurried along, and it was dark and cool under their low canopy.

"Ouch!"

A particularly scraggy, low-hanging branch had scraped my leg.

Darius glanced over his shoulder. "Be careful," he advised unhelpfully.

The gate Darius led me to was little more than a wooden door in the wall. He took a deep breath and knocked.

The door opened with a soft creek and a man stood in the doorway, silently assessing what he could see of us. His large frame blocked the dim yellow light from inside the room, and with the light behind him, I could not see his face clearly.

"We have need to enter the city," Darius told him.

Taking advantage of the available light, I glanced down at the scratch on my leg and held it out, twisting my ankle awkwardly so I could inspect the stinging wound. It was much worse than I thought, being deep and quite long. The branch had drawn blood. After a moment, I noticed the men were silent, and I looked up.

They were both staring at my leg.

"Where did you get that?" the guard asked.

Glancing down, I realized he referred to the onyx bracelet I wore on my ankle, which caught the flickers of light.

"My friend gave it to me," I said, trying to insert boldness into my voice. "Ammon."

The man moved aside so more of the light spilled out past him. After a long look at Darius, he slowly extended his hand. Dare readily accepted it and supplied the handshake, which seemed to be some kind of sign between the two. The man pulled Darius over the threshold. I followed quickly and the man shut and barred the door behind me.

Once past the door we entered into a small stone room, an old guardhouse maybe, lit by a shuttered lantern. When the door was firmly shut behind us, someone removed the shade from the lantern. I blinked in the bright light and looked around. There were four men in the small room, and I recognized all of them—or I thought I did.

The man who had opened the door was Elias. Ammon and Kish were on their haunches in the corner playing some kind of game of chance. And I thought it was Gideon who had pulled the shade from the lantern, but when my eyes adjusted, I could see that this man was much younger than Gideon. He was perhaps a year or two younger than me, but he was the size of a full-grown man—a strong, and powerfully built one with sculpted muscles in his arms and chest, visible even through his tunic—and he looked so much like Gideon, it was all I could do not to stare.

We all looked at one another in silence until Darius turned to me and said, "I believe you know everyone."

I tried to smile at the men, and I hoped it looked genuine.

Ammon grinned and slowly rose to his feet, but he made no move to come to me. Kish looked indifferent to our presence, but slightly annoyed that Ammon had abandoned their game. Elias was not exactly smiling, but he looked neither surprised nor upset to see Darius there. The other man was staring hard at Darius. They locked eyes for a brief moment, but it was long enough for me to tell they knew each other, and probably not from the Order of the Nehors.

"I have met Ammon, Elias, and Kishkumen," I said. "But I have not met the man who looks like—"

"Shad." Darius abruptly turned to me. "This is Ava," he said to the boy named Shad.

Shad glanced around at the others before he ducked his head a little and reached out a hand to my shoulder, not even completing a full step toward me, before backing away again.

I knew Shad was Gideon's brother. He had to be. But the look Darius sent me warned against saying it out loud. I thought quickly as I smiled at Shad and said a hello. If I was not to give away his relationship to the powerful Nephite chief captain, he must be working secretly like Darius was.

But were they working for the same cause?

Not wanting to give either of them away by a lengthy, questioning gaze, I quickly turned back to Ammon, which was something he seemed to be waiting for.

"What are you two doing out on a night like this?" he asked, his voice surprisingly pleasant, but his eyes darted between Darius and me with mistrust.

I felt Dare's hand at the small of my back push me a little toward Ammon. That was all, but I knew he wanted me to engage the other men in conversation, to distract them, while he got the information he needed.

"Dare said he had business with someone in the city he couldn't neglect, not even for a closed gate." I laughed a little, hoping it sounded natural.

"Dare works alone," Kish said from his position on his heels. He stood, and despite Dare's protective presence, I felt something heavy in my chest like a warning when Kish crossed the little room to be closer to me.

Turning back to Elias, Darius said, "I need supplies from the city and then I am to take the news of Pahoran to Coriantumr. His army sits west of Antionum."

This was obviously good news to the men.

"So he was able to assemble soldiers?"

"Innumerable soldiers," Darius affirmed and continued to talk to Elias in lowered tones.

Trying to slow the beating of my heart, I turned to Kish, who had leaned a shoulder against the wall at my back. I shifted to the side, but he leaned closer.

"What is this place?" I asked, glancing around the small room with its dark walls, low table, and half-shuttered lamp. A torch was nestled in a sconce on the wall, but it wasn't burning. A door on the opposite wall was closed and barred like the one we had come through, and a pile of weaponry was heaped in a corner.

He looked at me lazily for a moment. "A good place to hide." He stretched his neck. "But I'm getting a little..." he glanced down my body, "restless."

I had heard Kish speak before, but he had never spoken to me and certainly not in the sultry tone he used now.

"You associate with dangerous men." He chuckled low in his throat. "You should be careful."

Slowly, he turned his gaze, and I followed it to Darius.

"Even him," Kish said. "Be wary of that good boy act."

Then he lowered his lips to my ear and whispered, though it electrified me as if he hissed the words. "He can be very ruthless."

I believed him.

I believed Dare could be very ruthless. And I definitely believed the good boy act was a lie. But not the way Kish thought, and he was the one who needed the warning.

There was something almost evil in Kish, I could sense it in him as I stood so close, but he was charming, too, and very handsome. Like Darius, he was a contradiction. There was something in his tone that was almost friendly, and there was something in his warning that was sincere.

He did not trust Darius.

I leaned into Kish and looked up at him through my lashes. "I can be ruthless, too."

A broad grin spread over his face, making very dark eyes shine.

"Back off," Ammon said, shouldering his way in with a grin. "You're betrothed now, remember?"

Ammon laughed and Kish smirked, but a glance at Shad showed he was not amused in the slightest.

Suddenly Darius was next to me. He touched my waist and said, "Time to go."

Kish raised a brow slightly, but he moved aside and let me go.

Shad was opening the door, and I realized he intended to go with us. He slipped out, and as Darius ushered me toward the dark opening, I looked back at the others.

Ammon lifted a hand to give me a small wave. I shared a nervous smile with him. Kish gave me a slow nod. Elias leaned back on his heels and folded his arms across his chest. None of them gave any indication I would see them again. But they never had, and yet here they were again.

Outside in the dark, Shad was already making his way down the side of the dirty street. The moonlight was spare, and I hurried to catch up. Darius knew his way through the city, but I assumed Shad knew where the new patrols were and how to avoid them.

As I looked around, I saw that the secret gate was tucked into a far, forgotten corner of the city. As Shad led us through the twists and turns of narrow streets strewn with broken clay pots, old cloth, and thin, forlorn goats and chickens bedded down for the night, I guessed the old stone buildings were abandoned. I knew I would never find my way back through the derelict neighborhood, nor would I want to.

Shad proved his worth as we stole through the more dismal part of the city.

"In here," he whispered and pulled me into a darkened building just as a patrol of four men came around a corner. He pulled me down so we were crouching. A quick glance over my shoulder showed that Darius had ducked in behind us.

Light from the patrol's torch spilled through the window above us, but the men marched on, passing with no suspicion of our presence.

"I hate this part of Zarahemla," one of them said. "All the stray dogs are filthy and have disease."

"No different from the Nephites," another one of them laughed.

"What did they say?" Darius asked me when they were gone. "Something about dogs?"

It took me a moment to realize neither he nor Shad had understood the men and another moment to realize the sentries hadn't been Nephite soldiers patrolling the streets after curfew. "They don't like this part of the city," I whispered.

"Come on," Shad said, and he led us back out onto the street.

We must have walked a mile before I recognized the main city center. We were silent by necessity, but I got the feeling Darius was embarrassed for bringing me into the city the way he had. He wasn't proud of himself for exposing me to those men.

But that was silly. I had grown up with the High Assassin in the Order of the Nehors.

Shad slowed to a stop in the shadows near the main square of the city. His voice was low when he said, "You know the way from here."

"Yeah." Darius hesitated, but gave Shad the strange handshake I had seen him give the other men before Shad slipped off into the shadows alone.

The silence was uncomfortable as we walked toward the lane that led to the Estate of Alma.

"What do you think of Kish?" I asked, keeping my voice low in the stillness of the quiet night.

"Less than I think of Ammon," he said immediately, as if it was exactly what he had been thinking about.

"Do you know them well?"

He glanced at me as we hurried along in the darkness. The dawn was not long off, and I assumed he wanted to be safe within the walls of the Estate before the light rose.

"Better than I want to."

"Where are they from?"

"Zarahemla."

"But, I heard them speaking in Lamanite."

"They speak it well."

"Do you?"

He paused before replying. "No."

"I don't believe you."

He grunted. "I'm not trying to win an honesty contest."

"It hurts you to have to lie."

"What makes you think I have to lie?"

"You obviously have those men convinced you are something you're not. Even Kish warned me away from you, and Kish makes my skin crawl."

"You should take his advice," he said, but I could see the slight shadow of a smile on his lips.

"Do you see the man who is following us?" I said, lowering my voice even more. Shad had disappeared, but this was someone else. "They don't trust you."

Dare's step did not falter. "They don't trust anyone. I am doing as they anticipated. They know I am a guard here."

"But you're not. Not really."

"Being a guard on the Estate of Alma is what makes me useful to them."

I thought of Helaman, of the meal I had taken in his cozy home, of Dare sitting relaxed and at peace by Helaman's hearth. His smile had been genuine, the lines at his eyes proving he had once smiled a great deal. I thought of him pushing his hair from his eyes, catching my gaze, igniting something in me I had thought long dead, and I thought of how his eyes had turned to young Nephi, who wanted only to escape the bosom of his family, when Dare wanted only to return to his.

I thought of Ammon and Kish, of the lies they told every time they opened their mouths, their flattery and pretty words, their guile, not quite hidden from someone who could feel things she couldn't explain. I glanced down at the bracelet that had proved an asset in the darkest part of the city. I thought of the confusion I felt when I was around Ammon, such contrast from the peace I had felt on the Estate of Alma.

Darius had neither confirmed nor denied my suspicions, but I knew where his true loyalty lay.

We were soon upon the guards at Helaman's gate. Darius lifted a hand in greeting as we entered the low light of their lantern. Two young men flanked the gate, each leaning against the wall. They looked at ease, but I knew their weapons would be deadly if an enemy tried to breach the gate.

"Is Helaman inside?" Darius asked as we approached uncontested.

"With Pahoran dead? He is here where he's safe," the bigger guard boasted.

"How did you get in the gates?" The other guard was curious, not suspicious—which went to show how much the men here did trust Darius.

"Ava sweet talked the sentries," Darius laughed, and it sounded so genuine, even I believed him.

The eyes of both men swung to me, and I felt myself blush.

"You want to sweet talk your way past this gate?" one guard invited, a grin spreading over his face. He turned to

Darius. "Is this another one of your pretty sisters?" He came off the wall to stand straight as I passed him and then stumbled over himself to get in front of me, forcing me to stop just inside the gate. Placing a sweaty hand on my shoulder, he said, "I'm Tim. Timothy."

Timothy was clearly the younger of the two guards and had burnished brown hair held out of his eyes with a headband. Large bright eyes made him look even younger than he probably was.

"I'm Ava," I said. "Thank you for the pretty compliment, Tim." I offered him a smile but continued past him after Darius.

He hurried to cut me off again. "I meant it," he said earnestly.

"Well, thank you then," I said and looked down at my sandals for a moment before looking back up again into Dare's eyes, begging him to take me away.

But before he could say or do anything, the other guard called to Tim with mild reprimand. I didn't know whether the reprimand was for leaving his post or for teasing me, but when I saw a look pass between the older guard and Darius, I wondered if there was more reprimand in it than I had heard.

"Come on," Dare said and touched my elbow to urge me away.

"Don't mess with her. She's not his sister," we heard the older guard warn. "And while you're at it, don't mess with his sister, either."

"Are those men scared of you?" I asked, glancing back over my shoulder.

"If they're not, they should be," he teased but did not really answer the question. "Sounds more like they're afraid of Keturah."

Darius led me to the stone bench in the little garden. "You can wait here while I deliver the message."

As he hurried away, I sat and inspected my stinging wound.

He was back in no time.

"Time to go," he said.

"That's it?"

He raised a brow. "You could have waited outside."

"And risked a patrol finding me, a lone Lamanite with a bundle of weapons?"

"They're searching the inside of the city. The gates are locked."

"By now they must know the assassin could get out. I have seen myself that there are ways out."

"I wish you hadn't."

"But I did. You're embarrassed to have brought me in that way, to have exposed me to men who clearly conspire against the city."

A flush swept up his neck and his jaw tightened. I didn't know if he felt embarrassment or anger. He may have had Ammon and Kish convinced he was dangerous and not to be trusted, but he could not hide his true self from me.

"You deserve better than lies. I'm sorry for what I am, for what I have become. When I look at you…Ava, when I look at you, I wish I had never become embroiled in this."

"Dare," I said gently, "I come from a different culture."

He turned to look at me.

"My people don't have the same stigmas about dishonesty as the people of Ammon seemed to. I don't think less of you for your secrecy. When a secret is not yours to share, you have honor in keeping it."

He swallowed hard. "Sometimes, I am not so sure I haven't become the man Kish thinks I am. When I go home...when I'm with you..." He blew out a breath. "I find it difficult to move between my two worlds."

"But it is necessary."

He grunted, maybe in agreement.

"What you are doing with Kish and Ammon and those men, I think it is a cause you believe in deeply—or you would not do it. You *could* not do it. Your god helps you, I think, and he gives you your family and your home to go to when you need peace. There may not be many men with a foundation such as you have. Mayhap you have been prepared for this very assignment you are doing."

"Assignment?"

"You work here, Dare, but not as a guard. You work for someone—someone very important, I think."

"You are a very clever girl," he said, but in a way that was meant to end the conversation.

We passed quickly through the gate with little comment from the guards and hurried down the long lane. The shadow man was gone. Dare did not turn toward the city center we had passed through, but turned west and soon I realized he was heading for the west gate of the city.

I wondered what he meant to accomplish there, but he produced a missive. The head guard read it in the light of his torch and in a moment, the guards slid the gate open wide

173

enough for us to slip through.

"That was easier," I said. "We should have done that the first time."

"How is your arm?"

"I cleaned it at the stream and wrapped it."

"I want to see it in the morning."

"It is morning," I pointed out.

"So it is," he said, glancing east. "We need to go to ground."

"Are we not just travelers now?"

He shrugged, and we didn't speak for a while, just ran.

"We might as well camp here," he said when we were a fair distance away from the city. "It's hidden well, and we both need sleep."

I nodded and produced some nuts and fruits from my satchel while he prepared the two slim bedrolls that he carried on his pack. With little ceremony, we ate, tucked ourselves into the crevice of an outcropping, surrounded ourselves with brambles, and fell into sleep.

It was late afternoon when we awoke.

"We can still make a few miles if we get moving soon," Darius said as he tossed me some venison. "I will be more comfortable with your safety when we are out of the Land of Zarahemla."

"Because of the army?"

"In part."

"Do you think they will invade immediately or wait awhile?"

He squinted into the sun. "It is hard to say. Coriantumr's army was amassed already. He has no reason to wait. The longer he tarries, the more chance Moronihah has to amass his own armies. It is in his best interest to strike immediately."

"If that is his aim."

"Yes."

"And you think it is."

He let out a weary sigh. "I know it is."

CHAPTER 15

We found Chloe in the village, peeling vegetables and making preparations for the evening meal.

"He's at the tannery with Father," she said when Darius asked her where Tec was. She looked between us and her eyes took on worry. "What is it?"

Darius turned to me. "You can wait here while I talk to him."

It had been a tiring journey. He was being kind, offering me rest, but I knew what he wanted to talk to Tec about, and I wasn't so sure Chloe should be kept out of it. He would end up telling her anyway. Tec never glossed over the truth. He expected people to be capable of dealing with what life brought them.

I shook my head, and Chloe was already leading out anyway.

Tec greeted us with a smile, and as always, his eyes lingered on Chloe. I noted that today, her eyes lingered on him as well. Maybe he would make the relationship work. Maybe Chloe wasn't as wild as she had appeared.

We ducked under the awning of the small building with Tec. Darius wasted as many words on greeting Tec as he had on Chloe.

"There's an army to the west of Antionum. Thousands

of soldiers. We saw it ourselves." He paused and took a breath. "Lamanite."

Tec's eyes widened slightly, the only sign that he had even heard what Darius told him.

"The governor of Antionum says they are encamped there to protect their lands from the Nephites."

"We've amassed no army against them," Tec pointed out, and I wasn't surprised anymore that he aligned himself with the Nephites.

Darius gave his head a hard shake. "No. They are not here in defense of their lands. We've already sent runners to our major encampments, but Captain Moronihah will need to know where Coriantumr intends to attack and when."

Tec shot a look to Chloe, the look he used to shoot to me. It was a silly thing to be suddenly jealous of, but I was. I bit my lip and looked down at my hands so I wouldn't see Tec check his satchel for supplies or step from the shelter as if he would leave this moment.

Darius followed him. "Will you go?"

Would he go? He was already halfway there in his mind.

"Doesn't the army have their own spies?" Chloe blurted.

Tec glanced at her. He would explain it all, how he could disappear into the ranks of the army, how he wanted to show his loyalty to the Nephites.

"You'll take care of her?"

I heard Tec say the words and they stung, because he wasn't talking about me.

I looked over at the beautiful Chloe, who was staring

with sad eyes after them.

"You'd better hurry if you want to tell him goodbye," I said. "He won't wait."

But he surprised me when he said, "I'll make preparations and leave on the morrow." He held out his hand to Chloe and when she took it, he led her away.

Darius and I stood awkwardly together as they left the clearing. Darius dragged a toe through the dirt, and I tried not to watch Chloe with my brother.

Darius raised a hand to Hemni and Jarom, who were working in the tannery.

"I guess I should go say hello."

But he hesitated.

"Give them the terrible news, you mean." I smiled, tried to offer him encouragement. "I'll leave you to it. I know the way back."

He nodded, his eyes thanking me, and I turned and went back to the village alone.

Leah was smiling when I walked into the little yard. "Tecumeni said you were back. How was the wedding? Did Seth look handsome?"

Her eagerness for news of the wedding made me smile.

"He did," I said, "with clothing of fine linen and his bride in beautifully colored silks. Her bridal boots were beyond compare, crafted with thousands of opaque beads and opals and pearls at the rims."

"I wish I could have seen her. Is she lovely?"

I remembered her on the journey home, her hand in her husband's, making plans with Seth and Darius to take word of the invading army to the surrounding cities.

"She is fierce," I said.

Leah studied me for a moment, and I wondered if I had said the wrong word.

"A fine wife for a warrior," she finally said.

I studied her face—beautiful, but showing signs of age. Her skin was dark from a life spent in the sun. Wrinkles were beginning to form around her eyes, around her mouth. Eyes that had probably once been very bright like Chloe's looked as if they had seen too much, known too much pain. I looked at her hands—healer's hands, skilled, sinewy and strong, and as hard-working as my mother's.

When the men joined us for the evening meal, I studied Kalem, too. He was gentle with Leah, but I sometimes got the feeling he would defend her to the death. There was a hunger beneath his calm exterior, the basic need every man had to pick up a sword and defend what was his.

I had watched the two of them together for many months. I did not think he was the love of her life. When she looked at her sons, the softness in her eyes always declared that their father still held her heart. And yet, I thought as I watched her serve Kalem his meal and then stand near him with a hand on his shoulder, she loved him, too, and it was good. It was enough. And it was blessed.

I was pulled from my thoughts when Darius set aside his empty dish and took a deep breath. "I have to leave again."

"Darius!" Leah all but gasped.

"I'm to take the news of Coriantumr to the army at Ammonihah." He glanced at my brother. "Tec will run for Antionum and learn where Coriantumr intends to attack."

Tec was suddenly alert, not because this was the first

he had heard of it, but because he recognized the subtle deceit in Dare's words. Dare's friend, Lib, had already run for Ammonihah.

Kalem glanced at his wife. "Perhaps one of Hemni's boys could take the message of the army up to Ammonihah."

"Why ask them to do what I can do myself?" Darius looked down at his hands. "Besides, I could take Ava to the sea. She misses it."

Whether he meant it or whether it was cleverly crafted to appease Leah, the triumphant look in her eyes showed that it very clearly did.

Darius turned and spoke to Tec. "I'll take Chloe, too. You can meet up with us when you're done in Antionum."

Tec was quiet for a moment, wondering, like the rest of us, why the additional journey was necessary.

"I think Chloe would like that," he said at last and tossed a piece of bark into the fire.

Tecumeni took the time that night to shave his head in the Lamanite style and to find his old leathern kilt. I found his tunic folded on his bed when I awoke the next morning. He was right to leave it. He could have nothing on his person that might have the appearance of being Nephite in nature.

He had left before dawn and had probably passed out of the land of Melek before the rest of us had even awaken. Darius, Chloe, and I were a few days behind him, needing rest and preparation, but we were soon on the road again, this time traveling north.

"Where will Tecumeni meet us?" I asked as we put Melek behind us.

"He will meet us north of Hermounts, near the West

Sea," Chloe said. "He promised me. If he cuts across the east of Zarahemla, he will save days of travel."

Darius and I exchanged a look, biting back our smiles. She was well and smitten with my stinky brother.

"Will he need a great deal of time to get the information your armies need?" I asked.

Darius shook his head. "Tec was sure he could get it very quickly and get out."

I had not ever seen Tec as a soldier, nor as a spy, but I did not doubt it.

In the afternoon, we began to climb into the hills, and Darius slowed so we could journey into the mountains at a more leisurely pace. When evening came, he stopped in a flower-filled mountain meadow to camp.

"I'm going to go pick some flowers," Chloe said.

I looked at the unprepared food and the tent that wasn't set up. I thought she meant to weasel her way out of the work, but when I looked up at her, she widened her bright eyes and ever so slightly tilted her head toward Darius who had bent to work on the tent.

She was giving us time alone, and as the days went on, she found other ways to leave us alone together. I wished I knew what to do with it.

Our pace was so slow, with Chloe wandering off to pick flowers or "take in the view" so often, it was almost ridiculous. But Darius didn't seem to mind, because he didn't seem to be in a hurry to get anywhere.

On the third morning we hit our first summit. Rich vegetation fell below us and the land of Zarahemla was vast and pretty. The Sidon River curved through it in large arcing bends. Zarahemla itself sat on the valley floor far to the south.

"What is that?" Chloe asked.

A dark cloud sat low on the ground. It had been nearly two weeks since I had last seen it, but I knew what it was.

Darius was silent for a drawn out moment. Finally he said, "That is the invasion of the grand city Zarahemla."

Though we could not see in any great detail, Darius said the troops in Zarahemla were not nearly enough to protect against an army we had seen on the border.

I thought of Helaman's little children, and even I felt the weighty disappointment of the fall of Zarahemla.

"Do you wish you were there?" I asked quietly, gazing on the scene far down in the valley below.

"I could not let anyone see me fighting there," he said and took a long draw from his water skin. "It would be over by the time I got there, anyway," was all he said before turning his back and pressing on toward the north.

He wanted to be there fighting with his people against an attack that was clearly unprovoked.

"We're not going to Ammonihah to tell them about the Lamanites, are we?"

Darius glanced ahead at Chloe, who looked to be intently sifting through pebbles on the ground.

"Of course not. They've had the warning ten times over by now. Captain Lehi is moving to protect the pass already."

"You're not thinking you'll fight with Lehi, are you?"

He shook his head.

I worried a fingernail. If we weren't going to warn of danger and we were not in a hurry, what were we doing out here in the wilderness?

"Are you okay?" he asked after a while. "You seem upset by the invasion."

"Is there another way to feel about it?"

"It is your people against mine."

"I am beginning to think we are all the same people. I am afraid my brother is there. Caleb. And the men from my village."

"Well, they looked victorious."

"But Coriantumr has gone straight to the center of the Nephite lands. He is surrounded. I have been in the midst of the enemy, and I can tell you exactly what will happen."

He huffed. "The midst of the enemy?"

"Coriantumr will reconcile to the Nephite rule and leave in peace, or he will be brought down by the hand of God. Like the doctrine of your church. A man must humble himself or God will humble him. Either way, he must be humbled."

Darius hooked an elbow around my neck much the way Tecumeni had and laughed, though I did not see what was so funny.

Despite the laugh, his mood was somber after seeing the invasion. It became darker as the day wore on, as thoughts of Zarahemla sat heavy on our minds, as the road became steep and Chloe began to complain. Finally, Darius walked on ahead so he could be alone.

"Are you going to marry Dare?"

My eyes shot to Chloe as we trudged slowly up a hill together, our sandals crunching on the gravel of the road.

"That's what everyone is saying."

I told her the truth.

"I don't know."

Darius was waiting for us at the top of the hill. "We will hit the summit and begin to descend soon."

The descent was as steep as the climb had been, but when we were at last through the worst of it, Darius led us a distance off the road and said, "You two make camp here. I'll go get something to eat."

"Can you get a fire started?" I asked Chloe, my eyes on Darius as he disappeared into the trees.

She snorted.

"I'm going to follow him."

She snorted again. This time it sounded more like a laugh, but she made quick work of gathering kindling.

She had known Darius for a long time—her entire life. She had seen him in so many situations that I hadn't. I looked back to where Darius was no longer visible. I would be able to track him, so I let him get a head start.

"Chloe, has Dare always been so distant?"

She was already positioning stones for a small fire. "No. He used to be lots of fun."

"What do you think has made him change?"

"Guilt."

"Guilt over what?"

"He is doing something he shouldn't. His conscience is getting to him."

I knew that, but how did she? I started to ask, but she cut me off with a look that was almost smug.

"You are not the only one who has followed him." She looked down at her fire. "Go help him," she said.

Darius was not deliberately hiding his trail, but he left little trace. Still, my father and Tecumeni had taught me well and thoroughly, and I made a habit of noting signs and reading the forest wherever I went. Sometimes I had to be very alert to them, sometimes it was more like intuition, but I could always find the signs that led me in the right direction.

I followed him for a quarter of an hour and found him on his knees in the dirt in a dense thicket of trees. He knelt next to a small spring where the water seeped from the earth and struggled to find its way out of the thicket. At first I thought he was inspecting a kill or preparing to tie it to his belt. I held back for a moment, debating whether or not to approach him. If he wanted to be alone, I should let him.

I heard a quiet sob and knew instantly that it wasn't over a dead animal.

I knew I should leave him to his prayer, but I couldn't make my feet move away. I wanted to offer him comfort, but I knew I had none to give. The peace he needed would have to come from his god.

Still, my heart ached for the obvious torment of his soul, and I wondered how a god could impose such morals and rules on his people that caused them pain when they had to transgress them. It wasn't like he wanted to.

I made up my mind. I could be of no help to him if I did not go to him. When I stepped forward, I let my feet make noise. It took him a moment to notice my presence, which was a clear indication that he was truly pained.

"It is only me," I said quietly.

He scrubbed at his eyes with the heel of his hand. He didn't look at me.

I stepped to his side and rested my fingertips on his shoulder. I didn't want to break the silence between us, so I moved my fingers into his dark hair and let them play lightly there while I thought of what I should do. I saw tears slip down Dare's face anew at the gentle touch.

When was the last time he had felt gentleness? Had it become so foreign that he couldn't bear it?

If Dare's god, his Father, cared about Dare, wouldn't he instruct me how I could be of help to his son?

I found a cloth in my satchel and, kneeling next to Darius, I reached up to dry his face. He didn't move, just frowned deeply into my eyes and let me wipe away his tears. Wasn't that what his Father would have done if he were there?

I pressed the cloth into one of Dare's hands and took the other in mine. Then I bowed my head as I had seen his people do, and I prayed to his god for him.

"God," I called up softly. "If there is a god, and thou art God, won't you make yourself known unto this, thy son? Can you not hear him call for you? Can you not see he needs thy love and reassurance? Can you not send him some peace to his heart?"

I would have pled on, but a calm voice stopped me.

"I have sent him you."

Startled, overcome by a hot feeling that stopped the words in my throat, I looked up into Dare's stunned eyes.

After searching mine for a moment, he said, "You heard that too."

I tried to speak, but I couldn't, so I nodded, the movement jerky, and looked back down at our hands, trying to understand, trying to overcome the hotness in my chest. It was burning me alive, and yet I lived.

187

I swallowed hard past the lump in my throat and whispered, seeking more answers still. "What wouldst thou have me do?"

And in an instant I knew what I must do.

I squeezed Dare's hand and let it go.

Then I eased his bow off his shoulder, avoiding the question in his eyes, and got to my feet. Slinging the bow over my own shoulder, I said, "I will get the food. You need only come and partake of it when you're ready."

I could feel his eyes on my back as I walked away.

CHAPTER 16

Chloe and I had both eaten by the time Darius walked back into camp. I offered him a smile with as much warmth as I could put into it and got up to prepare the meal I had waiting for him in the coals. When I looked up to hand it to him, I saw Tecumeni in the distance.

At home in Ani-Anti, I might have run to greet him, but now I just said, "Chloe, Tec is back." I motioned beyond Darius when she looked up. The grin she couldn't hide was reward enough for holding myself back.

I saw Darius watching them when Tec took his young betrothed for a walk in the forest before the sun set.

"I think she is starting to like him," I said.

He laughed a little. "Starting to? She liked him from the first moment she saw him."

I wanted to ask him how he knew that, but instead I asked, "What did Tec say?"

After they had eaten, the two of them had walked slowly away from the fire with their heads bent together.

Darius was sitting on the ground with an arm resting on one bent knee. He sent me a sardonic look, a lock of his dark, glossy hair falling over his eyes. "Coriantumr plans to march on Zarahemla." He sighed and brushed the hair away. "Then he plans to take the narrow pass."

"Tell me one thing."

Darius looked up.

"Did he see Caleb there? He wouldn't tell me."

He held my gaze for a long moment. He didn't want to tell me, either, but he didn't want to lie. "Yeah," he said softly. "He did."

I turned away to set up the tent for the night.

The tent was Chloe's, one Leah had made for her. I could set it up easily enough, but Darius brushed me aside and set up the tent with an efficiency that spoke of having done it many times and under many circumstances.

When Tec and Chloe came back, the hour was late and we were all tired. Darius offered to take the first watch. He stoked the coals and put another small log on the fire in preparation for it.

I watched the embers float up through the night, up toward the heavens.

"We're going to offer a prayer." Tec's voice cut through my thoughts. He motioned toward the tent, where I had so often repaired to during their prayers in the past. "So, if you want to go in there…"

I brought my gaze down to Darius, who was staring into the fire he had just stoked. When he felt my gaze, he looked up and returned it.

My first prayer had been for him.

"No. It's okay," I said, and ignoring my brother's surprised look, I knelt in the firelight for the prayer that Chloe offered up.

"I can take a watch," I said when she was done. "It's silly for you two to lose half a night's sleep."

Darius started to protest, but Tecumeni spoke over him.

"Would you mind taking the second watch so I can get some sleep first?"

"Sure," I said. Tec had traveled clear to the southern mountains with great haste. Then he had reported to the captains at Jershon. I could see the exhaustion in his face.

I looked to Darius. "Will you wake me?"

Darius looked to Tecumeni.

Easily reading the question there, Tec gave a quick nod. "She can handle a weapon."

"Alright," Darius said. "We'll divide the night into three."

Chloe made a sound of protest, but before she could offer, or rather beg, to take a watch, Tec took her hand firmly in his and said, "You can share my watch. Ava will wake us."

I expected her to argue with him, but she agreed immediately, submitting to his wishes.

I was beginning to think I had been very wrong about Chloe. I had judged her based on what others said about her and a few extreme instances. But I had not given any credence to the times I had witnessed her acting to the contrary—taking food to the old man, the one they all called Zequinim; helping Leda, a woman of the village who was big with child, to hang her wash; entertaining the younger children so their parents could listen to their religious meetings. I had failed to credit the way her eyes both lit with pleasure and gentled when she looked at my brother.

I felt suddenly very foolish and when Chloe and I were in our bedrolls inside her tent, I told her so.

"I have misjudged you," I said. She remained quiet, so I continued. "And I'm sorry for it. I mean—"

"You don't have to explain," she broke in. "I have seen it in your eyes." I could almost feel her shrug. "Everyone has a certain judgment of me. Even my parents."

It was true, and I couldn't deny it.

"It's my own fault," she added sadly. "Tec helped me see the effect my actions have. He says it's something that is hard to reverse."

"Yes," I said uncomfortably. "People do watch us."

"Tec says he will help me reverse it, that he will help me show others the way I really am."

"Do you love my brother?" I asked, feeling instantly impertinent for it.

"Yes," she said before I could apologize. "But Tec says it is little more than infatuation. He says as we grow older together, it will grow into a deeper love."

We lay quietly for a moment on our sides, facing each other in the dark. "Tec said that?" I finally asked.

"Mm-hmm." She giggled, and I couldn't help a giggle myself. To think Tecumeni, my stupid brother Tecumeni, was offering this young girl advice, and to think she was believing his every word. It was unexpected.

I reached out and found her hand in the dark, and she let me grasp it. "Goodnight," I said.

Then I rolled away and went to sleep so I would be rested when it was my turn to take the watch. I wasn't so sure Darius would wake me for it, but the next thing I knew, he was holding back the flap of the tent and rousing me from sleep.

"It's time for your watch," he said, his voice low.

I rolled up onto an elbow. He was on one knee at the door of the tent. The moonlight floated around him like mist.

I crawled quickly from the tent. It was cool in the open air, so I reached back inside for my blanket and pulled it tight around my shoulders. The fire was small and gave off little light, but enough that I could see Tec rolled on his side facing away from it and the bedroll where Darius would sleep.

"May I borrow your sword?" I asked.

"Mmm...no," he said as if even he couldn't believe he was refusing to lend it to me for the duration of the second watch. "I sleep on it when I'm in the wilderness," he offered in explanation, but it wasn't necessary. I didn't know many men that didn't.

Instead, he passed his quiver and bow to me.

"Did you make all these?" I asked as I pulled an arrow out and inspected it with my fingers.

"Some. Muloki makes them. He's quite good at it."

"I can see the modifications he has made."

If I hadn't had his full attention before, I had it then.

"What do you mean?"

"Look," I said and indicated the tip. "There is no barb. It's a modification from the Lamanite style. Here." I tugged my pack closer and got Josiah's arrow out of it to show him the barbed arrowhead.

He stared at me for a moment, watched me in silence as I carefully tucked the bloodstained arrow back among my things. Then he turned to stare up into the night sky, and I felt foolish because of course it was not the first Lamanite arrow he had seen.

Sensing he continued to be troubled, and knowing that his people so often claimed to find peace from their God, I asked into the quiet night, "Do you feel the Holy Ghost on nights like this?"

There was a slight pause. "I used to."

"What is different now?"

"You know I can't tell you," he said on a yawn.

"Perhaps you can tell me something else, then."

"Perhaps."

"How is it that I, who am not even one of your people, can feel the Holy Ghost when I am near you, but you yourself cannot feel it?"

"You're one of God's people, Ava. It's not a surprise— it shouldn't even be one to you—that you can feel Him in your life. You can't tell me you never felt the Spirit in Ani-Anti."

I had never thought about it, and I was nearly lost in considering it, in searching the depths of my heart, when he said, "It is not the same out here, on the road all the time, involved in deceptions."

"Can you not feel it as well here as you can at home?"

"It is not that simple."

"Your teachers make it sound very simple."

"Because they have no life experience!" he shot out in a harsh whisper. "Because they sit in their synagogues in Melek where it is safe!" He took a breath. "Besides, how would you know? You don't go to church."

"I'm just trying to understand."

"I know," he said on a tired sigh. "Here." He pushed a small log toward me. "Keep the fire up. I'm sorry, really, Ava. The Gospel is not complicated. It is simple, like you said."

I had meant that I was trying to understand him, not the Gospel.

"You are complicated," I said. "Now, go to sleep."

But it was a long time before he closed his eyes to the vastness of the dark night sky. So quietly, I got Dare's scroll from my satchel, tilted it toward the fire, and read some of the words he had taught me to read from it.

"O then, if I have seen so great things, if the Lord in his condescension unto the children of men hath visited men in so much mercy, why should my heart weep and my soul linger in the valley of sorrow, and my flesh waste away, and my strength slacken, because of mine afflictions? Awake, my soul! No longer droop in sin. Rejoice, O my heart, and give place no more for the enemy of my soul. Do not anger again because of mine enemies. Do not slacken my strength because of mine afflictions."

I read it several times, my words no louder than the crackle of the fire, and then I listened to the sounds of the forest around me, the cool wind fluttering the leaves in the trees above me, the distant howl of the coyote, the call of an owl, and while I kept my eyes trained on the edges of the firelight, I wondered what Darius saw in the darkness.

I didn't put the log on the fire. My eyes would adjust to the dark better without the light, and we would be less visible to any other travelers. I wondered that Darius had even allowed the embers to remain. Was it for me?

My watch passed quickly, and when the moon had traveled a third of the way across the sky, I woke Tec. He rolled to a sitting position, stretched, and looked immediately to the tent.

"I'll get her," I offered.

"Chloe," I whispered and nudged her shoulder. "It is time for your watch."

After Chloe crawled out of the tent, I crawled into it and just as Dare had done, I lay awake and stared into the darkness above me. I thought of the things I had read in his book. I thought about enemies. I thought about nations dwindling in unbelief. I thought of his god's invitation to partake of the waters and the bread of life freely. And I thought most about the voice I had heard in the wilderness.

Tec and Chloe had the morning meal cooking when I woke. I tried not to stare when I caught them sitting quietly together waiting for Darius and me to awaken, her back fitted snuggly against his chest.

Despite everyone's growing fatigue, Darius said we could be at Ammonihah in two days if we made good time. We were on our way early, meeting other travelers of the road as we passed them, and Tecumeni and Darius played a game of ball as we walked along which kept us all entertained so that the day went by quickly. The next day passed quickly also, and soon we saw the city Ammonihah.

"Can I purchase a dagger in the city?" I asked Darius.

"Do you have money in your satchel?"

Was he teasing me?

"Yes."

"Then you can purchase a dagger."

I laughed. "I meant, are daggers available to purchase?"

"Of course they are."

"Will you take me to the market?" I thought of the last

time we had gone to the market together and tried not to look at the bracelet on my wrist.

"Sure," he said. "Lib will know the best place to get a good one if you want to wait until we see him."

"I think I can locate a dagger without him. Is Lib the reason we are going to Ammonihah? How do you know him?"

"Not exactly, and he was a soldier in Ket's unit." He waited a moment and added, "One of her many admirers."

"That must be nice," I said, but I wondered about the pretty Miriam I had met, of her hungry eyes and Lib's seeming indifference toward her.

"Mmm?"

"To have so many admirers. I have only had one, and that turned out to be a lie."

We heard a rattle in the grass—one of the many snakes we had come across in the past few days. We veered in the opposite direction, avoiding it.

"I'm sure she would tell you having many admirers is nothing but problem after problem."

"I'm sure she would be right. I do only wish for the affections of one good man."

"So you are looking for a husband."

"No. Well, yes, I guess."

"You're not sure? I assumed you didn't want a husband, and I know I'm not the only one who thought that."

I cringed. I had been making myself unapproachable, the same way Chloe had.

"I guess I thought that was over with Josiah, and here, I'm different and not very pretty. I'm not even very nice to make up for it."

He snorted.

"I'm looking for a dagger or even a short sword," I said to change the subject back to something I could handle, something that wasn't embarrassing.

"What do you need with a short sword? The only people who use those are—"

"Lamanites?"

"Yes, and they are not used for fair fighting."

"What about fighting is fair?"

"Nothing," he said quietly and led us into Ammonihah.

CHAPTER 17

I was not surprised when Darius knew the guard at the gates of Ammonihah.

"Eli." He greeted the man with what appeared to be a genuine smile. "How are Nelia and Ruth?"

Eli was dark and very handsome. He looked more like the Zoramite men we had seen in Antionum than any of the boys in Melek. He was dressed like a soldier and wore several weapons, but his eyes were kind and his smile looked genuine.

"Noisy," Eli laughed. "The baby adds her voice to it as well."

"Congratulations," Darius said.

"A girl," Eli informed us proudly, glancing at the rest of us. "What brings you to Ammonihah?"

Darius grimaced and told him about Coriantumr's army and the fall of Zarahemla. Then he motioned to Tec.

"Tecumeni was able to learn of their battle plans."

Eli's smile had long since disappeared. His arms were crossed over his chest. His sharp eyes flicked over Tec, taking in his leathern kilt and shorn hair. With furrowed brows, he motioned to one of the other soldiers at the gate.

"Tecumeni," he said. "Tell Dan all you have learned. He will run to the camp of Lehi." He clamped a heavy hand on Dan's shoulder. "My fastest messenger."

Tec stepped aside with Dan, and Eli excused himself, turning to the other soldiers near the gates. He was already barking commands about fortifications as he stalked away, scattering his men in all directions with orders.

When he returned, he asked, "How long do you plan to stay in Ammonihah?"

"We've come to see Lib on the coast."

Darius had never told us the real reason he needed to travel to Ammonihah, but I doubted it was to see anyone this Eli knew.

"You'll stay the night with us then. My home in Noah is not a long walk from here."

"Of course," Darius agreed, but when we had passed into the city, leaving Eli at the gate to complete his duties there, Darius said, "Noah is in the opposite direction of the sea. I'm sorry. I know you are all tired of travel."

"It's fine, Dare. I would like to see Nelia again," Chloe said.

"You've met that man's wife?" I asked.

"Sure. She's Eliza's sister. Eli brought her to Zeke and Eliza's wedding."

"Eliza of the large house on Helaman's estate?"

"Yes."

"I would like to meet her and perhaps she will be good enough to let us stay and rest for a few days. Are you in a hurry to see your friend, Dare?"

"No. We have time to rest."

And time to travel here at an almost leisurely pace.

"Looks like we're in luck," Tec said, indicating the

square before us. "We've arrived on market day." The streets were busy, and sure enough, the square was filled with vendors. "Darius," Tec continued, "will you take Chloe to purchase provisions? I want to talk to Ava."

Darius took a moment deciding, as if the decision were his, but it wasn't.

"Sure," he agreed finally. "We'll meet you at the main gate when we're done." He tugged on a lock of Chloe's hair. "Come on, mischief maker."

Tec and I watched for a moment. Chloe purposely bumped into Darius, and they both laughed as Darius steadied her with an arm over her shoulders.

"You'd think they were the twins," Tec said.

"She makes him laugh. It's good. I do not think he has known much laughter in a while."

Tec was silent for a moment. "But you hate it."

I turned to look at him, then away. "I wish I could make him laugh like that."

"If it helps, I do not think that was genuine." He gestured after them.

It did help a little, and I was not surprised he had noticed it.

"It's another one of his faces."

"I know," I said, sighed, and set off toward the main square.

The market was busy, but nothing like the grand markets of Zarahemla. Nothing was like the grand markets of Zarahemla.

"Are you making any progress with Dare?"

The question, though I had been expecting it or

something like it, made the tips of my ears hot. I thought instantly of Dare bending down to put his lips on mine.

But, *progress*? Why did he have to say it like that?

"No. But I can see you are making it with Chloe."

"So are you. She likes you."

That caused me a moment's pause. "Truly?"

"That's what she said."

"Maybe it is some trick to get you to do what she wants. Sometimes I do wonder which of you is in charge."

"No one is in charge."

"Meaning she is."

I thought he intended to punch me in the arm or wrestle me to the ground, but he restrained himself and just kind of growled his disapproval instead.

I thought I should change the subject. "So what did you want to talk about?" It might have been about my *progress* with Darius, but I still knew Tec better than anyone, and I didn't think so.

Tec slowed and pulled me to the side of the road as the crowds began to get thicker. He lowered his voice. "On my way to meet you I came across some men. They were heading west toward the sea. I camped with them for a night, but when I invited them to join with the rest of you, they wouldn't."

I had a feeling I knew who the men were, or at least who they worked with. I thought of the shadow man, of Darius almost making a show of going to the Estate of Alma.

"They didn't want to impose," I said.

Tec's eyes narrowed. "I got the feeling these were the type of men who impose whenever they feel like it." He shook his head. "No. It was something different."

"A feeling," I supplied for him.

He looked straight into my eyes.

"Your holy spirit gave you a warning."

Apparently, it had spoken to him as clearly as it had spoken to me.

I could tell something about his meeting with those men wasn't sitting right with him. He would have made himself fit in perfectly with them, whatever they were like, to pass the evening, to get information from them, but they had made him uneasy.

"Look there," I said, taking the opportunity to talk of something else. "A shop with weapons."

Tec didn't need any further coaxing to drop the subject or walk over to view the selection of weaponry.

We browsed until the merchant made his way to us and asked Tec if he was looking for anything in particular.

Tec looked to me.

"I am looking for a good short sword," I told the man. "I see you have some there."

The man glanced over his shoulder at the swords and then turned back and eyed me closely. He crossed his arms over his chest and motioned with his chin to the side of the shop. We all three stepped away from the others at the tables.

"What need does a pretty girl like you have of a sword like that?" he asked.

"What need does anyone have of a sword?" I replied.

The man turned to Tec. "If I sell your girl a sword, do you plan to teach her how to use it?"

"I know how to use it," I broke in, ignoring the assumption that I was Tec's girl. It was a common mistake.

"Do you plan to do a lot of fighting?" The slight smile on the merchant's stern face told me the idea amused him.

Tecumeni's very slight step back showed he was beginning to understand what acquiring this weapon would mean to me.

"I have been letting others protect me for too long. It is time I protected myself." I spoke to the man, but the words were for my brother.

"I can respect that," the man said, and he turned, picked up the swords, and arrayed them in front of me.

I inspected them. I touched the hilts of each. They were all just longer than a dagger, wider, and sharp on both sides of a forged blade. All were serviceable, none were beautiful.

"This is all you have?" I asked.

The shopkeeper considered me for a moment, glanced at Tec. "I do have a pretty piece I took on a trade. I was saving it for my son." He rubbed his stubbled chin. "But he's an ungrateful rogue. You might as well have a look at it. It is a little longer than these." He looked me up and down. "But it might fit you right well—long arms and all, like you have."

I knew I was tall, and I guessed I was gangly, but no stranger had ever remarked on it before. I just gave him a nod, and he got out the sword.

I knew it was mine the moment I saw it, so I didn't feel bad for taking it from the man's ungrateful son.

Tec knew it was to be mine too, because he got out his coin purse to pay the man. I placed my hand over his. We didn't even have to exchange a look for him to know what was in my heart.

I had to pay for the sword on my own.

While I paid, Tec asked, "Have you a scabbard for it?"

When the man retrieved one and laid it on the table before us, Tec looked to me, but I shook my head.

"That is a fitted scabbard. They are meant to go together. You can do nothing with that scabbard alone."

The man pulled the scabbard toward him. "I can draw a hefty sum for a piece of this workmanship."

"We will pay for the scabbard," I said.

Tec started to protest.

"We will pay for the scabbard *if* you include that dagger and *its* scabbard for free." I pointed to a small dagger, black as night, plain and unremarkable.

"Robbery!" the man bit out, but I knew I had him, so I reached for my coins.

Tec covered my hand with is. "You're robbing us!" he exclaimed. It was in fun, and some haggling was expected, but I still rolled my eyes. I had already done the haggling. "You couldn't sell that sword because of its odd length! You were stuck with it! And you think to overcharge us?"

The merchant feigned shock, but in a few moments, Tec had talked him into the scabbard for free and including the dagger for next to nothing. This was a blessing, because the price he had quoted me for the sword had been fair, not overpriced like Tec claimed, and all three of us knew it.

With the dagger wrapped and tied, we set off again, Tec shouldering his way through the crowd and me on his heels.

When we got out of the market square and the crowd was not so dense, Tec offered to help me tie my new scabbard to fit. It was meant to be worn on the back, and Tec helped me position it so that I could draw the sword easily from the leather.

"There," he said with one final pull on the knots. "Now you can draw it without slicing your head off."

As we started walking again, I screwed up my courage and said, "I am ready, Tec. Tell me about the Gospel of Jesus Christ."

I expected a reaction, and I received one.

Tec stopped in his tracks and slowly turned to me. He watched me closely to see if I was serious, and when he determined I was, he whooped and picked me up, lifting me high into the air and spinning me around.

"People are staring!" I laughed.

He set me back on my feet, and as we walked to meet Chloe and Darius, I told my brother that I had heard the voice of the Holy Spirit.

"Is that what persuaded you?"

I shook my head slowly. "No. I think it is that I am prepared to hear now. How do they say it? My heart is softened."

"Do you think Dare heard the voice too?"

"I know he did."

Tec's brow rose a little in surprise.

We sat in the shade of the wall near the gates of the city. Eli noticed us and waved, and while we waited, Tec told me of Jesus Christ and something he called the Atonement and how it was that "purchase" was in fact a good word for what Christ would do for the children of God.

"Darius didn't think I would understand this. He

didn't think I was ready to hear it when we left Zarahemla."

"You weren't. Does Darius know of your change of heart?"

"Why should he?"

But how could he not? Those moments of prayer we had shared were very vivid and the voice was undeniable, but we had not spoken of it.

"Ava, if you don't wish him for your husband, you only need to say so."

"We've been over this! I do!" I glanced around, hoping Darius had not come into hearing range without me noticing.

He frowned at me. "The Gospel is something you should want to share in with your husband. It will be a part of your marriage."

How could I explain that I wanted to be loved for who I was, the girl my past had made me into, instead of for the woman I might not ever become?

"I don't want to get it mixed up in my feelings for him right now." I might not be able to tell the difference. "It still feels...personal."

"Maybe you're right."

When we could finally see Darius and Chloe walking toward us, it was time for a late midday meal. Along with the provisions they carried, they brought food already prepared from the market, and we sat together and ate. Tec continued to tell me about the Gospel while Chloe interrogated Darius about Sarai and Isabel. Dare's attention was divided between the two conversations, and I had to admit mine was too.

"Why won't you tell me?" I heard Chloe say.

"I told you, there is nothing to tell."

They were very comfortable with each other, and they bickered like Tec and I did.

"Yes there is. Something happened with Sarai. That's why she went away, isn't it?"

She didn't already know?

Even if Darius had been inclined to answer Chloe, which I doubted he was, he wouldn't have when he noticed I was watching them and Tec had stopped talking. He glanced over at us and clamped his mouth shut.

"What is there to see in Ammonihah?" I asked quickly.

"I'm tired," Chloe said. "I don't want to see anything."

"I'll take you to see the writing on the wall," Darius offered with a note of relief in his voice. "It's supposed to have been written by the finger of God."

"Truly?" I asked, intrigued, and loving the idea of getting away alone with him.

"That's what they say." He stood and held out his hand to me.

We walked back toward the main square, which was still full of people at the markets, but we walked right on through and crossed the city.

We approached the temple at Ammonihah from the level of the street, unlike the hill from which we had observed the workings of the temple at Zarahemla. From this view, it looked like little more than the walls of an estate. Darius stood on his toes and peered over the wall, but I was not tall enough.

"What is over there?" I asked.

"A courtyard, just like the one at Zarahemla. Do you remember it?"

"Yes, I remember."

It appeared that many people came to look at the writing because the section of the wall that held the writing was ensconced in a cozy courtyard which was filled with flowers and bushes. It reminded me of the small park on Helaman's estate.

Darius led me to a bench. He didn't sit but removed his satchel and weapons and set them aside. Then he removed his sandals.

"Yours too," he instructed.

I did as he had done, ever more curious about this place, and then followed him to the wall.

Though the people here tried to keep the place special, evidenced by the garden and the bench, many people had traced the outline of the words. They were dark with oil and grime, but it only served to highlight them against the wall.

"When were these carved?" I asked.

"Nearly a hundred years ago I think."

I reached forward and traced the words with my own finger. The idea that they had been carved by the finger of God made the action irresistible.

"They do not look like the words in your book. What do they say?"

"They were interpreted to mean that Ammonihah would be conquered if the people did not repent."

"Repent?"

"Repair their wrongdoings. Stop committing sin."

I nodded and turned back to the words, still feeling the deep grooves with my fingertips. "And was it?" I laughed. "Conquered?"

"Yes. It was destroyed."

"And yet the temple remains?" I laughed again.

He didn't answer for a moment. When I realized I was making light of something he felt was sacred, my smile faltered. He shifted. Then his fingers were tracing mine on the wall.

I went very still.

"The people were destroyed," he murmured after a few moments. "The city remained, but it could not be inhabited."

I remembered what he had said about burying the dead at Cumeni, and I wondered if the people here had not been buried, if no one had remained to bury them.

Darius eased himself behind my back and placed his free hand on my ribs. Still I did not move except to close my eyes. Darius seldom allowed himself to show his emotions, and I did not want to interfere. He laced his fingers with mine on the wall and drew my hand down to my side.

"Ava," he breathed into my hair.

Even though I had learned to speak his language, I had not yet learned to understand him. If this moment had any reality in it, I had been misinterpreting Darius from the beginning, from the moment he had said I was pretty. How many of his words had I ignored or written off as impossible, patronizing, teasing, or even pity?

I turned my face to his, intending to search his eyes to determine his intention, but I could not read his feelings in his eyes. Perhaps he did not even know them himself.

Why? I wanted to demand. *Don't you know what I am?* "I have something for you," I said instead. "I got it in the market."

210

He pulled back and looked down at me. A small smile formed on his lips, one side, as usual, arching up higher than the other, as if half of him were more optimistic than the other half.

I drew away from him and went to my satchel on the bench. I withdrew the dagger and passed it to him.

He liked it, I could tell, but he gave me a funny look and said, "I have a dagger. It was my father's."

"I know. I've seen you use it every day." It was a beautiful, very distinctive knife. "You need this one too." Just as I had known the short sword was mine the moment I had laid eyes on it, I had known the black knife was for him.

"Thank you," he said with genuine gratitude and bent to tie the dagger to his leg. Embarrassed, I turned away. But I couldn't keep myself from peaking over my shoulder. Darius caught my eye and gave me another smile.

"Let me see your sword," he said.

I picked up the scabbard from the bench and tossed it to him. He caught it easily and pulled the sword from the leather.

"Somehow, it suits you," he said.

"Tec thought so too."

"Do you know how to use it? Do you want instruction?"

I did want his instruction, but I didn't need it. "I know how to use it." I folded my arms over my chest and took a small step back. "I know you have things you have to do. If I need anything, Tec can help me."

"I can help you."

"It is Tec's job, Dare, not yours."

He stared blankly over my shoulder until finally he

looked down at me and said coolly, "If that's the way you want it."

I couldn't blame him for his coolness. "That's the way it is." I searched his face and saw that the hardness had returned. "That's the way you need it to be."

"Can you find your way back to the gates?" he asked abruptly.

My skin prickled. I didn't need to steal a look over my shoulder to know who was lurking in the shadow of the trees behind me.

CHAPTER 18

As we traveled the short distance to Eli's house, I watched the troubled boy who strode next to me. He had waited until I rounded the corner of the temple walls before he spoke in low tones to whoever was there. It wasn't good of me, but I stopped to listen. All I could hear were low murmurs, mere hints of words, so I made my way back to Tecumeni.

Nelia fussed over us, fed us, and insisted that we rest. She was a pretty woman with curly hair and two curly-haired daughters. Her husband greeted her warmly with a smile and a kiss on the top of her head. He made no mention of Zarahemla or the bad news we had brought him.

Chloe obviously admired Nelia. "Have you seen the writing on the temple wall?" she asked the older girl as Nelia served us our food.

"Of course. Everyone has."

"What does it look like? Darius took Ava to see it, but I didn't go."

Nelia finished dishing up the stew and put the pot down. Then she straightened and stretched her back. "It just looks like old words no one can read, Chloe."

"Do you think God really wrote it with His finger like they say?"

"Yes, I do."

Chloe had three older sisters, all beautiful, kind, intelligent, talented, and righteous, and from what I could tell, this woman was the one Chloe looked up to. I had seen that she resented her sisters, but she showed none of that resentment toward this woman. The two seemed to have a rapport, a friendship even.

"Were you here when they burned the women and children in Ammonihah?" asked Tec.

What?

Nelia didn't answer right away. She took her own dish and sat next to Eli. "I was five when that happened. I didn't realize what was going on, but supposedly many of the men came here to Noah. It was such a terrible thing. The older people here remember it quite well, but to me it is more of a legend, like the writing on the wall."

"How could men be so cruel?" exclaimed Chloe.

I did not know the story, so I stayed quiet to listen.

Nelia bit her lip and tilted her head as she thought about her answer. "It was very cruel, to be sure, but perhaps it was not without some purpose. It was after this, because of it, that my father decided to disassociate himself from the Order of the Nehors and consider the teachings of the Church of God. He could not abide what had been done by his people."

Nelia's father had been of the Order of Nehor? Here in the north? I hadn't known its reaches were so far from Jerusalem. Something about Nelia's history with the Order made me feel a kinship with her and like her even more.

Eli and Nelia's home was quite large and they insisted we all sleep indoors with them. Chloe and I slept in a room with their young daughter, Ruth, who was delighted to have two women to entertain. She showed us all of her belongings, leading us around the room by our hands. Darius and Tec stayed in the large room for guests.

Just before I put out the lantern, there was a knock at the door. Chloe went to it and pulled back the curtain that covered the doorframe.

"I've come to kiss my girl goodnight," said Eli. His eyes went straight to Ruth in her bed and didn't wander to either Chloe or myself.

Chloe stepped back to allow him in, and I went to stand near the door with her to give Eli a moment with his daughter. Ruth giggled and jumped up to throw her arms around his neck when he bent to her.

"Papa!"

Chloe and I exchanged a smile.

When Eli was done and Ruth was tucked into her bed, he came to the door. Still managing not to look at either of us, he said, "Nelia is with the baby." I thought he might have blushed. "Do you need anything before I go?"

We told him no and he left.

"Your papa sure must love you to brave coming in here with us," Chloe said to Ruth with a small laugh.

"What do you mean?" I asked.

"Oh," she said, surprised, as if there was some secret everyone knew but me. "Eli is very shy."

I frowned. I had seen him talking and laughing half the day with his men at the gates of the city. He had boldly issued his commands. He did not seem shy to me. He talked openly to his wife and played easily with his daughter. He spoke quite candidly to Tec and Darius, especially Darius. True, he hadn't talked much to either Chloe or myself, but we were strangers to him. He wasn't shy. I shrugged it off and put out the lamp.

The morning brought deep gray and purple clouds with it, and anyone could tell with one look that it would rain. Eli invited us to stay and rest another day to wait out the rain, and Nelia enforced the suggestion by giving us all work to do around her home after Eli left for Ammonihah. Grateful to have a respite and a place to be still and to bathe, I was glad to stay.

"Darius and I are for the river before the rains come," Tecumeni told us before he trotted up the road toward his bath.

I helped Nelia mend clothing, and Chloe played with Ruth while the baby, Zinnia, slept swaddled in her cradle.

"You said your father was of the Order of the Nehors," I said to Nelia when we were at last alone.

"Yes, he was. Much to the displeasure of my mother's family."

"They did not like him just because of his religion?"

"Oh, I don't know. They liked him well enough. The Order, at least for my father, was more of a political alignment, I think. But marriage can be difficult. It can be so much easier if you both have the same beliefs. They only wanted Mother to be happy."

I nodded.

"Why do you ask? Does it have something to do with the handsome Darius?" Her eyes went cool. "Has his family not treated you well?"

Looking up from the tunic I was sewing, I told her, "My family is of the Order. My uncle, all my kinsmen. The whole village."

She relaxed back into her chair. "And are you?"

"I never gave it much thought."

"Do you know what they believe?"

Embarrassed that I didn't, I admitted, "No. Not fully."

"The main difference," Nelia said calmly while she sewed, "from the Church of God is that the Nehors do not believe in sin."

"Well, yes," I said. "We believe everyone will be saved regardless of their actions."

She looked up at me with raised brows, but quickly dropped her eyes back to her work. "But saved by whom and by what power?"

"The Great Spirit. I suppose that's what we thought."

She didn't say anything, and after a moment, she bit off her thread with her teeth and then smoothed out the fabric over her lap.

"But I have been learning about the Christ and how he will purchase us."

She nodded slightly, a slow smile spreading over her face. "And if Christ pays for our sins with his blood, don't you think we should commit as few as possible?"

"That is the conclusion I have come to over and over."

"Have you?"

"Yes," I said. "I have been pondering on it very much." I glanced around and shifted on my seat. "Zaaron, my uncle, talked once with a missionary from the Church of God. It was in Jerusalem. A man named Aaron."

"I have heard of this man," Nelia said. "He was to be the king over the Nephites, but he declined to accept the kingdom and instead went with his brethren to preach the gospel of Christ to your people."

"But why? I often wondered why the man, Aaron, had come into the land of his enemies. And you say he was of royal birth? Did he not have an obligation to his own people? Why would he do this?"

Nelia's smile put crinkles around her eyes. "I believe you have already pondered out the answer to that as well."

I was mulling the conversation over when Tec and Darius returned to the yard. Their hair glistened with river water, they smelled like sandalwood, and they were both smiling.

"The stream is cold!" Tec said as they approached, and he gave an exaggerated shiver.

Nelia laughed. "There are some buckets." She pointed. "There. If you will haul up some water, we can warm it for the girls."

The boys exchanged a look, one I knew all too well.

"But it would be more fun to carry them down there and toss them in," said Tec.

We laughed, but my laughter turned to squeals of protest when Dare threw me over his shoulder and headed toward the stream. I pounded on his back with my fists, though I didn't truly believe he would toss me in, but I realized I had completely misjudged him when I was sitting, stunned, in the frigid water and he was laughing on the bank.

I looked beyond him to see my brother hauling Chloe down the path in a like manner.

I wanted to laugh again, but those terrible boys didn't deserve to be forgiven so easily. When Darius turned to watch Tec and Chloe, I took a breath and slid under the water.

I heard Chloe splash in. I heard her surprised yelp at the coldness of the water. I thought she got out and delivered an ear-lashing to Tec which faded into the distance as she was likely chasing him back to Nelia's. She had her way, and I had mine. In a moment, I heard Darius calling to me. But I was a good swimmer with strong lungs, and I had a few more minutes to wait him out.

But it didn't take a few minutes. In an instant, I felt his hands pulling me out of the water. He was on his knees next to me, up to his waist again in the cold water. His look of worry faded to confusion when he saw my uncontrolled grin, and then with a growl he splashed me and got out.

"I'm going to freeze to death in here," I said, laughing because he was soaked again.

He tried to hide his smile and tossed me a chunk of hard soap tied up in a cloth. "Better hurry then."

He waited for me up the hill a short distance with his back turned. I kept an eye on him as I quickly washed, but he never once attempted to turn. He leaned against a tree with one ankle crossed over the other and I thought he might have been reading while he waited.

I thought of the times he had read to me from his scroll and of how he had been teaching me to read it myself. No matter what happened, I would cherish those times together always. I would hold them very close to my heart.

When I got out of the stream, I was soaked, dripping, and freezing.

Darius turned as I approached him, holding out a large, thick cloth that I recognized as one of Nelia's. It was damp—he must have already used it—and it took a few moments to warm to my skin even when he wrapped it around me and then wrapped me in his arms and pulled me close to his warm chest.

"That was not nice," I said, my voice muffled in his chest.

His only reply was a low chuckle I felt more than heard.

We stood like that for a long time, long after I was warmed and dry enough to walk back to the house.

His lips were in my hair when he said, "You scared me."

"That was the point."

"Don't do it again."

Tec was regaling Nelia with stories when we got back, and I noticed there was a vessel of water warming near the fire for his betrothed.

Nelia gave me a knowing smile and passed me a warm blanket. Tec was finishing up a story.

"So I had an arrow trained on Josiah, and Ava walked right between us and called us a couple of big babies. She told us to drop our weapons and told Josiah these weren't the men they were looking for."

Chloe's round eyes turned to me.

"It wasn't dangerous," I assured her. "I knew neither of them would shoot me."

"But what about the others? You didn't know whether or not my kinsmen would shoot you."

I shrugged. "We had been running for hours based solely on a feeling Tec had that someone needed our help. I wanted to help."

"But you didn't even know them."

"I wanted to help Tec," I clarified. I glanced at my brother, remembering that long-ago day.

"So you stood between two warring bands of men?" Chloe's eyes were lit with delight.

Darius was staring at me, his expression unreadable.

"I thought you were shy!" he burst out. "I thought that was why you never talked to anyone or tried to learn our language."

"Shy?" Tec laughed. "Ava is the boldest woman in the world! To stand up to Josiah, her old—" He coughed. "The village's most ruthless warrior?" He shook his head.

I hadn't realized he had been so impressed by my actions that day. He had only seemed annoyed at the time.

Darius glanced at Tec, but returned his hot gaze to mine.

Clearly my lack of meekness angered him.

I cleared my throat a little. "That was the first time I spoke to Josiah after...you know, and I made him listen."

Tec scoffed. "I should have put the arrow through him, and he knew it. I think he wanted me to."

I put my hand over his clenched fist and shook my head. "Josiah set me free, Tec. He set me free from a marriage that would have been terrible. I would have surely lost my boldness married to him. He set me free to come here and learn about the Atonement of Jesus Christ. Let us both forgive him."

To my great surprise, Chloe placed her hand over both of ours.

We took our leave of Nelia and the girls that afternoon after the rain had come and gone and bid Eli goodbye when we passed through Ammonihah.

"Send word, and we will travel to Melek for your weddings," he told us. Nobody mentioned there were only plans for one wedding.

It was another half-day's journey to the sea, but the sight of it would have been worth many more days of travel. It was utterly beautiful. Jerusalem was near the sea, and I had always loved to go there, but as I stood on the crest of a hill next to Darius, a look of hope on his face as he stared into the blue horizon, I thought it had never looked so beautiful.

We could see the large boats from the hill, larger than any structure I had ever seen.

"Why are they so large?" I asked.

"For shipping. They carry provisions to the lands northward and beyond, and these," he gestured to the ships, "will be full of people as well."

"What lies to the north?"

"A land like this, surrounded by water, but overused and barren of timber."

"But how can the people live without timber?" They would need homes. They would need fire. They would need medicines and food and shade.

"Shipping," Darius grinned.

I looked again at the ships. "How can such large vessels float on the sea?" I asked dubiously.

Darius chuckled. "Lib can explain it."

I shaded my eyes with my hand. "Is that the Sidon?"

"Yes. It has carved narrow gorges here over time and empties from them into the West Sea."

"They're pretty. Can we walk through them?"

"There's a good trail through that large one."

"Where does Lib live?"

"We will find him onboard the largest ship."

"When will the ship sail?"

"Soon."

"And what is the reason for our visit here?"

A corner of his mouth turned up. "Stop asking questions, Ava."

His wry amusement made me want to look at him all day, the warmness of eyes that were so often shadowed and the ease in the crease of his brow, but I just laughed and started running toward the beautiful gorge that would lead us to the West Sea.

As we wound down through the craggy canyon, the four of us felt the nearness of our destination and our steps were hastened by our excitement.

Chloe crossed the Sidon on large jagged stones that protruded from the water, and when there were no more stones, she dropped into the water and waded to the opposite shore.

"Be careful," Tec called to her, but it was only something he felt obligated to say. He barely glanced at her and turned back to his conversation with Darius.

I had been watching the two together. Generally they got on well enough, unless the subject of Tec's twin sister came up, and then the words became clipped, the looks turned hard, and the conversations were accompanied by a posturing I did not understand. Tec was proprietary—almost to the point of pushing Darius away. Perhaps it was because he was my brother, the only family I had here, and he felt protective. Perhaps it was because he was a man and felt a responsibility for his female relative. Or perhaps it was because he was Tec and he felt like being a jerk.

"Ava, come over here and see these flowers," called Chloe.

Only Chloe would cross a river just to look at some flowers. But I had seen the water was barely deeper than her waist, and though the nights were cool, the days of travel had been long and hot. Even now the sun was burning down on my dark hair. I slid off my sandals and crossed the rocks as Chloe had. The sharp edges of the stones stung a little, but not any worse than wearing the dusty, sweat-soaked shoes. The rocks were ridden with imprints of small sea animals. I anticipated the coolness of the water, and floating in it was something that had always given me peace when my mind was in turmoil. How many hours had I spent at the cistern in Ani-Anti after Josiah had come home? Hands on my hips, standing on a large stone in the middle of the Sidon, I looked up the canyon the way we had come, up the steep stone walls to the sky above, and down toward the sea where Lib would set sail in his large ship.

Then I bent my knees and dove into the water with the current, missing the muddy bottom by an arm span.

"Ava, that's dangerous!"

I expected some kind of reprimand, but not from Chloe.

I stood and tipped some water from my ear and heard Tec laugh. He knew it to be of little danger to me. I could swim in shallow water as easily as deep. I could swim in turbulent water as easily as calm. I could swim in the bright sun at the sea as easily as the dark echoing recesses of the cistern. Swimming had long come so easily to me that I seldom thought twice about the transition from land to water.

Tec knew of my proficiency because he had swum with me so many times, and it occurred to me then that this was how Tec knew what was dangerous for Chloe and what was not—he had experienced so much of it already himself. Hemni and Dinah lived in a sheltered world where they kept themselves and their family as safe as possible by limiting their experiences. Tec had hard-won knowledge and compassion and wisdom, and Chloe was just about the luckiest girl that had ever been betrothed to a man.

I looked back toward him and Darius on the other bank where they had both stopped to watch. Tec was amused and Darius was, if I read his face right, surprised.

I made my way to Chloe and looked at the flowers, which were quite unusual and pretty, just as she'd said. I had not seen flowers such as these before, and they grew straight from a crack in the rock.

We crossed back to Darius and Tec and had not traveled far before we were both dry and warm again in the sunshine.

CHAPTER 19

Lib was as tall as Darius, but as blond and light-skinned as Darius was dark. Lib was handsome, but I much preferred the darker complexion of my Darius.

It was too embarrassing to say out loud, but in my mind, I had begun to think of Darius that way—as mine. Maybe his mother's far-fetched wish wouldn't come true, but I had known small moments with him that made me think his circumstances would not prevent him from loving me.

At least a little.

And it was enough for me.

Me, who had come to think of myself as eternally rejected and unwanted.

When I thought of it now, of Josiah's rejection, I was severely disappointed in myself. How could I have let one choice of Josiah's change the way I felt about myself? I had once been so strong and confident. I had been kind and open and had empowered others to believe the same of themselves. It was all such a shame.

While the way Josiah had informed me of his choice had been abrupt, harsh, and devastating, his motivation had very likely been born of, if not love for me, at least esteem. I could see, now that my pain did not mar my vision, his choice had not been easy and informing my family of it had not been something he had relished doing. He had acted from a tenderness and compassion that I had been privileged to have seen, and it shamed me now that I had flung my opinion of his character away so very quickly.

It truly was I who did not deserve him, though not in the ways I had thought.

That would be one of the first things I repented of.

I wasn't sure how I would make the necessary reparation, but I did know that I would not repeat with Darius the mistakes I had made with Josiah. I would not do him the dishonor of thinking he enjoyed causing me pain. I would not do him the dishonor of thinking he pushed me away because he wanted to. I would graciously accept what he had it in him to give and not selfishly demand more.

Lib was excited to see Darius and seemed quite pleased to meet the rest of us. He was not warm, but he was polite, and his eyes lit when he greeted us.

"Zeke and Jarom were good friends of mine," Lib said when he placed his hand on Chloe's shoulder.

Chloe made a face, but said, "They speak highly of you and your talents."

Lib stepped back and nodded slightly, modestly accepting her compliment. He was talented and smart and he knew it. He was proud of his accomplishments but was clearly not boastful.

Which wasn't to say he was not eager to lead us across the ramp to the deck of the ship. The view was spectacular as the deck was the highest thing around, save the masts and sails, and all we could see in most directions was the beautiful water. When Tec questioned him, he explained what made the boat buoyant and how it would be able to transport both the weight of the provisions, which were even now being loaded onto the deck, and the people who boarded it to new lands.

"Of course, we have already identified the land we wish to populate. There are people and explorers there already."

"But Darius says it is a land without timber. What will you make homes out of?"

"Stone. Mud. Mortar. There are many things. And we will bring timber with us." He gestured behind him to the large trees that were stacked there, a task obviously completed with the ropes and pulleys that were still suspended over them.

He followed my gaze to the ropes. "This is a fantastic device," he said. "When you run a rope over this, it makes the lifting easier."

"Enos uses something similar in his business," observed Darius. "Your design?"

Lib nearly blushed, but nodded modestly again.

We toured the ship for a long time. It took so long because Lib couldn't stop talking about how everything worked.

"Looks like you found your mission," Darius said quietly, crossing his arms over his chest and giving Lib a pleased look.

Tec and Chloe were at the edge of the deck, holding to a polished railing and looking out to the west as the sun began to sink into the water. I stood a small distance away from Darius and Lib and debated joining my brother as the conversation between the men seemed to grow more personal.

"I have," Lib said. "I have found contentment in my work here."

"I am glad for that. Have you found yourself a wife?"

Lib took a deep breath and let it out. "Not yet."

Darius didn't say anything, and he might have grimaced a little.

"I will," Lib said. "Just...not yet."

Darius grinned suddenly. "I saw a lot of pretty girls on our way into the city."

Lib laughed too, the tension completely gone. "Not down here by the docks you didn't. And I don't know how you could see past the pretty girls you brought with you."

I flushed, feeling guilty for listening, feeling too obvious to leave.

"I can see why you have marriage on your mind," Lib teased.

Darius must have sensed my discomfort because he said, "Ava, come here," and he stretched out a long arm to slip his hand around my waist and pull me into their conversation.

But he cleared his throat, glanced over my shoulder to note that Tec was still a distance away, and said to his friend, "I am glad to hear that you are unattached, Lib." He licked his lips nervously and I felt his fingers flex. "I have a job—for the chief judges. You know of the recent assassinations, the unrest we saw in Zarahemla."

Lib nodded, and glanced at me, wondering what I had to do with it.

"Plans are in motion. I will have to leave the country.

Zarahemla, Melek, Bountiful—nowhere will be safe for me."

Lib folded his arms across his chest, and gave Darius his intense attention.

"I need to know Ava will be taken care of."

Lib blinked twice before glancing over his shoulder at Tecumeni and Chloe.

"Her brother has his own life to manage, and Chloe is..." Darius glanced at the couple too. "She's a bit of a handful."

One of Lib's brows went up.

"Of course Tec won't let Ava starve," Dare said, digging a thumb into his temple. "I just mean, she needs friendship. Companionship." A flush crept up his neck. "And more than she'll get in her brother's home."

Darius looked embarrassed, but I was embarrassed enough for both of us. Did he feel that bad for me? Or was his work truly that dangerous?

"Is this a joke?"

My cheeks went hotter, if that was possible.

Lib held up a hand before I could burst into tears, and he smiled at me, the warmness he had withheld earlier showing clear in the crinkles around his eyes. "I meant," he turned back to Darius, "because she looks so much like Keturah."

Darius looked down at me, and I could almost feel it like a touch as his eyes brushed over my features. "I hadn't noticed," he said at last.

Lib smirked. "Is she anything like her?"

Darius casually reached back and drew my short sword from the scabbard on my back.

Lib huffed, amused.

I snatched my sword back. "I'm quite spectacular all on my own, thank you," I sniffed.

"I see what you mean," Lib said.

I didn't know Keturah well. I wasn't sure I liked them comparing me to her. But one thing I did know: the men of their circles admired her above every other woman.

This was a compliment.

It only felt insulting.

"I did not know things were this way between the two of you," Lib said, his eyes dropping to where Darius still had a hand at my waist.

Darius took a quick step away. "They aren't. A dying man does not plan a future for himself."

Lib pulled a wrapped stick of charcoal from above his ear and twirled it in his fingers. He was thinking about what Darius had asked him to do, but he was frowning.

Finally, he cleared his throat. "I..." He cleared it again. "My heart is not as free as I led you to believe," he admitted somewhat sheepishly.

All of a sudden, I understood that Darius was not just asking Lib to see me married. He was asking Lib to marry me himself.

"No." I shook my head furiously. "You do not have the right or responsibility to make arrangements for me," I hissed to Darius, flashing Lib a phony smile which he returned with a real one.

"Your brother is terrible at it," Darius said. "And besides..." He pulled me a little bit away and his tone became very serious. "I do not think I can have my whole mind on my task until I know you will be taken care of and loved as you deserve. Lib has the capacity and freedom to see to both."

"But he does not have the inclination. And what if you don't die?"

"I will have to leave in either case."

I was lost for a moment in his eyes. Weary, worried, wondering if I would ease his mind by agreeing to let his friend see to my future.

"I will sail with you." My voice was soft, and I hoped it didn't sound pleading.

Lib took a small step back, and I knew that I was approaching a line Darius was not ready to cross. Traveling with him to Zarahemla or Ammonihah was one thing, but traveling to a new land together would be making a statement. Making a commitment.

"Ava."

Was that pity in his eyes?

Lib cleared his throat. "Two can board as easily as one." He laughed softly. "Be at ease. If you don't make it in time to sail, I will see Ava married to a worthy man."

My smile was slow, but by the time Tec and Chloe had covered the distance between us, Darius, Lib, and I were all laughing.

Looking at us strangely, making me feel guilty for agreeing to a marriage pact without his approval, Tec said, "We need to leave. We need to find lodgings or a camping site for the night."

"You can lodge on board," Lib said, his laughter subsiding.

"Alright," Tec said simply and led Chloe to retrieve

their travel gear. He glanced back at me over his shoulder and widened his eyes in question. He wanted to know what I had to laugh about with these two men. I shrugged slightly, offered him the phony smile, and he rolled his eyes the way he used to do with Chloe.

Arms crossed, Lib turned to Darius and me with a smile. "The girls can sleep in the large cabin, and you can book passage for yourself first thing in the morning."

Dare shifted and cleared his throat softly. "I can't be seen making the arrangements. Could you make them for us?"

"Sure, but who would see you—"

Lib trailed off when Darius just gave his head a small shake.

I was with Darius the next morning when Lib brought him the documents that would allow us to board the ship. A subdued thank you was all he offered his friend.

I thought of his tenderness at the temple. I thought of his arms around me at the river, warming me after my immersion in the water. But I knew he couldn't make a commitment, even if it seemed he was warming to the idea of it.

I vowed again to admire his willingness to do what had to be done and his loyalty to what he believed in. I vowed I would not resent it. It was what made him the man, the Nephite man, I was beginning to love. I would be the friend he could count on. I would be as strong as he needed me to be.

And if he thought I was so much like his warrior sister, he would know that I would not sit idly by waiting to see if he died at the hand of his enemies.

I shook the thoughts from my mind. The sea had been calling to me since I awoke to the sound of the waves crashing against the shore.

From the deck of the ship, I could see Chloe and Tec walking out on the beach. Tec was bending to pick up starfish from the sand and toss them back into the sea.

I turned and ran down the boarding plank and out toward my brother. Grabbing his hand, I pulled him into the cerulean blue waters with me. He grinned, and when the white caps were crashing against our chests, we dove under them together.

The others had a fire burning cozily on the beach when we finally slogged out. We were warmed and loved, and I was happy for the first time in many months.

When the week was done and we began the hike back up into the beautiful, narrow gorge, I overheard Darius tell Tec he had to carry a message to the southern cities, and he conveyed that there was some urgency to the task. The excuse had about as much substance to it as his reason for coming north.

Tec scrubbed a hand over his cheek. He was as suspicious as Leah and Kalem were of Dare's strange absences, and I didn't know how much longer he would put up with it. Tec would demand to know what Dare was up to or he would find out for himself.

He sent me a frown, but offered, "I'll take the girls into Melek so you can get on your way."

"No." I flatly, utterly, unequivocally refused. I would not let Dare go into danger alone.

"Stubborn," Tec muttered under his breath.

"Melek is not my home," I said quietly.

Tec's eyes narrowed. "What do you mean?"

"I can't live the life you have chosen. I have to build my own life."

"Ava, what?"

"I love you, but I have to build my own life."

Tec glared at Darius. "You will come home and be welcome always in the house of your brother."

"No. I have to build my own life." My voice was escalating, sounding eerie as it bounced between the high walls of the canyon.

"What does that even mean? You have a life with me. Do you mean to follow Darius on his, excuse me but, suspect travels?"

"I mean for you to trust me!"

"I do trust you."

Darius was not weighing in on the matter, and I knew that he intended to wait until his secret work was done before he ever spoke to Tec on the matter of two booked passages on the large ship.

I couldn't explain this to Tec, and I didn't want to argue, but it was clear Tec thought I was pining after Darius and Darius did not want me. He thought it was Josiah all over again, and he thought he was protecting me from it and that protecting me from it was a kindness.

But I couldn't tell him about the day at the temple, about the warmth I had found in Dare's arms. Darius needed time, and, eyeing Tecumeni, I really wasn't sure how he would like the idea of Dare having his arms around me.

"I need to be alone," I said and veered away.

"Ava!" His shout echoed through the gorge.

I stopped but didn't turn.

"Take Chloe with you. We need to...stick together. Something is not right in the woods."

I stayed still a moment and felt he was right. There was an eerie stillness in the air, so I nodded.

Chloe hiked beside me and kept up a steady stream of lighthearted conversation. She was being very sympathetic, and I wondered why I had ever disliked her.

When we had traveled a good length of the gorge, Chloe and I crossed the river to eat our midday meal in the shade on the other side, down in the cool air near the water. We hefted our travel packs off our shoulders and leaned them against a boulder, but Chloe seemed reluctant to let go of hers.

"We should leave." Her wide, worried eyes darted around the gorge. "Right now. We need to get back to Tec."

My eyes shot to Tec and Darius, hiking together on a path halfway up the canyon wall. They both went still as we all heard it at the same time.

I whipped my head around to see a swell of water pushing toward us, flooding the entire lower part of the canyon, ripping trees from their roots and breaking them into pieces against the rocks.

Chloe and I were right in the water's path. There was no way to safety and only seconds until the swirling, muddy water hit us. I registered Tec jolt and dart toward us, but my eyes were searching for something to hold on to, something to brace against. There was nothing. Nothing! So I grabbed Chloe in my arms and braced against the stones we were on.

The effort was futile. The surge of water was too strong. It picked us up and swirled us within it, knocking us against the jagged rocks and the walls of the gorge.

I held on to Chloe, and I could feel her clutching at me. I didn't want to lose her. I didn't know how far we would be swept down the gorge. We could be swept clear out to the sea.

I tried to keep our heads above water, but it was impossible. I was a strong swimmer, even in the waves of the sea, but without my arms free, I could do nothing.

"Pray!" I gasped suddenly into Chloe's ear when we emerged above the rugged waves. "Pray!"

And then we were pulled under again, but I knew we were both praying, and somehow, I knew Darius and Tecumeni, wherever they were, were praying for us too.

We swirled into an eddy, and when my hand brushed something hard, I grappled with it until I could hook an elbow around it and turn so we were facing downstream. The water rushed at us from behind, hitting the back of our necks and heads and streaming around into our faces. I took a moment to look at our surroundings, trying to determine how far down the gorge we had traveled. I couldn't tell, as mostly all I could see was sky and the top of the canyon walls.

Chloe's hand shot out and I looked to where she pointed. There did appear to be a small dry shelf just above the raging current. But could we get to it?

"Hold on!" I said, spitting out the water that filled my mouth when I opened it.

Chloe made a noise to affirm she had heard me, but she knew enough not to open her mouth. Her instincts were good.

I had one arm hooked around Chloe's chest and the other hooked around a limb that was caught up on something and felt like it might break free at any moment. The dry shelf was a straight shot downstream, but there were rocks between it and us. We would have to hit up against them, but they would slow us down and would possibly give us a way to brace ourselves to climb out of the river. I knew we were both already bruised, but the cold water made it impossible to know where or how severely. We were both surely cut up too.

But all that could be dealt with later. First, we had to get to that shelf, and we had to do it on our own.

I gave Chloe a squeeze, and then I let go of the limb.

The first hit was hard. I felt my head bounce off the jagged rock, but we went spinning away. Debris swirled around us. I had never felt so helpless in water, and I wondered if I should let go of Chloe, if our chances would be better if we separated, but I thought of how my brother loved her, and I held fast. After long moments in the dark water, we hit up against a rock that was narrow enough for Chloe to grasp with both of her arms and, working together, we were able to drag ourselves from the water and crawl up to the safety of the small lip that hung out over the water.

And then we lay on our backs and just breathed.

Finally I rolled over and hugged Chloe.

"You...were brave," I panted.

"And you...were...strong."

It was many minutes before we heard Tecumeni calling to us.

"Chloe! Ava!"

Chloe rose up to her elbow and searched for him. When

she didn't say anything, I sat up, too. Like her, I couldn't see him, but I called back.

"We're here!"

"Where?"

"We are on the north side!"

We kept searching, but we didn't see either him or Darius.

"Where?" he called again after a few moments. "I can't see you!"

The echo off the canyon walls and the sound of the still rushing water made it difficult to determine where in the canyon he was calling from, but I didn't think it was close.

At long last, I saw Darius running along the opposite bank maybe a quarter of a mile upstream. His eyes scanned the flood waters. He hadn't seen us yet.

I glanced quickly around and spied a long narrow broken branch near us. Grabbing it up, I said, "Rip me off a piece of your dress."

Chloe set to ripping a piece from the bottom hem of her soaked sarong.

"Mine is green," I said. "They will never see it."

She nodded, understanding. Her sarong was red, and they would see it easily waving about on the end of my branch.

It took a few minutes, but I saw the moment Darius noticed our flag. I could see his relief in the drop of his shoulders, and he sped up to get to us quicker.

"Are you all right?" he called when he was across the burgeoning river from us.

I had barely even thought about it yet. Casting a quick

glance to Chloe to see that she was in one piece, I called, "Just bruised. Where is Tec?"

"He ran to look downstream."

Our eyes met over the water. He looked safe and warm. He looked strong and capable. He looked like home.

"We are fine for now. Go find him. I don't want him to worry."

Darius hesitated, but nodded and turned to go find my brother.

CHAPTER 20

"Ava!" Chloe exclaimed. "You've got a gash on your head. It's bleeding."

The travel packs were gone, but we were fortunate we still had our satchels strapped over our shoulders, and she got some soggy bandages from hers. She gently wiped the blood away from my head and then pressed a bandage to it to staunch the flow of blood.

"I think it looks worse than it is," she said quietly. "Luckily the water is cold. Hopefully you did not lose too much blood. Hold this on tight against your head. Do you feel faint?"

"No."

"Alright. Lean back here. I will see if there is a way off this ledge."

But it was quickly apparent that there wasn't. Until the water went down, or unless we wanted to jump back into it, we were stranded here.

"The good news is we have plenty of wood to burn. Wait here and I will gather some for a fire."

I watched her limp to the base of the ledge and reach above us for the scrub oak that grew out of the steep, rocky hillside.

"You're hurt," I said quietly when she came back with her folded sarong full of dry wood.

"My knee." She didn't try to deny it. "It's twisted pretty bad. I don't think there is anything we can do for it."

We were quiet while we waited for the boys to come back. We needed rest, and we knew it. Fighting the river had drained us of energy.

When I began to feel the comforting warmth of the fire, I said, "You're pretty good with your flint."

She smiled a little. "Anyone can start a fire, Ava."

The fire did its work warming and drying us, and by the time Darius and Tec were back, we were ready to discuss our options.

The river was at least double the distance across it had been and twice as deep. It wasn't too far to call across to the men, and I suspected it wasn't so deep the boys couldn't wade across, but it was still running very fast and occasionally seemed to have sudden surges that were both dangerous and unpredictable.

"Could you climb?" Tec called.

I brightened at the idea and almost called that we could. "No. Chloe's knee is hurt."

"How bad?"

"Bad."

We all fell quiet for a moment.

"How long do you think the water will run high?" Chloe called.

Tec shrugged and Darius called back. "Could be a few days. Maybe more."

I didn't know when Darius needed to show himself in Zarahemla, but I did know he couldn't discuss it. He might have to leave and he wouldn't be able to tell Tec why. Even suggesting that he leave without us would bring up more than he was able to disclose to the others.

"I think we can swim it," I said to Chloe.

She shook her head as she looked out over the water. "It's too rough." Her eyes dropped. "And I can't use my knee."

I sighed. Even if we could get to the other side, she wouldn't be able to walk home.

"We're coming over!" Tecumeni called.

I wanted to shout to tell him no. It was too dangerous. But I knew if Tec had made up his mind, just shouting no would not stop him.

Both men stashed most of their gear on the opposite bank and then ran upstream. When the deemed they were at the right place, Tec jumped in without hesitation and Darius was right behind him.

Tec managed to avoid the rocks and landed right under our overhang. He easily hauled himself out of the water and, sparing only a small glance to see that Darius had also made it, he knelt near Chloe and began inspecting her leg.

Darius had a rougher time of it, hitting against rocks and overshooting the shelf we were on, but he grabbed a branch downstream, pulled himself out, climbed the steep hillside and slid down from above us in a light shower of gravel and dirt.

"How's the leg?" he asked Tec, but he came to me, knelt, and gently pulled back the bandage from my head. He winced when he saw the wound.

"Ava," he breathed, and I was sure there had never been a time when I had liked the sound of my name so much. "Are you sleepy?" he asked.

Droplets of water formed on the tips of his hair. His lashes were wet, too, and worry creased his eyes. I thought of how he had warmed me after my freezing bath in the river, the worry that had been in his eyes then, too.

"I'm exhausted, but not really sleepy."

"Good. How many fingers am I holding up?" He held three fingers in front of my face.

I rolled my eyes, just a little exasperated. Chloe had already treated my wound.

"Well that's not a good sign." He grinned.

I sighed melodramatically. "You are holding up three fingers."

He started to nod.

"And two fingers on your other hand." I nodded slightly to where he hid his other hand near his foot, but even the small movement made me dizzy.

He grinned again and reached over to lift my chin as if he might kiss me.

Tec cleared his throat. "The knee is hurt badly. Chloe can't walk on this, not home to Melek. It's already swollen." He reached over and knocked Dare's hand away from my chin. "And Ava is also mine to take care of."

Darius dropped his hand away from my chin but not until he was ready to. Then he glared at my brother. "Not anymore." Another hard look passed between them until suddenly Tec grinned and Darius continued. "What do you propose to do? Will you wait here until the injury heals?"

Tec and Chloe exchanged a look. And it was in that moment that I realized—and I thought Darius realized it too—that Tec and Chloe loved each other. They had established a bond. They had already formed a partnership. They were a team against the world. They were friends, and they respected each other. I suddenly understood what he had meant all those times when he said neither one of them was in charge. He didn't want to rule over her or make her submit to his wishes by force. He honored her and expected her to honor him in return.

The look in her eyes made it very clear that she did.

"We have actually been discussing the possibility of sailing with Lib and his friend, Hagoth. They intend to take people to colonize a large area to the north. There is much land and much opportunity."

That was new information to me, but not a complete surprise. I glanced at Dare, but he avoided my eyes.

"Do you mean you won't even return to the village before you embark?"

"Chloe can't travel, Ava."

"But you can't stay here," I indicated the ledge and turned to Chloe. "You can't leave without even telling your family goodbye!"

Chloe looked resolute. "Tec is my family now. My father willed it so, and it is done."

"But—"

"Ava." Chloe lowered her voice and gestured to her knee. "I have little choice."

"Darius," Tec suggested, "I know you have to leave. Perhaps you could stop in Melek and ask Hemni to come bid his daughter farewell. He could be here before we sail."

Darius bit his lip and ran a hand through his hair. His eyes turned to the south.

"Without the girls," Tec reasoned on, "you could make good time."

"I can run," I said into the silence when Darius didn't answer. He knew I could run. Tec knew I could run.

"But what for?" Tec scoffed. "It only takes one to deliver a message."

Did he think I would sail with him and Chloe?

I looked to Darius, but his eyes did not turn back to us.

"Alright," Darius said after a moment, but not as if he had even heard my offer to go with him. He looked to Tec. "What is the best way to get off this ledge?"

While Tec and Darius looked over the raging river, I shoved my supplies into my satchel, and I begged Chloe with my eyes to keep quiet, to smooth it over with my brother after I was gone. The only move she made was to pass me the rest of the bandages from her satchel.

I felt a small catch in my breath when I realized I no longer had Josiah's arrow. It had washed out to sea with the rest of my gear. I let my eyes fall briefly closed. I didn't need the arrow.

I leaned over to Chloe and whispered, "Our plan is to sail also. We have already booked our passage. Take care of my brother until I return." I squeezed her hand.

Chloe's eyes flicked from me to Darius and an immediate smile lit her face when she determined what I meant.

Darius turned to me. He put himself between me and my brother, giving his back to Tec. He scrubbed at the back of his neck and wiped some moisture from his forehead. Finally, he bent his head so he could speak into my ear.

"You know how I feel," he said quietly. "That is enough."

No I didn't.

And no it wasn't.

"If I don't return, sail without me. Go with Tec, he will care for you. You will be happy."

I shook my head. He could not command my happiness.

Placing his hands on my shoulders, he gave me a small shake. "Yes! If I don't return before the ship sails, I won't be returning at all. Do you understand that?"

If he did not return, he would be dead.

"I understand," I said as he pulled me into his chest for a hug that might have surprised us both. And had I really felt his lips brush my forehead?

"Good luck," I murmured, fully intending to see to his luck myself.

After he released me, he turned to the others.

"Goodbye, Chlo," he said, lightly kicking the foot on her good leg. "I will tell your family of your plans. You can probably expect a visit from the whole lot of them."

"Wait," she said, ignoring the mention of her family. "Can you, I mean, will you help Tec give me a blessing before you go?"

He nodded and knelt near her. After he gave some quiet instructions to Tec, they both put their hands on her head and my brother said a very simple prayer over her. Darius playfully tugged on her hair as he stood.

He turned and caught my eye, a sad, crooked smile touching his lips, and then he stepped to the edge and dropped into the river below us.

I looked at Tec and Chloe. This was a terrible place to leave them, but Tec would get them both off the ledge. I had no doubt of it. Tec was watching Dare's progress down the river when I placed my hand on his shoulder. His eyes shot to me in surprise.

But I could see he relented when he suddenly pulled me to him in a fierce hug. "I love you," we both said at the same time. He grinned and gave his head a quick jerk toward the water as if to say *go on before I stop you*, and I jumped in.

Darius was standing, dripping wet, on the bank when I got my footing in the water. He had his hands on his hips, and he looked less pleased than I had imagined he might. The water was so swift, I almost lost my balance when I tried to take a step toward him, but he was there quickly taking my elbow and helping me to stay upright.

"You little fool," he said, but when we were both firmly on dry ground he hugged me tight to him.

"I'm coming with you," I said, my voice muffled against his shoulder.

"I figured as much. What does your brother think?"

I stepped back. "He thinks he wants to be alone with his betrothed."

Darius smiled wryly. "Let's get going then. You can come as far as Melek."

We hiked back upstream along the bank which became so narrow in some places we had to wade through the river or crawl over boulders and soggy piles of debris. We stopped to collect Dare's things but left Tecumeni's so he could retrieve them when he could cross the river with Chloe. I looked back at Tec and Chloe. They both waved and called goodbye, but when I looked back again, I could no longer see them. Finally, the gorge fell below us. We turned south toward Melek and Zarahemla, and Darius set a quick pace.

"Will we have to run?" I asked.

He glanced at the sky. "Probably not." But then he amended, "Maybe for a while. I can't go too long without showing my face in Zarahemla and certain meetings. We are at best a week away."

So was it Zarahemla or was it the southern cities like he had told Tec?

"I know I said I could run, but the truth is—"

"The truth is you've got a gash on your head."

Stung by his harsh tone, I said, "I was going to say 'the truth is I don't feel up to running,' but you are right, the gash is probably a large part of the reason why I don't. I will slow you down. I'm sorry. I didn't think of that."

His jaw tightened. "My mother will look at the gash. It might need to be sewn."

"But if we don't run, your mother is three days away."

"We'll make good enough time. You've got long legs."

He meant it as a joke, to kind of smooth things over, but it only embarrassed us both.

We did make good time. We were traveling much faster than we had been with Chloe, and I realized Darius had taken a slower pace on the journey to Ammonihah to allow Tec to catch up. The afternoon slid away, but when the sun began to descend into the west sky, we were still walking.

"Is this how we are to make up the time I've cost you?"

"Hmm?"

251

"By walking for extra hours."

"I guess. If I were alone I would continue until the second watch ended, then I would find a place to sleep for the third and be on my way by the fourth."

"Oh."

"I thought we could sleep the second watch, too, since you're here to sit guard for one of them." He looked over at me. "We'll cover twice as much ground this way. How is your head feeling?"

"It aches." Actually it pounded with every step I took.

"Sorry," he said, and in a few minutes, when he found a nice place with water and shade from the evening sun, he drew to a stop.

"The ache is not going to subside. There is no point in stopping," I said.

"Make a small fire," he nearly commanded, and then he stalked off into the trees.

I stared after him for a moment, wondering in what direction my decisions of the day would send my life, and then I built the fire.

"Put on water to heat," I heard him call from within the trees and, smiling to myself, I did, pouring the last of the water from my water skin into the shallow dish I kept in my satchel.

Darius came silently back into our little camp and dropped a handful of bark and leaves into the water.

"Let it steep and then drink it."

"What is it?" I asked.

He shrugged.

"Something of your mother's? Please tell me it is

something of your mother's and not just a handful of grass."

I hoped it was one of Leah's remedies because I did feel pretty out of sorts. I ached everywhere and bruises were starting to show on my arms and my legs, and I knew they would be showing on my chest and torso and back too. But my pounding head and my lightheadedness were the biggest concerns.

He smiled. "It is. You'll feel better."

I believed him. Still, I sent him a wary glance and wrinkled my nose before I drank the disgusting, bitter tea.

He laughed while I gagged it down, but he passed me the cool, clear water in his water skin when I was done.

"Do you know many of your mother's remedies?"

"I know them all. I've written them all down."

"Really? In a scroll? Do you have it with you?"

He shook his head. "No. In a book that she keeps at home."

"She has much knowledge."

"She has spent her lifetime in study. She is very dedicated to healing others."

"A trait which she has passed to her children."

His brow rose in question.

I smiled. "You would spend your life in study I think, if you were not committed to ridding the world of the evil that infects it. Is that not a type of healing, too?"

"Hardly," he scoffed, but he looked as if he were considering it. In a quick motion, he reached out and moved the bandage from over my wound.

I realized how ridiculous I must look with a bandage tied around my head. I hadn't even combed my hair out, and

253

I probably smelled like fish.

But Darius didn't seem to notice. He was worried, but he tried to school his expression when he looked down at me.

"It's still bleeding," he said. "Why don't you lay back and rest for a little while."

I longed to do just that, but I looked toward the south. "We need to get on our way."

"Not before we eat. You rest while I rummage up some food."

"Okay. And thank you, Dare."

He grunted. "Wait until after you taste it to thank me. Nothing out here but rattlesnakes."

"I don't mean for the food."

"I know."

He waited until I lay back, and then he disappeared into the trees again.

I fell immediately asleep and woke to the smell of something cooking over the fire.

"Mmm," I said as I stretched, and then I caught my breath on the pain that shot through my ribs. I felt a warm hand on my forehead pressing me back.

"How are you feeling?"

"I don't know yet." I opened my eyes and slowly sat up. "Lots of bruises."

"I have some too."

"I know." I winced as I remembered watching him hit up against the rocks. "What are you cooking?"

"Snake."

"How did you catch it?"

"You don't want to know." He passed me some of it on

a skewer and made me chase it down with more of his disgusting tea.

When we were finally ready to leave, he helped me to my feet. "You'll feel better once we get moving."

"I hope so."

He studied my face for a moment. "You look pale."

I shrugged. As I took a step forward, I felt something brush against my ankle. Looking down, I saw that my onyx bracelet had fallen loose. I bent to retie it.

"I wish you'd leave that off."

I looked up at him. "Jealous?"

"No. You don't even know what it is."

"So tell me. And don't say you can't."

"I just wish you'd leave it off."

I pulled the knot tight and sent him a smile over my shoulder.

He sighed. "The group I'm infiltrating. They all have them."

"They are some kind of symbol?"

"Something like that. For the life of me, I can't figure out why Ammon gave you his. I have not seen it done before. But generally, Ava, when a man like that gives you a gift, he wants you to feel you owe him something."

That was exactly how I had felt—like I owed him my loyalty, my silence.

My eyes went to the bracelet Dare had given me. I remembered his fingers working the clasp. What did Darius think I owed him?

"It was a trade. I don't owe him anything."

Darius rolled his eyes.

"How long have you been in this group?"

"Over a year."

"And you don't know what this harmless bracelet means?"

He shook his head, opened his mouth to speak, then clamped it shut and shook his head. "No. There are—it's hard to explain—different levels of members, I guess. As you can see, I do not yet have an onyx bracelet."

"Would you give it to me if you did?"

A side of his mouth turned up. "No."

CHAPTER 21

We walked for most of the night and all of the next day. Leah was preparing the evening meal for herself and Kalem when we walked into the village. Her delight in seeing us glowed in her eyes—until she saw the wound on my head and the glow was replaced with concern.

"I need to talk to Hemni," Darius told his mother tersely after he kissed her on top of her head in the same way I had seen both of his brothers do. Then he motioned for Kalem to go with him, and they went to speak with Chloe's father at the tannery.

Leah urged me to a stool and inspected my wound. "What happened?"

I told her all about the canyon and the flash flood and Darius coming to our rescue. "He has been giving me a terrible-tasting tea, with willow in it I think."

She nodded. "Anything for the bruises? Poultices?"

"Just the tea."

Leah smiled but looked a little wistful. "If Chloe were here, I would send her to fetch some algae from the river. But I guess she is all grown up now—too old to run little errands."

"She has grown since she first left the village," I confided. "And during her betrothal. I did not think to ever say this, but she will make an excellent wife for my brother."

Leah began to cleanse my wound. Her ministrations stung and I winced but let her continue.

"And you? Will you be a wife as well?" She asked this calmly, keeping her hands busy and her voice soft. She wanted to know if I had gotten Darius to fall in love with me.

My instinct was to say no. We had not agreed upon anything, had not spoken of marriage. But then I thought of Dare's conversation with Lib. I thought of his exchange with Tec on the ledge, and I knew it had been an official transfer of both responsibility and privilege, at least in their eyes. I had stood next to him while he arranged passage on the ship for both of us. We had essentially planned a future.

Dying men don't arrange futures for themselves.

"I do not know what Dare wishes me to say on the matter," I finally said to Leah.

I felt her pleasure, though she made no sound and her fingers continued to prod at my wound. I felt like pond scum for letting her believe it, but I thought back to the day at the temple and wondered if I was truly misleading her or if there was truth in what I didn't say.

"This will need a stitch or two. Have you discussed a time for the betrothal?"

"No, and Leah." I touched her arm. She met my eyes as I wanted her to. "I believe Darius has some business in Zarahemla to complete before he can discuss it, before he feels at liberty to make plans for his future."

"What business could Darius possibly have there? Is he purchasing sheep?"

I gently pulled her hands away from my head and looked steadily into her eyes. "Leah, it is not sheep." She frowned, so I added, "It requires absolute secrecy and a complete commitment. I can't tell you where he goes or what he does when he is there, only that he needs your trust and your love." I squeezed her hands. "He needs to be bathed in the holy spirit when he is here. Bathed in it." And, taking a moment for a deep breath, I added, "I believe he will make the betrothal official when he is able."

She looked toward the path at the end of the village where he had disappeared. "When he is able?"

"Have faith in him to know what is best," I said.

Her eyes turned back to me.

"And pray for his safety," I added.

After a moment, she nodded and gave me a tight smile. "Wait right here." She went to the house, and when she came back, she had her needle and her salves. "This will numb your skin. You won't feel a thing."

It wasn't the complete truth, but what I felt did not hurt.

"Has my son kissed you then?" she asked quietly as she broke off her thread between her thumb and the edge of her little knife.

"Leah!"

"Your pretty blush says enough." She gave me a squeeze around my shoulders. "I will have faith in him then, and I will be patient."

"And you will not question him about his business."

Our eyes met and held for several moments before she looked again after her son. I knew she was disappointed, but I thought she understood what I was trying to tell her without betraying the trust Dare had in me.

Though I wanted to ease her worry, I didn't think telling her what Darius was into, even the small part I knew of his dealings, would ease her mind at all. And telling her what I suspected was out of the question.

"You are right to keep his confidence and paint him in the best light to others. You will make a fine wife."

Leah's compliment was pleasing, and I felt all the worse for keeping secrets from her.

I smiled, but over her shoulder I saw someone come down the lane of the village. I followed his progress with my eyes, and Leah followed the direction of my gaze.

Ammon stopped at the gate, gave me a sheepish smile and a small wave.

"What are you doing here?" I asked, a smile starting on my lips.

"I'm looking for Darius." He nodded to Leah.

"Leah, do you know Ammon?"

She gave Ammon a smile too. "We haven't met."

"This is Leah, Dare's mother," I said. "Ammon is one of Dare's friends," I told Leah. "He's from Zarahemla."

Leah's eyes lit at the thought of meeting someone from the part of his life her son would not share with her. "Then you've been traveling a while. You'll stay for the evening meal. Stay as long as you like."

Ammon glanced at me, a look Leah didn't miss, and I was afraid I blushed.

"I'll do that, thank you." He glanced around. "I always thought Darius must come from somewhere nice."

"Darius is with his friends. I could take you there," I offered.

Ammon grinned and shuffled back a step to let me through the little gate.

"I'll be back to help with the evening meal," I said to Leah.

"No need. It's already taken care of."

Her expression was watchful, as if she were trying to put together the pieces of a puzzle, and guarded as if she did not trust the way they were fitting together.

"Have you been traveling long?" I asked Ammon when we entered the small path that led to Hemni's tannery.

"You could say that."

I glanced over at him, suddenly wondering if he had been watching us on our journey back to Melek. My skin prickled at the idea of it. Had he been following us, like the shadow man? Had he been in Ammonihah?

"Darius brought news of unrest," Ammon said. "Zarahemla is not a safe place to be just now."

Coriantumr he meant.

I had a picture in my mind of Darius and his friends cutting their celebration short and running off in different directions to warn and protect their people.

"Did Elias and Kish come with you?"

He shook his head. "No. They chose to stay hidden inside the city."

But you chose to slink away to avoid the conflict.

The thought came into my mind, and there was a rightness to it. Suddenly Ammon didn't look quite as handsome as he had before.

"I hardly believe that," I said. "Kish seemed especially anxious to leave the guard house."

"The guard...? Is that what Darius told you it was?"

"I assumed. Wasn't it once?"

He shrugged. Suddenly, he held out his wrist. "I've still got it."

He did, indeed, have my bracelet tied around his wrist, and it did, indeed, still look better on him.

"It suits you."

He grinned at that.

"And I still have yours," I said.

"Has Darius seen it?"

"He'd have to be blind not to have seen it."

He grinned at that, too.

I stopped and twisted my leg a bit so he could see the onyx on my ankle.

I heard a sound in the brush ahead of us and looked up to see Darius coming through the trees. Our eyes met and then his shot to Ammon.

"Your friend is here," I said lamely.

Darius schooled his expression. It was dark and unwavering.

"Welcome," he said, but it was a welcome that was very clearly not one.

"Ammon just arrived from Zarahemla," I interjected quickly, thinking to dispel the awkwardness Dare's cool greeting had created. "I'll just...leave you to your business."

"Don't leave," Darius said, darting a glance beyond us, searching the path we had traveled.

"I'm alone," Ammon said. He gave me a funny look and asked Darius, "Don't you trust anyone?"

"If I did, it wouldn't be you."

Ammon laughed, and Darius let a smile touch his face, but it wasn't his real one, it wasn't the crooked one that was like his brother, Micah's.

"I've been invited to the evening meal," Ammon said, but there was a note of question in it.

"Of course you're welcome."

Again, it very much seemed that he was not welcome.

"Your mother invited me to stay a while."

Darius folded his arms. "Tell her you're passing through." It wasn't a suggestion.

Ammon laughed again. "Actually, I am. I've a message for you and then I'll be on my way."

"Good."

"Not before you eat," I said.

Ammon hooked his thumbs in his belt. "Of course not, Beautiful."

Kalem and Leah were polite and gracious to their son's friend, but Darius wanted Ammon to leave from the moment he arrived, and I wasn't the only person who knew it. His behavior bordered on rude, and he earned several warning glares from his mother.

After the meal, Kalem and Leah went across the road to visit at Hemni and Dinah's, and they were eventually joined by several of their married children and grandchildren.

Darius grumbled while Ammon bid me goodbye and then the two of them walked away toward the West Road.

It was late when Darius came back. Kalem and Leah had returned to sit in the firelight with me, and despite Leah's warm and sincere invitation for Ammon to stay with us until he was ready to travel again, Darius came back alone.

Leah and Kalem got up and went into the house, so obviously to leave us alone together. I might have been embarrassed by it, but Darius didn't seem to notice. He was frowning into the fire, and I knew Ammon had brought some kind of unsavory tidings.

When his parents were gone, Darius said, "I'm leaving again."

I was beginning to understand why Leah was so vexed when he left the village.

"I'll go with you."

"No."

The word was clipped and immediate. It was not up for debate.

"I have to go alone. I won't be coming back this time. I won't have time before the ship sails, and I have to be on that ship. If you still want to sail with me, you'll have to meet me at the sea."

He didn't need to say it was dangerous.

But did he question my desire to sail with him?

"Alright," I said slowly.

"I talked to Micah. He or Kenai will take you back to the sea."

I didn't want him to leave me behind. I didn't want to travel to the sea with his brothers.

"Will you tell Micah why he is to take me there?"

A smile touched his lips, the real smile. "He knows. They all know."

I kept that smile in my mind as I milked the goat the next morning and watched him prepare to leave. I stood with Leah and Kalem as he bid us a simple goodbye. They might not have known the danger he faced or how it weighed on him, but I knew, and I would not let him go alone.

I completed my chores and went to the stream to wash up. I braided my hair to the side, tying it with a length of rawhide, and I took a deep breath.

When I arrived back at the small house, Leah was wrapping food into bundles.

"My fool of a son thinks his mother does not know he's in trouble."

I watched her put the food into my travel pack and met her eye when she looked up.

"He does not want me there this time," I told her.

"Is it to be dangerous?"

"I don't know," I said honestly. "He is capable. I think this is a task he can do, but he needs all his attention for it. He cannot be looking out for me."

Leah cinched the ties on my bedroll.

"Then you will have to look out for yourself. You are ready."

Pleased by her compliment, I smiled and accepted the travel pack she held out to me. But instead of putting it on, I set it on the ground between us and hugged her fiercely.

"I love him," I said. "I love you all." I glanced across the road to Chloe's house, remembered her sitting there on the fence the night before her betrothal. Then I took the pack and followed Darius out of the village.

I was not sure where he was going. He had left toward the east, but tracks on the West Road were impossible to read because there were so many. Had he gone to Zarahemla or to the southern cities? There was a time when I would have relied on my own tracking skills, and in this case, I would have had to use my best judgment. But I didn't have to do that. A quick and sincere prayer gave me the answer I needed.

South.

I followed the West Road until I came to the road that went east toward the capital city. I stared down it for a long moment, but turned and continued on the path I had chosen.

I was only a half a morning behind Darius. Though I went fast, I was careful not to overtake him. But he was moving fast too, and it crossed my mind that he might know he was being followed. He might be trying to lose me.

I spent one night alone in the wilderness, but on the second night, when I was sitting near my small cook fire, I heard the call of the wildcat. I returned it, and Darius walked into my camp. He didn't say anything for a long time, just stared down at me with those dark eyes. He was fighting his anger, and I might have been flattering myself, but I thought he was also relieved. Finally he went to his heels near my fire, and I handed him a dish of food.

His eyes were troubled, so I left him alone in his thoughts, but when we had eaten and we were sitting quietly together as the forest fell into darkness, he finally spoke.

"Many of the families are thinking of going north," he said, as if it had been weighing on his mind all night, but I knew that was not what was weighing on his mind. "My brothers and even Kalem and Hemni have all considered it."

But this was their home! Did he mean they intended to leave Melek for good?

"The Ammonites are not new to seeking refuge in other lands, and we will if we must. The factions in the government are becoming detrimental to the peaceful life we have known. It becomes more dangerous to stay here all the time. The people the government sends as refugees to Melek are not always peace-loving people as they profess to be. They will say anything to save their skins."

"Wouldn't you?" I laughed.

"Not necessarily."

"But you would if there were another worthy purpose? Say anything, I mean?"

"What are you getting at?"

"What do they think you are doing? The bad men you associate with. What do they imagine you have been doing when you are away from them? What do they imagine you are doing now? Did they send you out here for some reason?"

Even as I asked it, I knew they had.

He considered me for a long moment, his gaze speculative and severe. "This is the final step in my initiation to their secret group. I have completed a combination of things, unlocking the way in, you might say. I am to murder the High Assassin at Jerusalem, and for that I am to get an onyx bracelet."

Maybe it spoke to my upbringing, but I wasn't as shocked over the nature of his mission as I was over who it involved. "What does the High Assassin have to do with anything at Zarahemla? He has nothing to do with them."

Darius looked down at me, eyes narrowed. "What do you know of the High Assassin?"

"Nothing," I lied.

"He is traitor. He does not recognize the new leaders. He must be eliminated because he can no longer be trusted."

"But he is a Lamanite."

He considered me, my flushed face and wide, worried eyes. "The Nehors, the Gadiantons as these men now call themselves, do not think of themselves as loyal to either the Nephites or Lamanites. They hate them equally and yet seek to rule over both."

"Will they? Rule?"

"I wouldn't fight if I didn't think so."

"But then you consider your fight futile."

He shrugged. "Not every fight can be won, Ava. It doesn't mean we shouldn't fight it."

"And you are willing to give your life for this fight?"

"I am not planning to die," he said. "I only said it is a possibility."

"You said it was a probability."

He laughed. "Listen to you! It's like you've been speaking Nephite your whole life."

I put my nose in the air. "I am quite intelligent in my own language, thank you."

"I didn't say you weren't."

"You clearly implied only Nephites were intelligent."

"I implied no such thing."

I laughed too. We could have a very fine life together.

If he did not get himself killed before it began.

Suddenly, he shifted closer to me and took my hand. He looked down at me with sharp, knowing eyes. "Even if the High Assassin was not your uncle, Ava, I would not kill him in cold blood."

I tried not to show my surprise, but I was not able to temper it.

"Not even to gain the trust of men whose trust I very much need," he added. "The followers of the man Gadianton do not send their assassins—nor their initiates—on assignments without detailed information."

I swallowed hard. "You will be initiated if you do this thing?" He had been working his way up in the group for over a year. This murder was to prove his loyalty.

He nodded slowly, but he was unable to hold my gaze. I could only imagine his remorse for some of the things he had been required to do, and it was clear he didn't like himself.

A huge lump formed in my throat, preventing speech for the moment.

"I hope to be on a ship to the northern lands before the Gadiantons know I have not killed Zaaron."

"Will you tell them you did?"

"If I want to live long enough to complete my true mission."

"Will they believe you?"

He shrugged. "They have no reason to distrust me. I have completed all my tasks so far."

"To gain their trust."

"Yes, but I find that quite suddenly the only trust I care about securing is yours." He touched my cheek. "I wish I knew more of your language. I wish I could speak to you in the way you understand best."

"I understand Nephite quite well now."

The breeze rustled the leaves, and sitting there in the night, with the vast sky above us, under the brilliant stars and their infinite glow, with the probability of death hanging over us and the possibility of a lifetime of love before us, he bent his head and kissed me until I forgot all those things.

"Do you understand that?" he murmured with his lips still on mine.

I took a shaky breath. "Now you are speaking to me in the way I understand best," I said and felt his smile.

CHAPTER 22

"We can still make a few miles if we get moving soon," Darius said as he tossed me some venison. "I will be more comfortable with your safety when we are far from the Land of Zarahemla."

In the days we had been traveling, we had already put a great deal of distance between ourselves and Zarahemla.

"Because of the army?"

"In part."

"Do you think they will invade other cities?"

He squinted into the sun. "Tec said the northern pass is Coriantumr's main objective."

"Is it guarded?"

"Yes."

"Dare, where are we going?"

Did he hesitate?

"Cumeni. One of the southernmost cities. It's not much father. Soon, you will see the walls of Judea through there."

It was an hour yet, but when I saw the walls, I said, "You know this land well."

"I did once. I have not been this way in quite some time."

Late that afternoon, we turned off onto a road which Darius called the Cumeni Road. It was long and narrow and surrounded by trees. I thought the city must be filled with trees—because how could they clear them all away? But the road opened up into a vast clearing filled with fields and crops. We crossed it and approached the walls of the city.

Darius was quiet as we crossed, and I wondered if he was recalling some long ago memory. I was quiet, too, and left him to his thoughts.

"What? You don't know the guards here?" I teased after we had passed through the gate of the city.

He glanced down at me in question, but his attention was on the busy city around us.

"You have known the guards at every gate we have crossed together."

"It is my business to know the guards. But as I said, I have not been this way in quite some time. Ah, there's the city building."

I looked in the direction he gestured. The building was large and made from stone and wood painted in bright indigo, green, and yellow.

"That building is atrocious," I said.

Darius laughed. "It's seen a new coat of paint since I was last here."

"When was that?"

"Not since the war."

"A long time."

"Sometimes it feels like it was yesterday."

A shiver ran down my skin when I thought of what he must be remembering.

"Let me see my contacts here, and then I will find you some accommodations."

I frowned, feeling suddenly like the tag-a-long I was. "Have I been so much trouble then?" I could sleep on the trail as well as anyone, and I was careful never to complain—to make complaints to Darius I might have made to Tecumeni just to be contrary and annoying.

The look Darius gave me was surprised. "Of course not. I like your company. I'm not going on to Jerusalem. We have some time before I am expected back, and we are free to do as we wish. I only thought to make you comfortable for the duration. If you don't want it—"

"No. I do," I said quickly, realizing he had meant to offer kindness not insult. "Thank you for thinking of it. I think I have my mind on other things." I tried to smile.

His eyes darkened. "I only planned to make a show of heading south, to lay low here in Cumeni for a time, but I could take you on to Jerusalem," he offered with clear reluctance. "If that's what you want."

I thought of the shadow man who had followed us to the Estate of Alma, and I wondered how far the band of Gadianton would go to be sure of Dare's loyalty.

"That offer is many months too late. Now, I will wait while you conduct your business."

At the top of the stairs of the government building we found a stone bench where I could wait for him.

"I shouldn't be long," Darius said as he shed his pack and set it near my knee. "Will you be all right here?"

I nodded. "Go on and take care of things."

When he was gone I spent a moment taking in the view of the plaza and the city, which was nestled back into the trees just as it had seemed to me that it must be.

Then I took out Dare's scroll and planned to read until he returned. I skimmed through it, for I was quite familiar with it by that time, until I found an account from the writings of Nephi which told how he had secured the plates of brass when his brothers could not. It did seem they were more rightfully his than his eldest brother, Laman's, but he had beheaded a man to get them.

And I was led by the spirit, not knowing beforehand the things which I should do.

The Lord hath delivered him into thy hands.

And I shrunk and would that I might not slay him.

Behold, the Lord slayeth the wicked to bring forth his righteous purposes. It is better that one man should perish than that a nation should dwindle and perish in unbelief.

When I looked up to mull this over, I caught the eye of a man who was ascending the stairs. Dark, but not Lamanite, he was handsome like Darius. He smiled and glanced in the direction of the entrance of the great building, but came directly toward me. I felt immediately uncomfortable as if he could not possibly be smiling at me, as if he could not possibly be coming toward me, but he was.

"Shalal," he said, surprising me by greeting me in my own language.

I smiled tentatively back at him. "Shalal," I replied, but asked in Nephite, for he very clearly was one, "Do you speak Lamanite then?"

He laughed and shook his head. "Not anymore."

Something in the man's eyes caught my attention and I felt like I couldn't look away. There was something familiar about the man. Had I met him somewhere in these strange lands? The sun was behind him and I squinted up to see him.

I stood. "I'm Ava."

"Jude," he said, and almost as an afterthought he placed a hand briefly on my shoulder.

Jude was my father's name.

"That is a name I've not yet heard in these parts."

His eyes glittered. "Like you, I am a foreigner here."

I saw Darius emerge from the building several pillars away. His eyes sought immediately for me, and curiosity filled them when he noted the man who stood before me.

"Here is my friend," I said. "It was nice to meet—"

The intensity of his stare made me stop.

"I'm sorry, Jude, but have we met?" I was almost sure we had never met, but he did remind me of someone. I searched his face, looking for signs of familiarity.

When my eyes finally found his again, he said softly, "Josiah was not the man for you."

The whole world went still. The people meandering about the square and the men bustling over the portico disappeared. My heart began to pound, the air spun, and surely even the sun stopped in the sky above.

"Who are you?" I whispered.

But Darius was upon us and looking at me expectantly, waiting for an introduction.

I licked my lips. "Jude," I said carefully. "This is my friend, Darius. He has brought me here to see my father's grave."

Darius held out his hand to clasp arms with the stranger. Jude stared at it a moment before he started a bit and remembered to take it.

The two men talked for a few moments about the city and the weather and their travels while my heart pounded in my chest. Darius was polite and friendly to the man, even open, and no one would ever have guessed at his secrets.

"I'm going to take Ava to find an inn. Would you like to meet us for the evening meal?"

Jude looked at me and then turned back to Darius. "I can't. But thank you."

Darius nodded politely to him and held out his hand for me, which I took. Could he feel my fingers trembling?

"Darius, I've something for you," Jude said before we could walk away.

Dare's brows rose, and turning back, he waited curiously.

Jude looked between us and then reached into the satchel he carried. He withdrew a slim scroll and passed it to Darius.

"I can see you are the right man to keep this," he said. "It was the highest pleasure to meet you both." Jude bowed in the way of my people, went down the stairs, and disappeared into the crowds.

"Nice man," Darius said as his eyes followed Jude.

I bit my lip as Darius unrolled the scroll. He read for a moment, and I watched his eyes scan over the contents. I told myself it was something for his work, told myself Jude was an informant or a member of the band of Gadianton, but Dare's eyes shot up to meet mine and he said, "Ava, who was that?"

"I don't know," I said softly. "Oh Dare, I don't know." But I felt like I should.

He gave me a long look filled with curiosity.

I wanted to ask him what was written on the scroll. I could see it was some kind of document, but probably none of my business. He looked down at it and read the words again.

"Did you give the officials news of the army?" I finally asked.

Dare took a breath. "The governor will send messengers to the nearby villages, try to round up more men, but with Coriantumr in the capital parts of the land, the urgency is not so great."

At least the officials had been informed now, and they could start to fortify against attack. But with the army of Coriantumr in Zarahemla, in the heart of the land and likely headed north to the pass, it might not even be necessary to assemble armies here. But it would be unwise to send all the strong men north.

Slowly, Darius rolled the scroll, fastened it carefully, and slipped it into his satchel. Then, placing a warm hand on the small of my back, he led me toward the grand stairs.

He found an inn so directly that I wondered if he had lied about not having been in this part of the country recently. Perhaps he had misled me, too, about not knowing the man Jude.

It didn't matter to me. I could trust him in matters that concerned me, and that was all that was important.

After we had secured lodgings, Darius led me toward the gate of the city. We had been on many journeys. I had walked many places with him, and so we walked together in companionable silence until, outside the city walls in a meadow at the base of a small, grassy hill, he stopped. He gestured to several other mounds around us. Then he took a small step back and hooked his thumbs in the straps of his satchel.

"If you want some privacy—"

"I don't," I said quickly, before he could go. I let my eyes rove over the mounds. "Stay with me."

I looked at the grassy hills tucked up next to the overgrown forest. It didn't look like much. No care had been taken of the graves. It was not the honored ceremonial platform that my father deserved.

But it was something.

I looked back at Darius. I wished he would stand next to me. "You helped bury them?"

He nodded, his eyes taking it all in too. "It took days."

The area was quiet and still, but there was no peace here. The men buried in this meadow had been prepared to die for their king, but they had not been prepared to meet their God.

I did not want to die like that. I did not want to live like that, never knowing where my true loyalty should be.

"Darius, thank you for bringing me here." I folded my arms. I felt the breeze against my face, and I turned to look at him again.

He rubbed a hand over the back of his neck and offered me a shrug.

"Do not shrug it off!" I stepped to him. "I invited myself. You could have told me to go home."

"And risk my mother's wrath?"

I flushed at that. Leah was becoming less and less subtle in her matchmaking schemes.

"Really, it's no trouble," he said uncomfortably.

I put my hand on his chest. It was warm and solid. "Whatever else you are or pretend to be, Darius, you are good." He started to back away again, so I fisted my hand in his tunic. "Your heart is good. You can hide it from Elias and Kishkumen and men who no longer recognize good from evil." My voice fell to a whisper. "But you cannot hide it from me."

I thought he might back away again, but he pulled me suddenly to him, crushing me to his chest. "Do you have any idea how much I've come to need you?" he mumbled into my hair, half embarrassed.

I shook my head into his shoulder.

"You are the only beautiful thing in my life."

"Your mother would be hurt to hear you say that."

I felt him smile. "My mother would understand. Do you think she does not pray daily that I will fall in love with you? My life was very bleak before you came to the village." He took a deep breath as if he might say more, but he didn't.

He couldn't.

So I would say it, but for the first time in many months, I didn't know the right words in Nephite.

So I told him in Lamanite.

"I don't know if you understand me or not." I suspected he did. I drew back to look into his face. "You must know I love you. You are my enemy. I was taught from birth to hate you, and I am a failure because I can't. The only place I have found refuge in many years is in your arms." I sighed when his expression did not change, and he just looked patiently at me with a slight smile, but not as if he understood the words. "I wish I could speak to you in the way you understand."

He didn't speak to me in the language of my fathers as I suspected he could, nor did he require me to speak in his language, just took my face in his big hands and smoothed his thumbs over my cheeks and brow as he had on the day I had asked Tec what pretty meant. And when he had gotten me to close my eyes at the pleasure of it, he kissed my lips. Long, slow moments passed as we stood there among the dead, both of us alive, really alive, for perhaps the first time.

It was strange to be kissing here at a forgotten grave in the soft light of evening. The meadow was wide open, and anyone passing outside the city or on the Cumeni Road could see us. But Dare's lips and his hands, the way he held me to him, and his soft breaths of air on my cheek made me forget to be self-conscious.

Dare pulled away and urged my head to his shoulder, but my head tipped there naturally, without coaxing.

I heard the smile in his voice when he said, "That is how to speak to me in the way I understand best."

I laughed and squeezed him tighter. Were we really far enough away from his secret combination in Zarahemla that he could let himself be like this with me?

When I opened my eyes, I saw the man Jude in the distance, standing with the guards near the walls of the city.

"Dare, is Jude involved in your work?"

"No."

Darius caught the line of my vision. Jude saw us notice him from across the field, raised a hand, perhaps in farewell, and set off down the Cumeni Road away from the city.

"It's just, I saw him with the guards and thought...But then he..."

"I don't know him, Ava. Are you sure you don't?"

I worried my bottom lip between my teeth. "You know, I feel like I should recognize him, but I know I have not met him. He said the strangest thing to me while you were in the government building."

Darius straightened slightly, and his arms no longer felt soft. "What did he say to you, Ava?"

"He said..." I could hardly believe I was repeating it. "He said Josiah was not the right man for me."

Darius turned to look at Jude again, walking down the road away from us, slowly as if there was nowhere he had to be before nightfall.

"That..." he held out the syllable, "doesn't surprise me. There's something I think you should see."

He set me free of him and retrieved the scroll from his satchel, the one Jude had given him, the one I had assumed was some secret communication for his work.

"Here." He passed it to me and watched closely as I unrolled it and looked at the words.

"What does it say?" I asked after I had looked it over.

"You can read."

I looked up. "I can't read in Lamanite." I paused. "Can you?"

A slow flush swept up his neck, and I tried to curb my triumphant smile. I knew it!

Taking it back, he pointed out the places in the document where my name was written. Then, giving me a guarded look, he pointed to the places where Josiah's name was written, and where it was signed.

My heart began to pound at the first sight of my own

name. "What is this?" I frowned up at him. "Dare?"

He cleared his throat softly. "It looks like your writ of divorce from Josiah."

I pushed the document back at him and started to cry—sudden, hot tears.

How could it be? How could it possibly, possibly be?

"Your betrothal is officially ended."

I wiped the tears from my face, but they were still falling in streams. "How can that be real?" I gestured to the document. I didn't want to touch it. "And who is that man?"

He shrugged and gave me a gentle smile. "Ava, I think he is just a man who wants to make things right."

When I didn't respond, just sniffed and wiped at my eyes again, embarrassed and confused, Dare pulled me back into his arms. "Maybe I shouldn't have shown you."

His embrace was comforting and right.

"Sometimes, we know things we cannot explain. You understand that now don't you?"

I nodded.

"And sometimes things happen that have no explanation. Now, let's go get a good night's rest."

He started to go, leading me by the hand, but I turned back to see the graves for one last time. He stood still, held my hand, and let me.

"He is at peace now," he said after a time.

I turned and offered him a small, watery smile. But I let the tears continue to fall because I had not cried nearly enough for my father. When the men from my village had come home, my tears had been for Josiah.

"Let your heart be at peace, too, pretty Ava. That is

what your father wants for you. He does not want you to be unhappy."

He raised our hands and kissed my fingers. Then, tugging slightly to get me to follow, he led me back to the inn.

We spent a week of perfect days there at the little inn, walking the lanes of the city and up into the mountainous regions to fish in the streams and forage. A part of me wanted to tell Leah of the look in Dare's eyes and the touch of his hands, the smile she had missed so much, but I wouldn't. I would keep it all in my heart.

On the last evening, I noticed he kept a close eye on the falling sun. We were alone in the hills with the smell of the fish we had caught cooking over a fire. I sat close to him with my legs curled to the side, leaning leisurely on one arm, close enough to reach the cooking stone, far enough to keep from burning my skirts.

"Are you anxious to return to Zarahemla?" I asked him as I tested the doneness of the rice dish I had prepared.

He sighed. "I am ready. I will do what must be done, but I wish there was another way."

"What do you have to do?"

His eyes held mine for a drawn out moment. Finally he shook his head. "I need more information. I haven't been able to uncover what I need yet."

"It has to do with Ammon, Kish, and Elias, doesn't it." I knew it did.

"Are *you* perhaps anxious to return to Zarahemla, Ava?" His gaze flicked away, and he wouldn't meet my eyes.

I flipped the fish from the fire and licked the heat from my fingers. "Why? Should I be?"

"Ammon is there. He is your friend."

I put my spoon down and turned to look at him. He was too close to the fire or he was blushing.

"The friendship I have with Ammon is a false one. I thought you knew that. It is as false as your own friendship with him."

Not to mention, I didn't think Ammon would be hanging around Zarahemla much in the near future.

Darius dropped his eyes pointedly to the onyx on my ankle.

"Neither he nor I am Nephite. Neither of us places the significance on this bracelet that you do."

"Then what is its significance to you?"

"It was meant to seal an unspoken promise. It is a sign of trust."

"What did you promise him?" A challenge had entered his voice.

"I promised to keep his secret."

"He told you something?" His interest was really piqued now.

"No," I said uncomfortably. "I overheard something."

He reached over and yanked the bracelet off my ankle. "Promise broken. What did you overhear, Ava?"

I drew my foot back and rubbed my ankle, but the sting wasn't anything I didn't deserve for keeping silent so long. I had made up my mind to tell someone if it came up— it just hadn't come up.

But now, there was nothing for it. I took a breath and said, "Elias, Kish, and Ammon were making plans to assassinate Helaman. I meant to tell—"

"What?" he hissed, and his eyes flashed. He dropped the log he had been about to place on the fire, sending sparks swirling up into the air. He stood. "We have to go. Right now, Ava."

And he was gone, disappearing into the falling darkness.

So much for the look in his eyes and the touch in his hands.

But that did not stop me from following him.

I abandoned our meal and collected my satchel. The forest animals would dine well. I poured water on the fire and then trotted into the twilight after Darius.

By the time I got to the inn, he had our gear collected and was making final payment to the innkeeper.

"But you can't leave now," the innkeeper's wife protested. "It's nigh on dark."

"It can't be helped," Dare said politely enough, but his movements were hasty and his eyes were angry and sharp.

"I should have told you sooner," I said when I was hurrying to keep up with him on the Cumeni Road.

He snorted.

I had all kinds of excuses ready. I didn't speak the language well. I thought I had misheard. I didn't like Nephites. I definitely didn't care about their prophet. It wasn't my secret to tell. But something told me none of those things was the right thing to say.

"Will you forgive me?"

My words brought silence as Dare's feet stopped jogging on the gravel road.

He turned to me. He put his hand into my hair and

drew me to him. He brought his lips to my forehead and breathed warm air onto my skin.

"It is already done."

The murmured words, sincere and miraculous, soothed the guilt I had been feeling.

Maybe forgiveness was as easy as Sarai said it was.

CHAPTER 23

I could see the lights of Zarahemla in the distance, the last rays of the sun catching the silver Sidon that snaked through the valley near it.

"Darius," I said carefully. "Do you think the men of Gadianton sent you from the city for a reason? I mean, besides what they told you?"

"It was timed during the invasion of Zarahemla. That was no coincidence. A man like Gadiantion does not wrest control by working off of coincidences."

"Did they think you would warn the Chief Captain or the city officials?"

"I never know what they think."

His voice was hard, so I stopped questioning him and we continued on until at last we came to the grand west gates of Zarahemla.

When we approached the gates, we saw that they were closed and guarded by three or four times as many men as before, and some of them were Lamanite.

Dare let out a breath. "I guess the takeover is complete."

I looked up at him.

He nodded toward the soldiers. "Coriantumr's army."

Despite the ominous feel, Darius led me directly to the

gate and hailed Kimner, who stood at his regular post.

"You should quit the army and get a wife," Darius told him.

Kimner laughed and glanced around at the Lamanite soldiers who guarded the Nephite guards. "I think I will take my chances with the army. Who's your friend?"

"This is Ava. You've met."

Kimner's eyes studied me for a moment. "Oh, that's right. You look different."

I looked like I had been traveling for a fortnight.

"It's okay." I smiled prettily. "You're forgettable, too."

Darius laughed. "Are the gates open?"

Kimner bit back a smile and shook his head. "No. No one is to go in or out."

"Has the army moved on?"

"They went north, aiming for the passage no doubt." He spit on the ground.

"We will continue on toward Gid then," Darius said, a touch louder than necessary.

"Safer to go south," Kimner said with another shake of his head. He crossed his arms over his chest. "Go to Jershon or Antionum. Even Nephihah or Moroni."

Darius nodded and clasped hands with his friend.

"Wait!"

Several soldiers were playing a game of chance near the wall, and Shad rose from among them.

He spoke to one of the Lamanite guards in very good Lamanite.

"Dare's a messenger. He's to be let inside at once."

The guard stared at him a moment and then just

shrugged and gave a hand signal to the two guards who lounged lazily on the gates. Pulling back a large latch, they created an opening large enough to pass through.

Shad beckoned to us, but it wasn't necessary. Darius was already steering me through the soldiers. Shad waited while we slipped through the gates and then followed us through, and the gates closed behind us with a clank as the latch fell closed again.

"Did you complete your mission? You're back too early," Shad said, his voice low, his eyes darting around the area, which was abandoned save a few soldiers near the gate.

"I don't report to you," Darius said, but he gave his answer with the slightest shake of his head.

Shad's eyes were sharp and bright. I got the feeling both of them were reading accurately into what was not being said.

"There is to be a meeting of the Gadiantons tonight, but I fear your presence would be somewhat...unexpected."

Darius was silent a moment. "You're right. It isn't wise to make my presence known to all."

Shad hurried through the darkening streets of the city, leading us, without asking where we intended to go, to the lane that led to the Estate of Alma.

"It has not been taken over?" Darius asked, eyeing the lane warily.

"No. It is no more occupied than the rest of the city."

"What do you mean?" I asked. "I thought the Lamanites had completely taken control of the city."

"The government has been taken over. It is a matter of who rules here. But Coriantumr needs people to rule over.

Other than the soldiers who guard against insurrection and the closed gates, it is mostly the same here."

"And the Lamanites do not view Helaman as a threat to their rule?"

Shad shrugged. "Apparently not. He will be allowed to judge according to the laws. Coriantumr declared it on the steps of the government building."

"Helaman is the chief judge here now," Darius clarified for me.

"Oh. So he is not in danger?"

"Not from Lamanite soldiers."

"Were you here when the takeover happened?" I asked Shad.

"Unofficially."

"What does that mean?"

"Nothing," Darius broke in. "Those men, at the gate, they're Helaman's men?"

"Yes. Your entry should be simple." Shad hesitated.

Darius stopped and turned to him. "What is it?"

"Let me do it."

Darius studied him, but I didn't miss the glance he gave me before he asked, "Who is it to be?"

"Gadianton has designated Kishkumen."

Darius breathed a sigh that, though bleak, sounded like one of relief. But he said, "Haven't you been helping in the search for his betrothed bride? Paanchi's daughter?"

Shad's eyes blazed. His voice was low and secretive when he said, "I found her. Let me do it."

Dare's eyes dropped closed and he shook his head. "Is she safe?"

A muscle in Shad's jaw tightened. "He found her first."

Dare straightened his shoulders, shook his head. "I'll do my job. You do yours." He put his hand out to Shad.

Shad's face clouded with disappointment, but he gave Dare the strange hand shake and, turning to me, he said politely, "Nice to see you again, Ava," before he disappeared into the recesses of the city.

"Who is Paanchi?" I asked as we walked down the lane.

"He was a candidate for the judgement seat. His supporters did not take it well when he was not voted in."

"And his daughter?"

He glanced at me. "She has gone missing."

"But Shad found her?"

"You have learned my language entirely too well."

I laughed quietly. "Is she all right?"

"You saw the fire in his eyes. Either she is not all right, or he isn't," Darius said.

We were upon the guards at Helaman's gate. Darius lifted a hand in greeting when we were in the low light of their lantern. I recognized Tim, but I didn't know the other guard.

"Darius?" Timothy asked.

"Yes," he replied.

"Did you bring Ava to sweet talk your way through the gates again?" he asked, coming off the wall.

This brought a laugh from the other guard, and even a chuckle from Darius.

"I am more likely to draw my sword and demand entrance," I said in Lamanite, tossing my hair over my shoulder and giving him what I hoped was a deceptively sultry smile.

Darius had to stifle a laugh.

"What did she say?" Timothy asked.

"That's a dangerous language to be speaking just now," said the other sentry, more guarded than his companion.

"On the contrary," I continued in Lamanite. "I believe it is the language that rules here."

"She lives in Melek for asylum from her countrymen," Darius informed them. "Can we enter the estate?"

"Oh, sure," said the second guard, but he added, "If your girl can think of a nice way to ask."

I stepped to him, casually drew my sword, and held it next to his nose. "Open the gate," I said clearly in his language.

He laughed, maybe a little nervously, stepped back, and opened the gate.

"It doesn't surprise me he ended up with a woman so much like his sister," I heard him say before they closed the gates behind us.

Timothy laughed. "Well, if my sister was like his, I'd think about it, too."

The man's words were loud enough that I knew we both heard them.

"Am I like your sister, Dare?"

The moon was dim, but the light from a million stars lit the sky. Despite the intrigue of the night, I felt safe within the walls of Helaman's estate. I felt safe with Darius, and the walk through the gardens, quiet and private, felt romantic.

"Do you mean are you like her or do I think of you the same way?"

I knew he didn't think of me the same way. Though I had tried to guard against this very thing, I could still close my eyes and remember his kiss. But I said, "Both."

"I hadn't really noticed you were like Ket."

"But I am?"

He adjusted the strap of his satchel. "The more of your true self you show—yes, you're like her."

"When have I not shown my true self?"

"That shy little doe who came to live with my mother?"

Doe?

"I wasn't shy. I didn't know your language."

The look he gave me was almost stern. "You were skittish and heart-sore." We drew to a stop near Eliza's house.

"It looks like there are people staying here." I pointed to the travel packs that were stacked near the door.

Darius took my hand. "We'll stay at the cottage until morning, then get settled in. I don't...I'm sorry, I don't know how long we'll be here."

"Helaman won't mind if we stay?"

"You know he won't."

I followed him in through the darkened door and strained to see.

"There is a bed over here," he said quietly. I heard him shuffling around and then saw him spreading some blankets on a low pallet in the corner. "Tired?" he asked.

"Very." But I couldn't have been more tired than he was. We had been traveling for much of the past month and especially hard over the past week.

I lay on the pallet and Darius sat next to it, leaning his back up against the wall.

"You need to sleep," I said softly.

He grunted.

I touched his arm, and felt the reflexive tightening of his muscles.

"You are safe here," I told him. "You got us here, and we are safe. Sleep, Dare."

He sighed, but slid down until he lay on his side on the hard floor with his back to me. He fell quickly into sleep, and after I said a silent prayer for him, I slept too.

I woke to an empty, dark room. Darius was not on the floor near me, and as my eyes adjusted, I saw that he was not anywhere in the room. He was going to that meeting.

And I wasn't going to just sit and wait.

The air was unusually still outside of the cottage. The half-moon lit the night, but the shadows were dark. Movement caught my eye near Helaman's family home.

I strained to see as Darius slipped inside without knocking on the door or announcing himself. I waited, doubting his intentions for the merest of moments, but I pushed those thoughts out of my mind and darted in that direction. I stopped in the shadow of a hedge and watched the door. Reaching up, I touched the hilt of my sword.

It wasn't long before Darius emerged from the house and moved quickly toward the gates of the estate. I wondered how I was going to follow him off the estate without the sentries noticing. Could I go over the wall? Saying a quick prayer in my heart, I ran to catch up.

When I reached the gate, the sentries were occupied with changing the guard and I did miraculously manage to slip out unnoticed into the nearly dark lane.

A shadow moved purposefully down the lane, and while I wondered if I should follow, I was already doing it. I followed as he turned from the lane onto the road that led to the heart of the city. My breath caught when I saw him turn near the granaries. Was this where the meeting of the Gadiantons was to take place? But no one else arrived. As Zarahemla lay blanketed in darkness, Darius paced over the hill beyond the two large structures, and I stood silent and still in their shadows and watched him do it.

I could see he was worried. He stretched his fingers and clenched his fists, shook his arms out, folded and unfolded his arms. He stretched his neck, bounced his shoulders, and rolled his head.

I smiled, thinking of the times he fidgeted when he was talking to me, but my heart caught and wept for him when he went to his knees and retched.

And then he bowed his head.

It was all I could do to keep from going to him. I would give him water from my water skin. I would kneel beside him. Press him close to me. Add my prayer to his.

But that would embarrass him. For that reason alone, I shouldn't have come. But had he really expected me to wait at the cottage wondering what was happening and fearing for his life?

He turned and came toward me. It felt a terrible betrayal to stay hidden in the shadows. I contemplated stepping out, but another shadow converged with Darius as he entered the main road.

The men hailed each other. I crept closer so I could hear, pausing to remove my sandals to make my tread absolutely silent, for the feeling in my stomach told me silence was absolutely essential now. Getting caught here would lead to more than embarrassment.

"No," Darius was saying. He folded his arms across his chest and stood stock still. "I was just at his house. He is still at the judgment seat."

It had been hours since Darius checked at Helaman's house.

"It is the last night he will have to work late," said the other man, the man I recognized as Kish by the sound of his voice and the shape of his shadow.

Darius burst out with a laugh. "Come. I will take you to him. Perhaps you would like an introduction."

Kish chuckled.

It sounded so normal.

A memory of Uncle Zaaron flashed in my mind—chuckling the same way with the village men.

I closed my eyes and remembered watching them gather with their weapons, congregate in the center of the village. Papa moved past me and tousled my hair.

"Bring Tecumeni," Zaaron said when my father reached them. "It is time."

Papa turned and called, "Ava, go get your brother."

And I had done it, never thinking that I shouldn't have, never suspecting what Tec would be taught to do.

But then, Tec's work with Uncle Zaaron and the Order of the Nehors and the Lamanite army, all if it, had brought us here—to Melek, to Kalem and Leah's, to Chloe and Darius. Zaaron had helped us leave the village because he had sensed the same spirit about the band of Nephites he had brought to the village as Tec had. The same spirit, to be honest, that I had sensed in Sarai. Zaaron might have been bad, but he was so good, too. It was impossible to know where the line was. It was impossible to say he was all one or the other. Maybe he did bad things for a good, greater purpose.

Like Darius did.

But unlike Darius, maybe Uncle Zaaron had not been taught the right way. But that wasn't right either. I knew he had met the missionary, Aaron, in Jerusalem.

I gave my head a small shake, and when I opened my eyes, Darius and Kish were gone.

Cautiously I ran to the place they had been, knelt, inspected the ground, and determined they had gone toward the city.

To the judgment seat then.

I remembered the way to the government building. Darius had shown me. They weren't difficult to find as so few people were out this time of night. When I caught sight of them again in the darkness, they were walking across the great plaza, nearly to the grand steps of the building. I saw Kish slow and stop. Darius turned in question.

Kish's voice was low, and maybe I felt it more than I heard it. "Give me your knife."

Dare's hand went to the hilt of his blade. "What? Haven't you brought your own?"

Kish made no audible reply, just let his dark gaze rest on Dare.

After what looked to be a tense moment, Darius passed his knife to Kish.

I knew Kish didn't trust Darius. He had warned me

not to trust him either. Was he afraid to be alone with Darius? Or did he plan to use Darius's knife tonight? Any of the soldiers he knew would recognize it. It was distinctive—even I could picture it in my mind.

Either way, Darius was now without a weapon and walking with the man who, if I had pieced everything together well enough, was hand-picked to murder Helaman, the Chief Judge of Zarahemla.

And Darius had been hand-picked to lead Kish there, to get him in to see Helaman. Was he to assist in the deed? Was this just another one of the terrible things Darius had to do to keep his membership with the men of Gadianton?

But it couldn't be. He planned to retreat to the lands north, to leave his homeland and his family. Surely he meant to betray the band of Gadianton. Surely he meant to betray Kishkumen.

But how could he do that without a weapon?

I darted toward them, as silent and invisible as I could make myself, and I drew my short sword from my back as I went. I would make my sword available to him should he need it. I just had to get close enough and let him know I was there. He would be angry that I had followed him, but better angry than dead, captured, or wounded.

They were moving off, and I didn't get there in time for what happened next. It was so fast. In one moment they were walking together. In the next, Kish was in a heap on the ground with the plain handle of a dagger protruding from his ribs.

I stopped. Darius glanced at me, but looked away, disgusted or ashamed.

He went to his heels and reached a hand to feel for a pulse at Kish's neck. Apparently establishing there was none, he picked up his knife from where it had fallen, leaving the one I had bought in the market of Ammonihah in the ribs of his enemy. Rising, he gave one last long look to Kish, and then he turned and walked briskly toward me.

"Come on," he said as he brushed past me. And he threw back over his shoulder, "Are you always going to be disobedient?"

CHAPTER 24

His words brought a flood of relief. It was done, he hadn't died, and there would be a future for us.

Hurrying to catch up, I said, "I'm afraid I am."

"I guess you are like Keturah, then."

"Something you hate?"

"No. I like Keturah."

We were moving quickly back toward Helaman's, paying little heed to secrecy now, but still Darius moved through the darkest shadows when he could. Suddenly, Darius whisked me into his arms in the middle of a road. He began kissing me and didn't stop until a small patrol of drunken Lamanite soldiers had passed us, laughing and jeering.

"Good thing they were drunk," he said when we were on our way again.

"Was that necessary?" My head was still whirling.

"If I had been alone, they might have enforced the curfew."

The sentries at Helaman's gate cast each other a somewhat alarmed glance when we arrived out of breath at the gate, but they opened it with a simple, if suspicious, "Evening, Darius." They tried not to look at me.

"Wait here with Timothy," Darius said.

His voice was so calm and natural it took a moment for me to realize he was speaking to me.

"Wait here?"

He took me by the elbow as if to draw me aside, but an impatient glance at the open gate told me he didn't think he had time to speak to me privately. "I need to inform Helaman of tonight's events." I thought of Kish still lying in the grand plaza. "Timothy and Abnor can keep you safe if it comes to it."

He kissed me sudden and fierce. Then he punched Timothy in the shoulder and called, "Watch my girl," as he ran through the gate.

I felt both sentries' eyes on me then as I watched Darius run through the courtyard, ducking a low limb and disappearing into the night.

"There is a stool here," one of the sentries said. "If you would like to sit," he added.

Turning to him, I thanked him and sat.

"Are we likely to have to protect you from someone?" he asked.

"I don't know," I responded. Was someone waiting for Kish's return? How long until someone came across his body in the plaza? They would surely send for the Chief Judge. "Maybe."

He only nodded and went back to his quiet conversation with Abnor, whatever Darius and I had interrupted.

But when the minutes passed so slowly, I cleared my throat and asked the guards, "Does Darius ever work here at the gate?"

They turned to me.

"Oh, no. Darius doesn't work on the estate."

"But I thought—" I looked between them. "Doesn't he work for Helaman?"

They shared an uncomfortable look that made me sure they would tell me no, but Timothy said, "He does. But he does most of his work away from the estate."

I felt my brows come together, but I nodded. They seemed to know as much about Darius's whereabouts as his mother did. The question seemed to make them uneasy, because they fell silent and were watchful of the shadows along the lane.

I didn't hear the gate open, but suddenly Dare was moving swiftly between the sentries. When he turned and our eyes met, his were less troubled but still held a steely glint of determination. Tonight's adventures were not yet over. I took the hand he held out to me. Without a word, he led me in the opposite direction we had come, sending only a quick and silent wave to the men behind us.

"There is a way out of the city to the north," he informed me quietly when we were away from the sentries.

"Is this gate held by the Gadiantons, too?" I asked.

I hadn't intended to sound distrustful or accusing, but he looked slightly chagrined when he shook his head. "This is not a gate, and it is held by a member of the Church of God." He paused before adding, "We will be slipping over the back wall of his home."

By this, he meant that the drop would be far. I had seen the homes built into the city walls. And I also knew from his words that we would be passing through the more mean parts of the city. But I was not afraid. It would be a waste of my energy to fear when I was at the side of this tall and skilled Nephite warrior.

Twice we saw Lamanite patrols, but miraculously, they didn't see us. In the past, I would have thought we were lucky, but now I knew the truth. God helped us escape through the city. God made us quick and invisible.

"Here goes nothing," Dare said as he slipped inside the home of a merchant. I was to wait, quiet and still in the darkness outside, but it wasn't long before Darius swept back the heavy mat at the door and beckoned me inside.

A low lamp had been lit and it had shields at the sides so very little light escaped, but it was enough to see our host's eyes widen when he saw me. He was middle-aged, of average height, and leaning slightly on the table that held the shuttered lantern when I drew up beside Darius.

"My friend Helaman sends me a very compelling mystery this night," the man chuckled. He reached a hand up to scrub at his short beard.

"This is Cael," Dare said to me and then turned to Cael. "I wish we had more time to explain."

The man shook his head. "There is no need. Helaman can regale me later. It is best for you to drop over the wall and go to ground. Get some rest and start your journey tomorrow at dusk." He picked up the lantern and moved toward the back of the home. "I will send my boy out to warn you if it is not safe to continue."

"Thank you." Darius took my hand and followed the man.

"Judith, arise and pack our guests provisions for a journey."

It wasn't until he spoke that I realized the room we entered was a sleeping chamber and a woman slept on a wide pallet to our right. The light was so dim I couldn't see what was to our left. The woman sat up, took one quick look at us, and rose to do her husband's bidding. As she passed me, she gave me a soft, welcoming smile. Her husband had passed the lantern to Darius and was hauling a rope from a large chest in the corner. He set it on the floor while he and Darius removed a set of heavy wooden shutters from the small window.

I swallowed hard when I realized he intended for us to go out through it.

"Beautiful views," he said as he casually secured one end of the rope around his waist with a knot I had never seen.

"I'll go first," Darius said. "Watch closely."

"I can barely see you."

I felt his laugh, but he spoke to Cael. "There will be soldiers searching the city before long."

"Looking for you?"

"No, but there will be false ones who are."

After the man gave Darius directions to find the place we were to hide, Darius stepped outside the window and disappeared. Cael braced himself against the wall until the rope went slack. Then he turned to me and repeated his instructions, reminding me to hold tightly to the rope and walk backward down the wall one step at a time.

"Push your satchel around to your back so it doesn't get in the way now," he said. "That's a girl."

I didn't hear anything from Darius below, and peering out, I couldn't see him, just a dim outline of the mountains to the west where Melek was.

"What if I fall?" I whispered mostly to myself.

"That boy will catch you," Cael said with a wink. "Go with God, the both of you."

I took a deep breath and did as instructed.

Crawling down the wall was actually fun, and I felt an exhilaration as I descended. When I was nearly to the ground, I felt Dare's hand grasp my ankle to let me know he was there, then his hands around my waist lifting me down.

There was as short owl call I barely noticed, but Darius looked suddenly up and, stepping away, caught the bag of provisions.

That was it. We were out of Zarahemla, and we couldn't go back. I watched the rope disappear as Cael hauled it up and through his window. After the quiet click as he set the shutters back in place, all was silent.

Darius didn't wait for the silence to get weighty. He hefted the bag of provisions over his shoulder and started to walk away from the base of the wall, taking a moment to cup a hand around the back of my neck and kiss my forehead, showing me without words that I had done well.

"I think Chloe might like that wall climbing," I said after a few moments.

He huffed, amused. "Where do you think I learned it?"

I laughed and wondered if it was true. I thought of all the things I had done with Tec and the other boys from my village, the girls too. "You've known her a long time."

He didn't say anything for a minute. "I'm glad to let Tec have her," he said finally.

"*Let* him?"

"Oh, no. I mean, Tec is the right one for her. I'm glad it is him and not me."

"I shouldn't have said that. I was just missing the friends I grew up with."

"Josiah?"

"Yes," I said honestly, though in truth, he had been quite a bit older than me and had never joined with my friends. "And others."

"Were you close to Tec growing up?"

"Always."

"You would miss him. I mean, if you were ever separated."

"But he and Chloe will be sailing with us."

He turned to me with a slightly raised brow. "Because your brother would miss you. He can't stand the thought of you sailing away without him."

I frowned. I had never thought of Tec missing me, only that I was not sure how I would ever live without him. Something inside me had known he wasn't coming back to Ani-Anti, and that was why I had followed him all those months ago. I knew he felt guilt over leaving our family to fend for themselves, but I had never thought he might be in turmoil over leaving me.

"What makes you say that?"

I heard a smile in Dare's voice when he said, "The murderous glint in his eye when I told him I was taking you to Zarahemla." His use of the word murderous caused us both a moment's pause, but Dare pressed on. "I told him I meant to marry you, but that only seemed to make it worse." He shook his head. "For an easy-going guy, he is extremely protective when it comes to you, Ava."

I didn't know if easy-going was the right way to describe Tecumeni. He was kind and fun, but when he wanted something, he was focused and intense. "He feels bad about what Josiah did, maybe even responsible for it, though he isn't. I never talked to Josiah after that, but I think Tec did." We walked quickly on in silence. "But wait," I said, breaking it. "You talked to Tec of marriage?"

"How else did you think I persuaded him to let you go to Antionum?"

"He didn't tell me that," I said slowly.

"I asked him not to."

He shoved a hand through his hair, and I took it and held it. "Why?"

"I thought I could, I don't know, make you fall in love with me, or at least like me, if we had some time together. I couldn't do it in the village. I couldn't stay in the village long enough. Even when I have time to, I don't like to be there. But since you came, I found myself…" He sighed and reluctantly went on. "I found myself stopping there between my assignments." He jerked his hand to push it through his hair again, forgetting I held it, and it made me smile. "Even when it wasn't on the way," he admitted.

"Did you tell Leah this?"

"No. But she knew. She knew with my brothers and my sister, too."

"She is wise."

"Do you remember that night you burned your hand at the cook fire?"

I remembered it very vividly.

"The large pot was in the coals, and you were rubbing it with ashes to clean it. I tried, but I couldn't take my eyes off of you."

"I felt them," I said quietly, and he squeezed my hand. I did remember the night he was speaking of.

"I was angry about it, confused by it, and frustrated that I couldn't even talk to you. I wanted to get up and walk away. I couldn't. And then you burned yourself."

"And Leah got up to get me some salve, but you stopped her and withdrew a container of it from your satchel."

We were both silent while we remembered what happened next. Darius had gone to his heels next to me and, taking my hand in his, smoothed the cooling, opaque salve over my wound.

"Later, after you went to bed, Mother came to sit by me. I thought she would chide me for not coming home enough or maybe beg me again to tell her what happened with Sarai. I know it caused a rift between her and Dinah." He paused. "Or deepened the one Keturah caused."

As the wall started to curve east, Darius veered west.

"What did she say?" I asked when he didn't seem to want to continue.

He led me down a rocky hill and around some brambles until we were in a sheltered copse of trees. Tucked in the southwest corner, just as Cael had promised us, was an area cut into the rocky hillside. It was cut back about ten cubits and was not tall enough to stand up in.

We had made it in time. Nearly dawn now, the light was rising, and it was time to be hidden. Darius surveyed the small cave and then turned to me. "Tired?"

"What did Leah say to you?" I persisted.

"Come here." He pulled the strap of his satchel over his head and, stooping to walk inside, dropped that and the bag of provisions in the corner. He held out his hand for my satchel, which I gave him. Setting that beside the others, he took my hand and drew me down to sit beside him. Awkwardly, he positioned us so he leaned back against the wall and I leaned back against his chest. I wondered if it was so he didn't have to look at me while he talked.

Finally, he took a breath. "Mother sat beside me and said you were a pretty girl."

I couldn't help a smile.

"I was sullen and told her you were too pretty for me. She said, 'Maybe.' It made me laugh, and she said, 'I've missed that smile so much.'"

I knew the one she meant.

"I told her again that I couldn't stay in the village, but she said, 'Your smile is the only way I can still see your father's.'"

I placed my hand over Dare's.

"And then she told me she would arrange my marriage through Tec when I was ready." He huffed. "I guess she knows me well enough to know I wasn't going to let my mother arrange my marriage."

His arms tightened around me, and I relaxed back against him.

"Wake me if you get uncomfortable," I said on a yawn.

"On a rock floor? Impossible."

"You're relieved to have it over," I realized, though it shouldn't have been a revelation.

I felt his smile and another tight squeeze. "I wish there had been another way, but yes, I am relieved."

"Do you think we are safe now?"

"Gadianton's men will comb the streets for a while, but they will be the first to realize it is possible to get out of the city. They will suspect it was me that killed Kishkumen." He took a breath. "But yes, if we lie low and then move quickly, we should make it to the ship all right."

"And after that?"

I felt him shrug. "Go to sleep, Ava."

I knew he needed sleep more than I did, but I let my eyes drop closed. He woke me in the afternoon and I sat watch, reading the scroll he had given me, while he slept until dusk. I had food prepared when I woke him and we both ate hungrily. Our eyes kept meeting. We were almost giddy with the success of the previous night's escape, so relieved to have our freedom, so relieved to have each other.

The journey to Ammonihah was different from the last trip. Dare was much more open and talkative. He said funny things just to get me to laugh. He told me all about himself and about growing up in the village. One night, he even told me about Sarai and Isabel.

He finally felt free to plan a future for himself, and I felt lucky to be a part of his plans. He let himself trust that there would be a long life ahead of him, and I let myself trust in him and in the God who showed himself to me more every day.

CHAPTER 25

"You don't want to stop in Melek to say goodbye?"

"Of course I do, but we don't have time."

It was dawn and I could see we were nowhere near Melek. We had jogged through most of the night, and Darius had led us north up the east side of the valley so we had bypassed Melek completely. We were so far away from it, stopping there wasn't even an option now.

"But your Mother!"

His jaw tightened, but he said, "She will be all right. I explained what I could to Kalem and Hemni. When I told them about Chloe and Tec leaving, I told them we were leaving also and a little about why it is necessary." He squinted up at the sky. "Kalem will...help her see."

We had stopped for the morning to eat and to rest. We both needed to sleep again, and Darius didn't want to travel in the daylight until we were farther from Zarahemla. The second day we traveled deeper into the morning before finding a place to sleep.

"I miss my bedroll," I said as I tried to get comfortable on the ground.

"That is a bed of pines!" Darius said. "Soft as downy feathers."

I smiled up at him. I knew he had tried to find a

comfortable place for me to sleep. I reached out my hand to him and he took it.

"I know. Thank you."

He smiled too, but then a worried look crossed his face. I squeezed his hand.

"Something is wrong. What is it?"

He grimaced. "Ava, we don't have any bedrolls. We don't have anything. I have some money, but I don't know how much use it will be to us when we get where we're going."

I sat up. The needles were poking me anyway. "Dare, that doesn't matter."

One side of his mouth turned up. "You like me that much?"

"I trust you that much." I leaned over and lightly kissed his lips. "And I like you that much."

He kissed me back, so sweetly, but he wouldn't be distracted. "I mean it, Ava. We will be starting out with nothing. We don't even have an official betrothal contract." He looked down at our hands and entwined his fingers in mine, almost as if he were asking me to take a chance on him anyway. "We won't even have time to visit the market on the way, unless we get really lucky."

I placed my other hand on top of our clasped ones. "Lib said they are shipping supplies. We can purchase what we need when we get there or we can glean it from the ground. I can keep a home, or I can procure food in the wild. And I have infinite trust in your abilities. We will be fine. I only wish we could stop in Melek. You need to tell your mother goodbye, and I need to thank her."

"She loves you, you know," Darius said.

"I love her too. She was very kind to me, even when I refused to accept my circumstances. I was self-absorbed, even rude sometimes, and she just kept loving me."

"You were never rude."

I laughed. "How would you know? You've not spent four days in a row in the village since I arrived."

"Not that you saw."

I eyed him. Had he been in the village without me knowing? "I was beginning to think I smelled or something."

"You do. You smell good."

I rolled my eyes when he leaned over and nuzzled my neck, sniffing loudly. I pushed him away, and his eyes were glittering with mischief. "Don't get silly. We are not safe yet."

He did sober as he glanced at the position of the sun and turned his eyes to the north. "If you throw your lot in with me, you may never be safe."

I sighed and lay back down on my downy soft bed of pines. "There are those who would kill my brother for his betrayal. I've long known fear will do me no good. Throwing my lot in with either of you is not up for question."

He just nodded.

"Do you know what mahseh means in my language?" I asked him.

"It means to trust."

My brows rose a little even as I closed my eyes. "I believe you have made a greater study than you have let on of the language I understand best," I said, hearing the sleepy warmth in my voice.

"I have made a great study of many languages, and..." I almost opened my eyes when he hesitated, but thought better of it. "And I might have misled you a little about how much of your language I understood."

"I might have suspected that."

"You did not," he protested. "When?"

"Ammon and Elias and…Kish moved easily between the languages. I began to think it might be a requirement for your job." He tugged on my hair and I smiled but kept my eyes closed. "How much of what I said in the village did you understand?" I asked, already knowing the truth.

"All of it," he said guiltily.

I took in the weight of that, thinking back to many things I had complained about to Tec when I thought no one could understand. One specific thought that kept replaying in my mind was complaining to Tec how all the Nephite men were ugly.

I felt Darius's fingertips on my face. "You never said anything that made me dislike you. The very opposite happened," he said. "So don't be embarrassed, because I can see you are."

"I can't help it."

"You offered to help Mother in all of her many daily tasks and then kept her home while she saw to the needs of others. You told beautiful stories about your homeland and your loved ones. And you befriended Melia with your Lamanite words. Those things are nothing to be ashamed of."

Touched by his compliment, I replied, "Melia is the one who befriended me."

"No. She has many friends in Melek, in the city, I think, but when she comes to visit Kalem, Muloki does all the talking and she sits quietly and talks to no one."

I wanted to say he was wrong, that I had seen Melia talk to his mother many times, but he was right. When she came, she spoke the formalities, but quite often did separate herself from further conversation.

"She loves Kalem and Mother, but she is not as comfortable with them as they wish she was," Darius said.

I sighed again. "Why are relationships so complicated?"

"They are, aren't they?" he asked quietly, and I felt him lean back onto his elbows. I knew the pine needles would be digging into them.

And I knew he was thinking of Isabel and her marriage to his brother Kenai, of Sarai and her disastrous feelings for him, of his family, his mother, of Kalem—the man who had killed his father—and of Tec and me.

"Will it be complicated for us?" I asked.

"At times."

"Is it now?"

"No. I love you, Ava, and you love me. That's all there is. I am done with secrets and your heart is free. Here, rest your head in my lap." He sat up and moved closer to me. Grateful to take some of the pressure off my shoulder, I moved to him and did as he suggested, feeling instantly better. "It is catching that boat that will be complicated if we are delayed in any way."

"Maybe it will sail late."

"And maybe it will sail early."

I tried to laugh, but I was too tired. It just came out as a hum. "I will trust you to get us there in time."

He didn't reply.

"I mean it." I tried to lean up, but his large hand pressed me back down at the shoulder.

"Sleep now."

"I mean it," I said again. "I trust in the strength of your arm. I trust you to get us to the ship and to provide for us once we have settled in the new land."

I was surprised to hear him choke up. He tried to hide it, but I could hear it in his words. "I thank you for that. It has been a long time since someone looked at me without mistrust, questions, or accusations in their eyes."

We didn't run into anything that held up our progress toward the sea, and in fact, we made very good time. We avoided the trail through the gorge, though it appeared that, other than some debris, all had returned to normal within it. Bypassing the sea village, Darius walked me toward the ship on the beach. I took off my sandals and waded through the shallow surf.

When I caught Darius watching me, I blushed a little. "I miss the sea," I said. "Even after Father died, Mother would take us to the sea to swim and to fish. It wasn't far, only a day's journey, and we would camp on the beach. I miss the sound of the waves and the smell in the air."

"And swimming."

I grinned and nodded.

"I want to find out when the ship will sail, but after that we could come back and you could swim."

"I would love that."

"Tomorrow with the morning tide," the man in the shipyards said when we asked him when the ship would sail. "It will be a sight to behold."

318

"How long of a journey is it?" I asked him.

"A fortnight to the first stop, or so they tell me. A month to the second."

"Is there a place we can purchase supplies for the journey?" Darius asked, casting a nervous glance to me.

The man eyed us both, travel weary with dust, grime, and fatigue. "Aye," he said after a moment of thought. "You've missed the market, but if you have money, my brother-in-law will sell you all you need. He's an honest man, won't rob you blind like some."

The man told us where to find his brother-in-law, we thanked him and went to purchase supplies.

Good to his word, Darius returned with me to the beach, hauling all our provisions along, and sat in the sand to watch me swim.

"You come too," I said.

"Ava, this is all we own in the world. I am not going to leave it on the beach unattended."

Seeing the wisdom in that, I kicked out of my sandals, tossed him my satchel, and ran into the breaking waves. I swam out into the sea and glided back in to shore on the underside of a beautiful wave. It crashed over me and I came up laughing. I knew we had time to burn, so I swam out and did it again.

I could see someone sitting with Darius when I finally waded from the sea. He was blond and light in his blue tunic, but straight and strong like Darius.

They both stood when they saw me, and when I drew close, Darius tossed me one of the warm blankets we had just purchased. I wrapped myself in it and grinned back at the two men who were grinning at me.

"I've never seen anyone do that," Lib said to me.

I shrugged. "I'll teach you how."

He nodded. "I was just telling Dare I've never been so unhappy to see him."

I frowned, looking between the two of them.

Lib was so light-skinned that the flush on his neck showed immediately. "Alive and well, I mean," he said, even though it clearly embarrassed him to say so.

Understanding he was referring to the silly pact the three of us had made before Darius and I had left a fortnight ago, I smiled at him.

"Would you really have courted me?" I asked as we walked along the beach toward the large ship, Darius and Lib carrying the bulk of the supplies.

"Of course. I'd do it now if I couldn't see the way Dare looks at you."

The comment managed to embarrass all three of us.

To break the silence, Lib asked us if we had purchased all our supplies here on the coast.

"We did. We didn't have time to stop anywhere. And we had to leave our travel packs during the course of the mission."

"We came here so immediately, we did not even have time to stop in Melek to bid Dare's family goodbye."

"What do you mean?" Lib asked. "They are all waiting here for you. They are on board, or possibly roaming the village for a last feel of solid ground beneath their feet."

"On board? So they did decide to sail?"

Lib looked from Darius to the ship, still docked but

ready to sail. "Kalem, your mother, Muloki and Melia, Micah and Kenai and their wives, and Zeke and his family."

"Jarom?" Darius asked hopefully, eyes wide in surprise.

"Yes. The whole family. They have all booked passage. They are all on board, waiting to depart, and waiting for you."

Darius and I took that in for a moment. "Even Ket?"

Lib looked down. "Kalem sent word, but they haven't shown up here yet. Gid didn't want to leave the farm. Or more accurately, he didn't want to leave his parents. He never did want that farm."

Darius took a deep breath and let it slowly out.

His arm was still around me, and he pulled me close so he could kiss my temple. "Maybe we won't be starting with nothing. At least we will have family."

"With the government the way it is, seeking refuge up north is just wise," Lib said.

"Is there a government in place already?"

"There is. It is minimal but carries out all the necessary functions."

"Marriages?" I asked.

Lib smiled a little sadly. "Yes. You will be able to marry Dare when you get there."

"And does this government have need of a scribe?" I asked when Lib had managed to embarrass us all again.

He laughed, and the tension broke. "I have already recommended Darius to the governor of the more distant colony. Which reminds me." He rummaged in his satchel until he came out with a piece of vellum. "A kind of letter of introduction," he said and handed it over to Darius. "I was going to save it until you disembarked, but here. The man's name is Lachoneus and you will find him by asking around. Anyone will be able to tell you where he is at."

"Thank you," Darius said, and I could see he was truly grateful. I knew he was worried about providing for a family in the strange new land. Even if Lachoneus had no need of him, he held in his hand hope that he might be able to use the skill he loved in his new life.

Lib hooked his fingers around the strap of his satchel. He cleared his throat. "You two must be ready to rest. Go on up. I know your family is anxious to see you safe aboard with them."

"You're coming, right?" I asked Lib when we had begun to climb the boarding ramp.

"Of course I am. I have a lot to do before we sail, however. I will see you on board."

"Until later then," I said and turned back to the ship.

"Ava!"

I had no sooner turned back than I heard Chloe at the ship's rail. I looked up and waved to let her know I had heard her.

By the time we reached the deck, she had called for all the others, and soon the deck was filled with people hugging and crying and laughing.

Darius went straight to his mother and enfolded her in his long arms. I watched him as he greeted each member of his family, including Hemni and Dinah's children who had grown up alongside him like brothers and sisters. I couldn't help watching for regret when he placed his hand on the shoulders of Isabel and Sarai, but I didn't see any.

"He doesn't love them," Chloe said, drawing up next to me. She still had a limp. "He never did."

"I know. How is your leg?"

Her lips curled into a snarl and then she sighed, and it was only slightly more dramatic than necessary. "I wish we would sail already. Tec and I have already been on the ship long enough to have made it there by now. I'm glad you are finally here. The accommodations aren't fancy, but I kind of miss bunking with you."

"I missed you too, little sister," I said and hugged her.

She grinned at me, and when she sighed this time, it was much more dramatic than it needed to be. She had a huge crush on my brother, plain as the nose on her pretty face.

That night I stood at the rail with Darius, watching the sun sink into the ocean.

"Sky's pink," he commented. He stood behind me and held me loosely in his arms. His voice was muffled in my hair. "It will be smooth sailing tomorrow."

I took a last, lingering look to the south toward my homeland. Squinting, I saw five figures hurrying along the beach.

"Look there," I said, pointing them out to Darius. We watched as they grew closer, but before we could see who they were, they were hidden by the ship, and we nearly forgot about them until we heard a woman call out to Darius from behind us at the boarding ramp.

When we turned, Keturah and Gideon, who carried baby Gabriel, were just coming aboard. The crew had begun to light the lanterns, and in the light I could make out Dare's friend, Seth, and his new wife behind them, along with the girl, Miriam, I had met at their wedding.

Darius drew me forward with an arm around my shoulder to greet them, unwilling, I guessed, to let anyone think we meant less to each other than we did. Our travels had been long and arduous, and I knew that he felt the same closeness to me that I felt to him. I didn't sigh as dramatically as Chloe did, but I felt the same way. I had a big crush on this boy who greeted his only sister and his friends with all the love I knew he had in him.

"You made it," he said as he clasped arms with Gideon and then Seth.

"Just. I hear we sail on the morning tide," Gideon said.

"It will carry us away to a better place, or that's what they say." Darius grinned at his sister.

Keturah went up onto her toes and stroked her baby's head with a gentle, curved hand. "I do hope it is better there."

CHAPTER 26

I knew things would be better, at least for me, when I climbed up to the deck from the passengers' hold the next morning and saw Darius pitching in with the crew to get the anchors raised. And I knew by what power I felt the sureties I did.

I have sent him you.

An ugly, divorced, Lamanite girl.

I might have been ugly, divorced, and a Lamanite, but I knew those things didn't matter, not really. Darius thought I was pretty, and before long I would be married to a very good man, one who knew what it meant to keep his word. And I would have the advantage now of understanding why Josiah had done what he had done—at least I would not have the sorrow of his rejection to follow me into my future. His rejection had prodded me here to meet Darius. Darius was exceedingly brave and strong like Josiah, but he also knew what it was to kneel in humility. And as for being Lamanite, that one was mine to keep, and it was a heritage I would treasure. Yes, there were a lot of wicked Lamanites, but there were a lot of really good ones too, I thought as I watched Kalem and Leah emerge from the hold.

The spirit had touched me, as soon as my heart was ready, as easily as it touched any Nephite. And anyway, I had learned that there were as many wicked Nephites as Lamanites. Being Nephite alone was not enough to make a person good.

Leah's smile was bright as she came toward me. I peered around her to watch Kalem approach Darius. Soon all four of us were standing near the bow of the enormous ship as it set sail. When we were under way, Leah nodded to Kalem, who took a scroll from his satchel and passed it to Darius.

Darius opened the scroll and began to read after he cast a curious glance to both his father and mother.

"We had these papers drawn up after you two left for Zarahemla," Leah began. "They only need signatures to be binding. I thought…" She stopped to lick her lips. "I thought we could have the ceremony on board." When Darius and I both looked at her in confusion, she added contritely, "If you want to." But she seemed to straighten up when she declared, "I can see you have fallen in love. I won't apologize for wanting the best for my son."

Darius passed me the scroll. I smiled to myself, thinking of those many nights by the fire he had taught me to read the symbols I now saw before me.

This was a betrothal contract for Darius and me.

I slowly rerolled the scroll and fastened it closed.

I looked up into three expectant faces. They wanted to know if my answer was yes. Darius knew what I felt, of course, but he was as surprised by this as I was. Maybe even a little annoyed by his parents' presumption.

I tried to keep my face neutral, but it was very hard. I couldn't help clutching the precious scroll to my bosom. "I would like to have my brother present for this discussion."

Leah, understanding, closed her eyes in relief, but it did nothing to prevent her happy tears from escaping.

"I'll go get him," Kalem said. He gave his wife's arm a squeeze and turned to find Tecumeni in the crowds of people who now stood on deck and watched the land fade slowly into the distance.

"Would it be too soon to hug you?" Leah asked.

I laughed, suddenly unable to hold in my happiness. "No."

I caught Dare's eye as his mother hugged me— complete satisfaction with the turn of events in his life.

When Tec arrived, he tried to stay formal, as a decision of this magnitude called for, but like the rest of us, he couldn't. He rolled his eyes and said, "It was a done deal the moment you jumped into the floodwaters, Ava. Of course I agree to this."

I went into Dare's arms, still clutching the scroll in my hand.

"I wish there was a place I could kiss you in privacy," he mumbled into my hair.

"There is, behind those pallets of provisions stacked near the stern," Tec said, and then he actually flushed, embarrassed. "Not that I would know."

I hugged my blushing brother tight, then Leah again and Kalem. Then I let Darius lead me behind the pallets of provisions.

"Talk to me in the way I understand best," I said and, taking me in his arms, he did.

About the Author

Misty Moncur wanted to be Indiana Jones when she grew up. Instead, she became an author and has her adventures at home. In her jammies. With her imagination. And pens that she keeps running dry.

Misty is the author of *Daughter of Helaman*, *Fight For You*, *In All Places*, and other novels in The Stripling Warrior series. Her stories are filled with tenderness and humor, and her characters are real, endearing, and memorable. Her LDS fiction titles will inspire you.

Misty loves to read anything with a romance in it, edit, type, stare out the window, and hang with her family. She lives in a swampy marshland and spends her evenings swatting mosquitoes.

PLEASE ENJOY THE FIRST CHAPTER OF
BEYOND THE WEST SEA

CHAPTER 1

My arm came up to shade my eyes as I stepped from my dim quarters and picked my way across the unfinished deck of the massive ship. Already I could hear the hammering and the shouting of the workmen.

"It is the sun's reflection off the water," one of the crew explained when he saw me squinting. I didn't stop to listen, just flashed him a tight smile before I headed for the far corner of the deck where I thought I might be able to find a little privacy away from all the men, many of whom had halted their work to stare at me. I stepped over some thick ropes and found a seat on a crate, and there I sat watching the men work on building the deck, the rails, and the rigging while I waited for Ethanim to come for me.

He had been disappointed that it was nearly dark when we arrived, and had awakened me before dawn to tell me he was going in to the market to replenish our supplies. Certainly we had used them up on our journey from Orihah, but we both knew it was an excuse to go exploring. He hadn't thought he would be back before the morning meal.

"You get some more rest," he said, even his whispered voice unable to conceal his excitement to explore the coastal town.

I smiled into the dark after he left. I didn't mind him leaving me alone for the morning. He had been kind to bring me here and such a pleasant companion on the journey. I doubted he would even be back before the midday meal.

A man who looked to be in charge was scrutinizing some drawings and directing the placement of some large beams. It looked like a huge and complicated job that required many men, but it was all happening down at the other end of the ship. If the work moved to this end, I would have to move. Hopefully, Ethanim would find me first. After a while, I got bored of watching the action, so I lay back in the ropes and made myself comfortable.

I became aware of a man's voice near me. I must have fallen back to sleep.

"I think we have a stowaway."

I opened my eyes and looked for the position of the sun, which told me it was nearly noon. The four day journey must have been more exhausting than I thought. I rubbed my palms into my eyes and then looked around.

Two men worked near me. The one who had spoken was the man I had seen holding the plans and giving orders to the work crew. I knew immediately the other man was Lib, Ethanim's friend, but a quick glance around didn't produce Ethanim. Lib was tall, blond, slender with strong and square shoulders, and looked to be preoccupied with building the ship. When the other man spoke, Lib stopped what he was doing to lean back and peer at me around a stack of lumber, but clearly with little interest.

"I'm not," I said sharply. "A stowaway. I'm not."

The man laughed and smiled kindly. He was older than Lib, maybe in his thirties. I took in his strong shoulders, thick arms, rough hands, wide nose, and smiling eyes. He looked excited. Happy. Exuberant even. He either loved this boat or he loved me, and I was betting it was the boat.

"I know," he admitted in a kind of apology. "Just looking for some solace, eh?" he asked, going back to his work. It looked like he and Lib were making an adjustment to the large sail. "It can be nigh unto impossible to find peace and solace around here."

"Something like that," I mumbled, tucking a piece of hair behind my ear and gazing out at the sea—shimmering blue as far as I could see.

I thought the man intended to leave me alone then, but I heard him say, "She your sister?"

Lib barely glanced at me and didn't bother with a response beyond a shake of his head and humorless laugh, as if to say that someone like me could not possibly be related to someone like him.

I could see how the man might think it, though. My hair was nearly the same golden color as Lib's, and while he was tall and broad-shouldered and I was so small and thin I looked like a little girl, we did share other similar features—long fingers with bony knuckles, light skin that tanned easily, freckles on our arms, and eyebrows darker than our hair. I would have thought the same thing.

"Lib is a terrible brother," I said.

I had his attention then.

The other man laughed. "Teases you mercilessly, I suspect."

I shot a quickly calculating look at Lib. He looked like he could take a joke. "Once when I was small, he held me upside down by my ankle over the latrine, and when I tried to spit at him, it ended up in my hair." I stood and stepped toward the man. "I'm Miriam," I said.

"I'm Hagoth," the man said.

My eyes widened. I had heard of Hagoth. "You're younger than I thought you would be," I said.

"Did this young pup tell you I was old?" he laughed as he gave a last hard pull on the rope he held. Turning to Lib, he said, "I didn't know your sister was visiting."

Lib stared at me for a long moment. "Neither did I."

"I didn't even know you had a sister."

Suddenly looking from me to Hagoth, Lib said, "I don't. Miriam and I are not acquainted."

I had misjudged him. He couldn't take a joke.

"We met last night," I said, not sure which one I was informing.

Lib's eyes narrowed as he looked back to me.

"I came with Ethanim," I told him, hurt that he didn't remember. It wasn't like there were any other visitors sleeping in the new cabins, and from what I had seen, there were no other women on board either. I sighed and turned to Hagoth. "I guess I am the one who teases. Lib speaks the truth. We are not related, but I did grow up in Orihah, not far from Lib." Not far from Lib's home. Lib hadn't been there, not much anyway since I had been seven.

I felt Lib's eyes on me. He was studying my face, trying to decide if he recognized me or not. He obviously didn't.

Hagoth observed us both for a moment, and then he sort of smiled to himself and winked at me. He seemed to understand something I did not.

I thought Lib, a boy I had looked up to when I was young, a man whose bravery and faithfulness I had heard tell of, was just this side of rude. He was not living up to the stories I had heard of him.

I should have known better, I thought, sighing to myself.

Hagoth made some excuse and said he had to go, and before I knew it, he was gone and I was standing awkwardly with Lib.

He brushed some imaginary dirt off a pallet, kicked it lightly, rubbed the side of his nose, and looked longingly over my shoulder at his friend's retreating back. I clasped my hands behind my back and looked out to sea.

"I was kind of preoccupied last night," he said at last, maybe a little apologetically.

"Ethanim says you have been very busy." Actually, what he had said was Lib was too busy for his friends. I tucked my hair behind my ear again when the sea breeze blew it free.

"Yeah." He bent and picked up the thick rope. He wound it into a tidy coil as he said, "I can't wait until she's ready to sail."

"How long will it take?"

"Another year."

"A year? But it looks almost finished!"

I might have imagined it, but I thought his eyes

lit up. "There's—" He broke off and shook his head. "There's a lot to do still," he finished. Then he started to edge away. "I guess I will see you later," he said and followed Hagoth across the deck.

"I guess you will," I said, watching him go. I watched as he approached Hagoth, watched Hagoth say something, watched Lib's face turn red as he untied a huge knot that freed a large beam.

"I think he's a snob," I told Ethanim later when we were eating the food he had brought from the market.

Ethanim chewed thoughtfully and finally pushed the food to the side of his mouth. "That will make being married to him hard." He took another bite of his fish stew, scooping it into his mouth with his fingers.

I took another bite too. It was good, but I thought it was seasoned too heavily. "You still think I'm crazy."

"To want to be Lib's wife? No, not at all. To travel all this way to try to snare the heart of a man you've never met? Yeah." He chewed for a minute and then added, "Really crazy."

"That's pretty much what my parents said."

"What did Noah think?"

My oldest brother. I squirmed a little on my seat. "He talked you into taking me, didn't he?"

He laughed. "It didn't take much talking. Escort a pretty girl on a week long journey to the sea? I had to think on it for about a second, Miriam."

I flushed and squirmed again.

"Don't worry," he said, a little more gently. "You're not my type." He took another bite, chewed for a moment, but then pushed the food to the side of his mouth and said, "I'm all for Lib getting married. I just think you might have your work cut out for you."

"Because of Keturah, you mean?" The girl Lib had been in love with for eight years, married now to someone else.

His face hardened and he looked down into his stew. "Yeah."

I didn't know much about the situation, only that Lib had fallen in love with the only female warrior in Helaman's army during the war and that Ethanim did not approve of his friend's feelings. "I met Hagoth, today," I said to change the subject.

"You did? I haven't met him yet. What is he like?"

"He loves this boat."

"I bet he does. Did you know Lib helped him design it?"

"You told me." I looked around. "This has been in the works for a long time."

Ethanim nodded. "Lib has a very gifted mind for engineering. He has been drawing plans for things like this since we were kids." I detected a note of pride in his voice. "He knows everything about everything."

"He doesn't know much about being polite."

Ethanim barked out a laugh, but more generously allowed, "He is hurting, but I can't believe he was impolite—especially to a little girl."

"I'm not a little girl," I argued.

"Okay." But his amused smile said he thought differently.

"I'm sure getting this ship seaworthy has been very stressful for him."

"I'm sure it has been like a fun game for him," he disagreed, still looking amused, "but even if it was stressful, it would be no excuse to be rude to a girl."

"He wasn't exactly rude," I admitted, wishing I hadn't brought it up. He wasn't impolite. He just didn't like me. Didn't like the way I looked, the way I smelled or walked. He didn't like me on his magnificent boat.

"Hey, listen." Ethanim waited until I looked over at him. "I think what you're doing here, well, it's pretty remarkable. The Holy Ghost impressed you to come here and marry a man you hardly know. You acted on it. You did it. You're here. The Lord wouldn't lead you astray. I don't see that man's disposition getting sweeter anytime soon, but then I don't have the wiles of a pretty little girl with which to sweeten it."

Warmed by his words and the wink that accompanied it, I only said, "I am not a little girl."

He cleared his throat. "About that," he said. "It will help if you just let me think of you that way. I am not the one you need to convince you're a grown woman anyway." He leaned forward, putting his elbows on his knees and regarding me more seriously than he ever had. "I can see as well as any man that you are not a little girl."

I swallowed hard and looked down at my hands.

"When I refer to you that way, I'm not trying to degrade you or put you in your place. I'm trying to keep an appropriate distance. I need to think of you as my little sister and the young wife of my best friend, not as the beautiful woman I can see you are, not as a temptress I am aching to put my hands on, not as a woman who is prepared to become a man's wife."

Oh Ethanim, I thought. It hadn't occurred to me this task might be hard for him. I felt suddenly very guilty, but I was grateful for his blunt speaking and also for his faith in what I was doing.

"I will help you with Lib as much as I can," he went on, a soft determination in his voice. "I'll help you do what you feel you must, but I ask you to help me too." He caught my eye. "Alright?"

I nodded. "Alright."

I saw Lib standing alone on the deck that night when most of the work crew were sleeping—or trying to. I didn't know how anyone could sleep down in the stuffy hold.

I wasn't afraid he would see me. He hadn't

seemed to take note of me in the daylight, so I didn't think he would take note of me in the darkness.

After a long time of staring out into the blackness of the sea, only moonlight on the calm, quiet ripples to show it was there at all, he sighed, pounded his fist lightly on the rail, and went down into the hold.

I knew my first impression of Lib had been bad. I had tried not to have any expectations of him, but I knew I had expected a lot. How could I not? Keturah and Gid said he was wonderful. My brother, Noah, had always spoken very highly of him and had the utmost respect for him. Ethanim was his best friend and, though frustrated with his recent depression, loved him like a brother.

I looked at the stars.

God, I prayed. *How can I do this thing? He doesn't even see me, and he is ever so much more hurt than I was prepared for.* I smiled. *But heavens, is he ever handsome.*

I had only vague recollections of him as a boy. I had been only seven when he had gone to war, but he had made enough of an impression on me that I remembered him. But to be fair, I had memories of all Noah's friends. Noah, my oldest brother, was eight years older than me and had joined Helaman's army when he was just fifteen. I recalled that time vividly—the messenger who came to recruit the boys from Orihah, their excitement and determination to go, the words about their departure during the Sabbath meeting, the other boys who walked out of the town with him headed north to a training field near the city Melek. Both Lib and Ethanim had been among them.

Noah was home now, married to Sarah, a girl who had grown up near us. He worked with my father on the farm, and he was content there. He would have brought me here to the coast himself, but Sarah would soon give birth to their first child—any day now. There was Jed, my other brother, but he had his work and his newly betrothed to tend to. He might have taken me, but Noah had thought to ask Ethanim, Lib's best friend, to bring me here. Ethanim was glad for the excuse to visit his friend and had agreed easily.

And so I was here, and I was wondering what my next step should be. I had felt so strongly of the Holy Spirit that I needed to come here and marry Lib. I still felt it, but just showing up and stepping onto his boat was not accomplishing the task. I guessed I needed some kind of plan. So for days, I watched him and tried to come up with one. Sometimes, as often as he could, Ethanim would include me in whatever he and Lib were doing—meals, hunting, building—but Lib never paid me any particular attention. Maybe I had been expecting too much, but I had thought Lib would at least be friendly towards me. I knew Ethanim had thought this too. But it was almost as if Lib were deliberately looking through me like I didn't exist.

But I secretly took heart in this because ignoring me so thoroughly had to be taking a deliberate effort and a certain level of awareness of me.

Well, I decided, the first thing I must do was make him see me, and the things that interested Lib, the things he did see, were all related to the engineering and construction of that big ship.

www.ingramcontent.com/pod-product-compliance
Lightning Source LLC
Chambersburg PA
CBHW020224180626
46810CB00006B/2037